PRAISE F ...
QUEEN OF THE JEWS

"I challenge you to read The Prologue and the first paragraph of Judy Petsonk's *Queen of the Jews*. You will be drawn in immediately to the remarkable story of a queen history nearly forgot."

-Richard Scott,
Board Member and Conference Chair, The Historical Novel Society

"In *Queen of the Jews*, Judy Petsonk boldly pushes aside the curtain covering up the violent history behind the Maccabeean romance, exposing the palace intrigues and internecine religious struggles that almost swallowed up Israel in the wake of the Maccabeean victory over the Greeks. Her sexy passionate heroine, Queen Salome Alexandra, known to her adoring people as Shalom-Zion, possesses the brains, hutzpah, and vision to save Israel not only from the many enemies seeking to destroy it but also from its own conflicted nature. A marvelous window into a neglected and little-known chapter of Jewish history."

- Ellen Frankel,
Former Editor in Chief, Jewish Publication Society

"Judy Petsonk has captured the life of an important – yet overlooked – Jewish leader who serves as a model, especially for women, and for all who seek insight and inspiration. A novel, a history lesson, and a spiritual map, all rolled into one book."

-Rabbi Kerry M. Olitzky,
Executive Director, Jewish Outreach Institute

QUEEN
OF THE
JEWS

A NOVEL BY
JUDY PETSONK

Published by Blair Books
Highland Park, NJ

ISBN-13: 978-1470160937

DEDICATION

To Steve, my anchor,

To Hope and Ben

Lee, Andy and Carol

And to Ed and Jud Petsonk.

I hope they would be proud.

ACKNOWLEDGMENTS

Thanks to Susan Leviton for her lovely cover, to Jim Remsen for copy editing and incisive comments, to Marilla Wex for web-site design, to Tammy Reid for interior design; to Michele Alperin, Anna Beck, and Elise Gonzales for proofreading; to historian Kenneth Atkinson for help in getting started; and to the many wonderful friends who read the manuscript and gave valuable feedback at various stages in the evolution of the novel: Judy Koslowski Kirsten, Roselyn Bell, Harriet Katz, Rabbi Nancy Fuchs Kreimer, Carol/Annie Petsonk, Dena Seidel, Barbara Gordon.

Thanks especially to my teachers Katherine Taylor, Russell Rowland, Dalia Pagani, Diana Spechler and Lisa Reardon and my fellow students at Gotham Writers' Workshop.

KEY

1. Temple Mount
2. Temple
3. Women's Court
4. Tomb of Alexander Janneus
5. Royal Caverns
6. Tombs
7. Siloam Pool
8. Gate of Essenes
9. David's Tomb
10. Aqueduct
11. Wealthy & Priestly Residential Area
12. Upper Market
13. Lower Market
14. Hasmonean Palace
15. Tomb of John Hyrcanus
16. Hezekiah's Pool
17. Commercial-Industrial Quarter
18. Street along Tyropean Valley
19. Street
20. Tower Gate

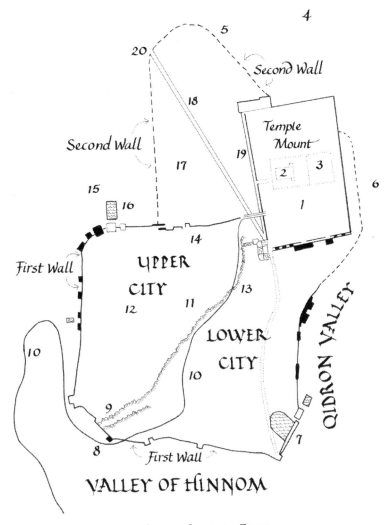

JERUSALEM AT THE TIME OF QUEEN SHALOM-ZION

Adapted and redrawn by Susan Leviton from Lee I. Levine, JERUSALEM: Portrait of the City in the Second Temple Period, C. 2002, used by permission of The Jewish Publication Society, Philadelphia, PA.

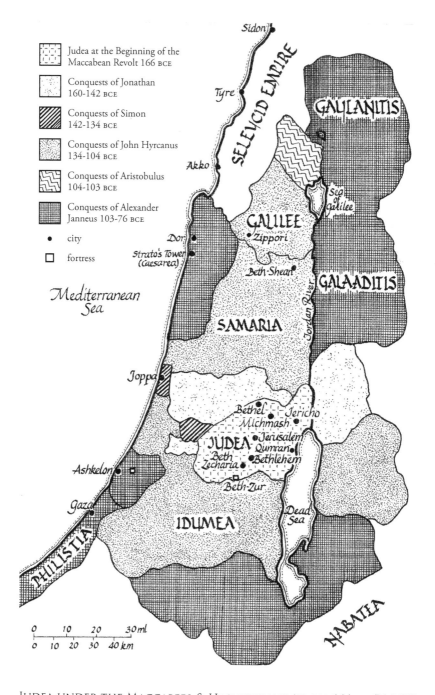

JUDEA UNDER THE MACCABEES & HASMONEANS (FROM 166 TO 76 BCE)

Adapted and redrawn by Susan Leviton from H. Shanks, ed., Ancient Israel: From Abraham to the Roman Destruction of the Temple, C. 1999, used by permission of the Biblical Archaeology Society, Washington, DC.

INTRODUCTION

Just after I'd met my husband Steve, but before we'd started dating seriously, I made a trip to Israel. I wanted to see the Sinai before it was returned to Egypt. It was astonishingly beautiful: ribbons of multicolored rock rising above vast sweeps of desert sand. But I couldn't go to the Sinai without spending some time in Jerusalem. I was walking down King Solomon Street toward King David Street, when suddenly I found myself looking at a sign that said, in Hebrew, Queen Shalom-Zion Street. A Jewish queen? Why had I never heard of her?

I married Steve a year after I came back from that trip. We've lived together for nearly thirty years. I've spent the last thirty years writing two books, raising two kids, and getting ready to write the story of Shalom-Zion.

For seven years, I've been researching, writing, rewriting, and rewriting. I've traveled to Jericho and walked through the scant remains of a palace she built. I stepped on a mosaic floor I'm sure she stepped on. There was a bench where she must have reclined, alongside twin swimming pools where she probably swam. The only witnesses were my guide, a goat nosing among the weeds, and the sand sifting across a pattern of pink and blue stones.

Hasmonean palace, Jericho, courtesy of E. Netzer, Hebrew University of Jerusalem and the Jewish Publication Society.

I've looked for references to Queen Shalom-Zion in Jewish sources and found almost nothing. So little remains of her reign that I've wondered if all traces were deliberately wiped out. When you hear her story, you may agree with my suspicions. Yet the Judaism we know today, the Judaism of the rabbis, might not exist without her intervention.

The Maccabee family led a rebellion that freed the Jews from Hellenistic Syria in the second century BCE. The events of this book take place largely in the first century BCE when the grandchildren of the Maccabees ruled Judea (modern-day Israel). If you don't know who the Maccabees were, or what Hellenistic means, or if you just want to know more, check out the ***Background*** section, which is, appropriately, in the back of the book. If not, onward to the tale itself.

MAIN CHARACTERS

*Boldface name indicates character appearing in the novel. Italics
indicate a fictional character or fictional nickname. Actual names of
Janneus's (Yannai's) younger brothers and Boethus's son (Zadok) are
unknown.*

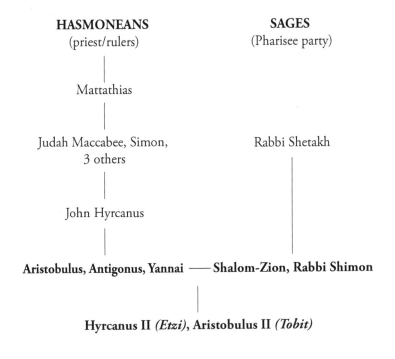

HASMONEANS
(priest/rulers)

SAGES
(Pharisee party)

Mattathias

Judah Maccabee, Simon,
3 others

Rabbi Shetakh

John Hyrcanus

Aristobulus, Antigonus, Yannai —— **Shalom-Zion, Rabbi Shimon**

Hyrcanus II *(Etzi)*, Aristobulus II *(Tobit)*

Miri, Queen Shalom-Zion's lady-in-waiting

SADDUCEES
(party of the wealthy nobles and priests)

**Ambassador Diogenes, Phiabi, Boethus,
Hanin, Ishmael, Zadok, Jonathan**

TIME LINE

Note: This novel follows the Jewish custom of dating events BCE (Before the Common Era) or CE (Common Era), rather than the frequently used BC (Before Christ) and AD (Anno Domini: Year of Our Lord). Italics indicate that date of event is unknown, or that nickname is fictional.

166-165 BCE Revolt of the Maccabees against Antiochus IV of Syria.

164 BCE Temple rededicated (origin of the Hanukkah holiday).

160 BCE Judah Maccabee dies in battle.

1st year of Hasmonean dynasty (140 BCE) Jews choose Judah's brother Simon as high priest. Shalom-Zion born.

6th year (134 BCE) Simon assassinated. John Hyrcanus becomes high priest. *Shulamit – later known as Salome Alexandra or Shalom-Zion – betrothed to Judah Aristobulus (Yudi), oldest son of John Hyrcanus.*

7th year (133 BCE) Siege of Jerusalem by Antiochus VII of Syria. Judea forced to pay tribute but retains autonomy. *Shetakh dies (father of Shalom-Zion and Rabbi Shimon).*

15th year (125 BCE) Birth of Alexander Janneus (Yannai).

36th year (104 BCE) John Hyrcanus dies. Aristobulus I *(Yudi)* becomes high priest and king. Shalom-Zion becomes queen.

37th year (103 BCE) Aristobulus I dies. Alexander Janneus (Yannai) becomes king and marries Queen Shalom-Zion.

64th year (76 BCE) Alexander Janneus (Yannai) dies. Queen Shalom-Zion is sole ruler.

73rd year (67 BCE) Queen Shalom-Zion dies.

77th year (63 BCE) Pompey of Rome conquers Jerusalem. End of Hasmonean dynasty.

Prologue

My people call me the Queen of Peace, but their memories are short. I am proud and grateful for the last nine years of prosperity here in Judea. I worry about the next life. My heavenly Father may call me to account for the twenty-seven years when I refused to drive my second husband, King Alexander Janneus, into exile.

I would feel at peace even now if I believed Judea would remain at peace after my death. But the seeds of war have been planted. They are the king's seeds, and they grew in my womb.

BOOK ONE

CHAPTER 1

Jerusalem, 37ᵗʰ year of the Hasmonean dynasty (103 BCE)

I was feeling peaceful the day of the murders. Lounging on the silk couch in my sitting room, I congratulated myself. I had persuaded my husband that no one planned to kill him.

Then came a drumming at my door. Who had managed to slip unnoticed through the phalanx of door guards and bodyguards with their swords and lances? Surely not one of the turbaned nobles, gifts in hand, who loitered in the Audience Chamber to ask favors of the king.

Miri, the plump little lady-in-waiting who had been my companion since we were girls, peered through the small window in the cedar door. "Is not your business with the king?" said Miri. "Her Royal Highness is at rest."

The knocking came again. "One of the king's bodyguards, My Lady," said Miri.

She opened the door, gasped and shut it again. "Your Highness," she said, "you do not want to see this."

I pushed past her. The guard's uniform was soaked with blood. His hands and his dagger dripped red. "Your Highness, come see who we caught in the Tower," said the guard. "All dressed in his murderous best. General Mattathias Antigonus!"

I ran down the corridor. Amid the greenish dimness of stone walls and floor, torchlight gleamed on bronze armor. My brother-in-law Matti lay on his back, his head tilted at an angle, his left eye a puddle of blood.

I felt sick. How could this happen?

A second guard stood looking down at the corpse. "He was a good man," the guard said. "But the best soul can turn foul, when tempted by a throne."

A few feet from the body lay Matti's severed right hand, fingers and wrist caked with crimson. Matti had always kept his hands so clean. In swordplay, that hand had swooped like a dancer's.

I swayed. Miri caught my elbow and held me tightly. On impulse, I pulled off my headscarf and covered the orphaned hand. Blood seeped through the embroidered seven-branched menorah of the royal crest.

Sandals slapped on stone. My husband Yudi – King Judah Aristobulus – knelt. He stripped off his white tunic and used it to wipe the blood from his brother's face. As if by that tender gesture he could bring back his beloved companion.

I remembered Matti, at six, catching an over-ripe fig in mid-air as a merchant tossed it away. He bit off the rotting spot and handed the rest to Yudi.

"You got red juice on your face," said seven-year-old Yudi. He wiped his brother's smeared cheeks with a corner of his tunic.

"I wanted to give it all to you," said Matti, "but I know you don't like the mushy parts."

* * *

Yudi flung himself full-length on Matti's body. He vomited into the pool of blood. He clanged his forehead against his brother's armored chest. My husband is going mad, I thought, or he would never permit himself – the high priest – to be polluted by a corpse.

"I'm sorry," Yudi wept. "I'm so sorry."

"You killed him?" I screeched. "I told you only to keep him out of sight for awhile – to send him on a mission or put him in jail."

Yudi sobbed. He scrubbed with his tunic at the mess of blood and vomit. How could I possibly comfort my husband in the face of this horror? I put my hand on Yudi's bare bony shoulder. He threw the sopping tunic into my face. "Get away from me, witch!" he screamed. "You made me kill him!"

I wiped blood and vomit from my eyebrows. "I told you to keep your brother from the public eye," I said. "Not to kill him."

"You made me fear him. You said the Sadducees would use him to displace me."

Yudi might have been named for his great-uncle Judah Maccabee, but he was no master of strategy.

"You did not see your brother strut at the victory parade," I said, "while you lay ill in your chamber. You did not see the wealthy Sadducees fawning on him. Or the children trying to touch his armor as he marched by."

"He deserved to strut," said Yudi. "He was the real hero of the Iturean war. The Sadducees were right. He deserved to be king."

It made sense to ban weapons from the palace. But why had I let my husband issue the order? All his life Yudi had been a blunderer and a blamer. I remembered running through the market when I was six and Yudi five. He slammed into a huge jug of oil. Sitting on the floor of the merchant's stall, bloody knees covered with oil, he screamed, "You pushed me!" When he'd been *following* me.

* * *

One of the guards retrieved a bronze helmet from the corner. Matti must have been carrying it. No need to dress for combat in the palace, his brother's home.

Two guards stripped the shiny vest and greaves from Matti's body. They heaved him to their shoulders. The third guard looped the helmet and armor straps over his wrist. He picked up the severed hand, still shrouded in my blood-soaked scarf. The three guards clanked down the stone corridor toward the underground chamber where the dead are prepared for burial.

Three opponents: not overwhelming odds if Matti had expected them. I had seen Matti keep three challengers at bay. He had darted among them like a mosquito.

Was this slaughter my fault? Was I wrong to warn Yudi against his brother? I had been intent on protecting my husband's throne. I had suspicions, but no real proof that Matti planned to usurp it.

Yudi pushed past me and ran back to his chamber. He slammed the bolt shut. He howled like a wounded dog. "Yudi, open the door," I shouted.

Crashing sounds: glass and pottery jugs shattering against the door. I feared my husband would cut his own wrists with the shards.

"Get my brother Shimon," I ordered Miri. "Tell him to come to my sitting room at once."

I hunched on the blue silk couch in my sitting room, biting the knuckle of my thumb. *Lord,* I prayed, *do not let Yudi hurt himself.*

Another hammering at my door. Yudi's valet, Jason. His brown hair was rumpled and his Greek-style tunic awry. He blinked rapidly, as he always did when he was nervous. "Queen Salome

Alexandra!" he shouted. "Come quickly! King Judah Aristobulus has taken poison! He kneels on the spot where his brother fell, vomiting blood."

Running after Jason, I tripped over the hem of my gown and slammed into the stone wall. I wiped grit from my scraped forehead and plunged into the corridor. Yudi thrashed and retched. Bloody bubbles oozed from his lips.

"You!" he bleated. He swatted weakly at me. "You pushed me."

The valet stood as if paralyzed. "Help me!" I shouted. "Summon the doctor. Bid him bring acacia juice. Tell him the king has swallowed poison."

I sat on the stone floor. I dragged my husband onto my lap, face down. Blood dripped down my skirt. I pounded Yudi's back. "Vomit it out!" I screamed. "Save yourself."

A twitch. A shudder. I turned Yudi's face toward me. I tried to put my finger in his throat. I had to make him vomit.

Yudi's head jerked back. His body thrashed. "Yudi, lie still," I begged. "Let me help you."

Yudi convulsed for what seemed an hour. I turned him over. I rocked and cradled him. His shoulders wrenched away from my hands. He arched backward. I saw only the whites of his eyes.

Jason and the doctor ran down the corridor toward us. Yudi's throat gurgled. His beautiful eyelashes fluttered and were still. He gave a hoarse, gasping breath. I waited for the next breath. It never came. His cheeks sagged. He was gone.

I did something Yudi had never permitted me to do in our married life. I held my husband's hand to my lips and let the tears wash over it as if they could bring that sweet, pious and ineffectual man back to life.

The valet Jason stared at me with narrowed eyes. His cheek jerked. "He thinks," I realized with a startled chill, "that this poison came from me."

CHAPTER 2

Creaking ropes lowered the coffins into the pit. Except for my brother Shimon, I had known Yudi and Matti longer than anyone else in my life. I remembered the day I met them. Yudi, the future high priest and my betrothed, was a year younger and a head shorter than I. Only five: a baby. He had pale skin and long eyelashes. He whined. Matti, red-cheeked, sturdy but graceful, was only four, but as tall as his brother and stronger.

Yudi and Matti tried to make an arrow and bow from green sticks and the broken rawhide thong of a sandal. Yudi, who had the better mind, realized that the bowstring would not hold. He notched the stick. Matti had the strength to bend the stick into a bow. What did they do with their handmade bow? They took turns shooting handmade arrows at me. They did not hate me. But they had each other. They had no need of a sister.

I did not need a bow. I fired rocks at them. Their mother Judith clenched my arm. It was not ladylike, she said, to throw rocks. Why was it more ladylike to let oneself be hit than to hit back? I demanded. I knew then that I would never become a daughter in that household. Over Judith's objections, High Priest John Hyrcanus had betrothed me, the daughter of his revered teacher, to their eldest son. Judith considered me a beggar, like the pigeons that pecked at our feet in the public square. Food was scarce during the siege of Jerusalem. She glowered each time she handed me a bite of bread. The Law, and her husband, High Priest John Hyrcanus, had forced her to feed me. Then Father died, transforming me in Judith's eyes from unwelcome guest to permanent intruder.

I'd always thought of Yudi and Matti as my two little brothers. Now they were two shrouded corpses, disappearing forever into the earth. The ones who had planned these assassinations would seek my death next.

Standing on the dais above the weeping crowd, I spoke loud enough to be heard through the widow's veil. "Judea has suffered a terrible loss," I said, "with the deaths of our king and our general. I have lost my precious companion, my husband King Judah Aristobulus. It appears that this tragedy began with a misunderstanding. General Antigonus seems to have assumed that he was not subject to the ban on weapons in the palace. The guards believed he was plotting violence and killed him. King Judah Aristobulus appears to have died of grief at the loss of his beloved brother. I will not rest until we are certain of the truth. I beg you not to indulge in rumors and idle speculation. All Judea must stand together and continue to follow the Lord's way. Members of our representative assembly, the Sanhedrin, will meet shortly to name the king's successor."

My brother Shimon kept glancing at me, his lips pursed, his eyes unreadable. Passing through the gate back into the city, I tugged his sleeve. I whispered, "I must talk to you. Come to my sitting room."

My sitting room was my sanctuary. Blue silk couch and

draperies. A small false window that looked out, winter and summer, on an imaginary garden. Shimon stomped in, gray side-curls flapping like the ears of a goat refusing the halter. He thrust aside the blue drapes as if parting the Red Sea. Miri raised her eyebrows and slipped out the door.

Shimon glared at me, his face a mirror of mine: thin lips, nose like an eagle's beak. *At least my hair is still dark*, I thought. *And I have not lost any of mine.*

"You arranged those deaths," said Shimon.

My chest tightened. How could my brother accuse me? "I did not kill Yudi and Matti," I said.

"You ordered the king's guards to kill anyone bearing weapons in the palace," he said.

"After the Iturian war," I said, "Yudi was near madness. He saw knives in every shadow. You know that he refused to leave his chamber. I thought banning weapons might calm him."

"Then you told General Antigonus that he was exempt from that order and should show off his new armor to the king."

"Never would I say such a thing," I snapped.

"Who did?"

"The Sadducees, I am sure. If those rich priests and landowners can persuade the people that I plotted these deaths, the Sadducees can execute me and put their own man on the throne."

My brother laughed harshly. "They may do it regardless. You should have thought of that," he said.

He paced from the couch to the window. I followed.

"You do not believe me?"

"I do not know who to trust," he said. "Who provided Yudi with poison in his moment of despair?"

I felt like weeping.

"Shimon," I said. "I grew up with Matti and Yudi. How could I arrange their deaths?"

Shimon's mouth tilted in a wry smile. "I hardly know you anymore. I am just a poor teacher and linen-weaver. You have lived in the palace for thirty years, feeding on politics with your dinner. How do I know what you're capable of?"

"If Father were alive, he would defend me," I said.

"You were good at manipulating him."

I held my head with both hands. "Are you still angry because Father taught me to read and write?"

"Not appropriate for a female," Shimon sniffed. "You manipulated Judah Aristobulus, too. Why did you push him to declare himself king? He would have been content to be high priest, like his father and grandfather. You wanted a throne."

I tucked wayward wisps of hair into my headdress. "I did not worm my way into the palace. Our father arranged this betrothal, for your sake as well as mine. So that you could become the respected Rabbi Shimon son of Shetakh, head of the Sanhedrin. So that you and the other Sages would have a place at the royal table. If becoming a commoner again would bring Yudi and Matti back to life, I would do it. You know that."

Shimon turned to go. I grabbed his sleeve.

"Shimon, save my life. Who will help me if not my brother?"

I stroked his hand – a linen-maker's hand, red and cracked from kneading the soaking flax. "When I was little, I followed you like the caravan master following the eastern star."

Shimon raised one eyebrow. A smile tugged at the corners of his mouth. "You followed me as a flea follows the goat," he said. "I will try to protect you."

"Thank you!" I threw my arms around his neck. I stepped back to arm's length. "One more thing," I said. "You are not going to like it."

"Probably not."

"Would you ask the Sanhedrin to appoint me as ruler?"

"What?" He threw up his hands. "You are a woman. You can never be priest or king."

"Neither can you. We are both commoners. But they could appoint me regent."

"You have no children."

I sat on the blue couch and folded my arms. "I consider the people of Judea my children."

Shimon snorted. Without my invitation, he plopped himself on the couch beside me and folded his arms. "High Priest John Hyrcanus had five sons," he said. "Alexander Janneus is next in line for the throne. He will be high priest and king."

"Alexander Janneus?" I said. "Yannai is a wild man. He grew up in Galilee. He has never seen a Temple service."

"The other priests will teach him."

"I will agree to Yannai as king – if you tell the Sanhedrin that I must marry him."

Shimon leaped to his feet, his tunic billowing. "Preposterous! You are fifteen years older than he is."

"You know the Law," I said. "It is the duty of every man to marry the widow when his brother dies without offspring."

"A high priest must marry a virgin."

I stood. "I have never known a man."

"In twelve years your husband never touched you?"

I pinched the headache growing between my eyes. "Yudi was obsessed with purity," I said. "He could not bear even to think about the sexual act."

"Why would you want to marry Yannai? As you said, he is a wild man."

"With Yannai in the palace, you will need me. I care about our people. I believe in the traditions of the Sages. I am on your side. If I am forced to leave the palace, you will soon see naked statues in every square in Jerusalem."

Shimon pursed his lips. "So you are doing all this for the sake of our traditions?"

"Yannai could give me children – as Yudi never would."

"Are there no other women who could produce an heir to the throne?"

The question was an insult. I set my jaw. "I have legitimacy, because I am already queen."

"And you want to remain queen."

"Would you want to give up being head of the Sanhedrin?" I said. "You judge the Law fairly; I govern Judea for the benefit of our people."

Shimon strode to the door. I gripped his shoulder. "Think of Father," I said. "He loved our mother more than his own life. Yet, knowing he could not take more than two on a single horse, he left her to die in Modi'in, and carried you and me to safety in Jerusalem. Have you ever wondered why he did that?"

"Many times," said Shimon, frowning.

"I will tell you why," I said. "He intended you and me to be partners."

"Partners?"

"You in the Sanhedrin, interpreting the Law, and me in the palace, carrying it out. I am sure that is why he betrothed me to the son of the high priest."

"What was this partnership supposed to do?"

"Defend the poor from the rich, and the true Jewish way from the Hellenizers. The Sadducees in the Sanhedrin promote the interests of the nobles and priests and the merchants who want to trade with the Greek world. But you are the only remaining Sage, the only man learned in the Law of Moses. The only man left in the Sanhedrin to defend the interests of the common people."

"I am well aware of that," said Shimon.

"How have you managed to stay in that position now that all the other Sages have been expelled?" I said. "Without my support, you won't last a week."

"What are you saying?"

"Have you heard the Sadducees ridicule the party of the Sages? They call you Pharisees, separatists. They try to persuade people that you are fanatics who give a false, extreme interpretation of the Law."

"You think I do not hear the Sadducee slanders?" said Shimon. "But I am only one man."

"If I marry Yannai," I said, "I will restore the Sages to the majority in the Sanhedrin."

"You think you have that power?" said Shimon.

"Yes, I do. If I release Yannai from prison, he will be indebted to me. The common people support me. My women give out clothing to the poor. My workers plaster the cisterns. The people of Judea know what I do and what I stand for."

Shimon chewed his lip. "I will do what I can."

"Thank you."

"Like any woman making a disputed claim to virginity," said Shimon, "you will be questioned by the court. People must not say I bent the Law for my sister's sake. And you must bring your bloody bed sheets to court, to confirm that you told the truth."

After Shimon left, Miri and I climbed to the topmost tower of the palace. Through the stone-mantled window, we looked out at the city, and over the massive wall to the barren hill beyond. Women balanced baskets on their heads. Men leaned on their staffs, leading donkeys, goats, and camels up the hill toward the city gate. "The Lord placed this land in my lap as if it were a child," I said. "I must take care of it."

I loved and hated this city: Sun-gilded squares and ancient archways. Alleys smelling of puddled waste and pigeon droppings.

"Jerusalem is the crown of the world," I said, "and Jerusalem is a jabbering commotion that makes it impossible for anyone to think clearly and reasonably."

"Your Highness, you think more clearly and reasonably than most," said Miri.

"I am glad you think so," I said, facing Miri. "Because you may think I'm insane when I tell you what I have decided to do. I am going to marry Alexander Janneus."

"My Lady," said Miri, "for the twenty-three years it has been my pleasure to serve you, I have never known a man or a woman who had more sense. But now I think you are insane."

"What else can I do?" I said. "Yannai will be king with or without me. He will be a better king with me beside him."

If Shimon can persuade the Sanhedrin to accept this marriage, I thought. Shimon was a reluctant advocate. But he was the only advocate I had.

CHAPTER 3

The stairwell to the dungeon was dark and smelled of mildew. I longed to linger by Jerusalem's sun-gilded walls. But I had made my choice. My guard lit a torch. Step by step Miri and I descended. I twisted the corroded key. The barred door creaked open. The rust on my hands looked like blood.

"Light penetrates the asshole of Jerusalem," said a man's voice. The torchlight shone on Yannai, clad only in dirty breeches, sitting on the damp floor of the cell, leaning against the lichen-covered wall.

I gaped at his bare muscled shoulders. I turned away and composed myself. I hoped that my burning cheeks had not betrayed the rush of desire that coursed through me.

"Alexander Janneus," said my guard, "stand. Her Royal Highness Salome Alexandra, Queen of Judea, wishes to speak with you."

"What a surprise!" said Yannai, rising slowly to his feet. "The holy queen has descended into the pit to greet the viper!"

He gestured around the bare stone cell. "Please excuse my surroundings, Your Highness. I wish I could offer you a chair."

I ignored his sarcasm. I'd made my choice. "I am going to release you from prison," I said. "And crown you king."

"How kind of you," said Yannai.

"But only if you accept my terms," I added.

"You're the queen. I am the prisoner," shrugged Yannai. "What are the terms?"

"I will remain queen, in fact, not only in title. You will be called king and high priest, but I will rule the land of Judea."

Yannai snorted. "You are tough! Is that all your terms?"

"One more. You must marry me and give me children."

Yannai hooted with laughter. I stared with grudging admiration at the boldness of the man.

"You want me to marry you, old woman?" said Yannai. "You think you can still bear children?"

"Children should be no problem," I said. "I am not sure I can bear *you*. Judith was older when she bore you than I am now."

"The less said about that bitch the better." Yannai spat.

"Your mother never mothered you; I lost my parents before I turned seven," I said. "We have much in common."

Yannai howled with laughter. He clutched his belly as if he might burst with mirth. "Much in common? I'm a man, you're a woman. You grew up in a palace in Jerusalem, I grew up in a foul army outpost in Galilee. You lived in my father's house for thirty years. I lived there for four. You learned to read. I learned to use a spear. We both hated my mother."

Yannai folded his arms and leaned against the wall. "Let me think about this offer," he said. He paced up and down the small cell. "As I understand it, you remain the Queen Bitch and I become your puppy."

"It is inspiring," I said, "to meet a man so careless of his life that he talks that way to a queen. The queen who holds the key to his prison cell."

I waved the key.

"You expect me to jump up and down and lick your feet because you are offering to let me out of the dungeon? Why did you lock me up?"

"You were your mother's tool. Judith tried to steal the throne from your brother Yudi, Judah Aristobulus. She claimed that your father had named you as his heir. And her as regent for you."

"You have gotten rid of my mother and my older brothers, and you want to make me *your* tool. Generous of you."

A clever man as well as daring. *He is posturing*, I told myself. *Has he any choice?*

I blinked. Where Yannai's head had been a moment ago, his feet were now waving in the air. He was walking on his hands.

I stifled a laugh. Not many people could keep me off balance, but Yannai did. The flickering torchlight made stripes of flesh and shadow, outlining the muscles of his arms and torso.

"You did an amusing thing here in Jerusalem when you were four years old," I said.

Yannai sprang back to his feet. "I have no memory of ever being in Jerusalem before we got word that my father was dying. What did I do?"

"You grabbed my breast and said, 'I am going to marry you, Shuli.'"

"I said that? I had no taste when I was four. Nor many options."

He strode up to me. His arm shot out; he grabbed my breast. My arm parried Yannai's as instinctively as a swordsman wards off a fatal blow. Yet a flame of lust shot through me. My guard leaped forward, his sword drawn. "It is all right," I said.

A lifted eyebrow and a toothy grin: Yannai exulted in both my outrage and my lust. I drew a breath. "Apparently this is how they betrothe people in Galilee," I said.

"I guess we are agreed," said Yannai. "See you in bed."

"You will sign a marriage contract and make your vows first."

"You will have to introduce me to these strange Jewish customs," said Yannai. "I grew up among pagans, you know."

As I locked the gate behind me, my heart swelled like a wine-skin newly filled. I laughed out loud. After twelve years of marriage to a man who never touched me, I was about to link my life to a man who would bed a she-lion.

Then I panicked. At four years old Yannai had bashed a stone table so hard he gouged it. He had kicked me so hard my shin still remembered the blow. Did I think that almost two decades of living among mercenaries in a wilderness fort had improved his character?

As I did nearly every day, I asked myself what Father would have wanted me to do. He would never have chosen Yannai as a husband for me. But he intended me to be his voice in the palace. To remain on the throne, to carry out Father's goals for our people, I had no choice but to marry Yannai.

I climbed the moldy stairs, into a day turned cloudy and chill.

"Your Highness, that man is insane," said Miri.

"He has the muscles of a Greek statue," I said.

"Your Highness," said Miri, "you have always been a remarkably clear-headed woman. What has happened?"

CHAPTER 4

I recognized the voices drifting through the latticed windows and drawn drapes. They were the four Sadducees who hated me most: Diogenes, our ambassador to Rome, who always sounded as if he were addressing a foreign monarch, even when talking about a broken pot. The landowner-priest Boethus, who always spoke as if his mouth were full (which it usually was). The merchant-priest Phiabi, smooth as silk. And Hanin.

I shifted from buttock to buttock, trying to get comfortable on the squat mourning stool. It must have been designed to provoke weeping. I would have to sit on this unyielding wood all day for seven days, while people who wanted to kill me pretended to "comfort" me. With its windows and tapestries shrouded in black and its high ceilings lost in shadow, the Audience Chamber was as gray as a tomb. I motioned to Miri to open the window a bit wider, and leaned forward to listen.

"Why go through these formalities?" grumbled Hanin. "The sooner we get rid of her the better."

"Nothing is as simple as we would wish," said the silky voice of Phiabi.

"Silence," said Diogenes. "The walls are thick, but the windows are wide, and there are many ears on the other side."

Miri left to usher in the visitors. "I am sorry to disturb you, My Lady," she said. "Four members of the Sanhedrin have come to offer their … condolences."

She rolled her eyes. She knew how I felt about the Sadducees, and they about me.

The four leaders of the Sadducees advanced, a choreography of sympathy. The priest-ambassador Diogenes strode erect in the gold-trimmed toga he adopted for formal occasions.

Bald barrel-bellied Boethus, who owned fields, vineyards and groves in Galilee, waddled, almost hobbled by his brocaded gown. His lips and cheeks worked to mold the proper expression from his triple jowls.

The trader Phiabi glided, sighing, in a blue silk tunic and turban copied from the garb of the high priest. I could smell his perfume when he was ten paces away. "I know you must be suffering, My Lady," said Phiabi. "I am concerned for you and for our people."

Black-browed Hanin, the oil merchant, scowled and said nothing.

"Kind guests," I said, "we have prepared a meal of consolation. I hope you will partake."

Shimon led them to the adjacent room. Miri closed the door loudly, then quietly opened it a handsbreadth. "Brethren," said my brother, "after you have eaten, we must retire to the Chamber of Hewn Stone to name the new government. Queen Salome Alexandra reminded me that since her husband left no heir, King Alexander Janneus is obliged to marry her and produce an heir in Aristobulus's name."

"While the blood of King Aristobulus and General Antigonus congeals on the Tower floor, shall we let the queen bask on the throne?" sneered Hanin. "We should hang the vixen."

I gripped the seat of the mourning stool. Its sharp edges etched the pads of my fingers. Hanin had hated me since I was six years old and broke one of his jugs of oil. He was Judith's cousin. He would have borrowed hate from her if he hadn't found his own reason.

"We live in a land of laws," said Shimon. "There is no evidence indicating that Queen Salome Alexandra is guilty of murder."

"So claims her brother," scoffed Hanin.

"She is a Jezebel," blurted Boethus. "It is obscene for a woman to have such power!"

"Queen Salome is popular with the people," said Shimon. "If the people lose their king, their general, and their queen in little more than a day, they will suspect a plot and rebel against whatever government takes their place."

Silence.

"She is a vixen and an upstart, but she is popular," said Diogenes.

"I would like to get rid of her *and* Janneus!" hissed Hanin. "And put someone on the throne who comes from the high-priestly line."

"Her taste is as narrow as her nose," said Phiabi.

"I do not like living in the most backward outpost of the world of the Hellenes," said Ambassador Diogenes.

"Queen Salome is as much a Pharisee – a separatist – as the rest of you so-called Sages." I recognized the voice of the barrel-bellied priest Boethus, embracing the chance to insult my brother as well as me.

"She thinks it is a sin to own sculpture, go to the theater, or play in the games," sniffed the worldly priest Phiabi.

"If she had her way, she would wall off the whole of Judea and not just Jerusalem," said Boethus.

"But friends," said Ambassador Diogenes, "this is not the right moment to unthrone the queen. The common people will not accept her removal. Not right now."

The ambassador had traveled the world. By their silence, his friends acknowledged his judgment. He was the leader of the Sadducee faction in the Sanhedrin. I respected Ambassador Diogenes. I wished he were my ally instead of my enemy.

"We are not talking about letting Shulamit rule," said Shimon. "We are talking about letting her marry Alexander Janneus, who will be our new high priest and king."

"A high priest can only marry a virgin," said Boethus.

"A priest may not marry a barren woman," said Phiabi.

"My sister says she is capable of bearing a child," said Shimon. "She says that her marriage to King Judah Aristobulus was never consummated. She is a virgin."

"A virgin?" said Hanin. "Why should we believe her?"

"You may inspect Shulamit's bedsheets after the wedding night," said Shimon.

"And does she know the penalty for lying about such matters?" insisted Phiabi.

"She knows that if there is no blood on the sheet, she will be brought to the city gate and stoned to death. She is not afraid."

It was humiliating. Men I hated discussing the most intimate details of my life as if I were a brood mare. But they were no longer talking about putting me on trial for the murder of my husband.

"I refuse to allow that woman back on the throne," said Hanin.

"Don't worry," soothed Phiabi. "Yannai will get rid of her soon enough. He is used to having a different whore every night. How long do you think he'll be willing to take orders from that harridan?"

"So it is settled," said Ambassador Diogenes. "Alexander Janneus will inherit."

"He is a superb horseman," said Hanin. "Maybe he can rein in his bitch of a queen."

"That will be our job," said Phiabi.

"We will have an even harder job," said Ambassador Diogenes. "To rein in the king."

* * *

The day the mourning period ended, Miri rose in the gray hour before dawn to help me dress to go to the Temple. I said, "How can I appear before the Lord? Yudi was right. I had no real proof that Matti was plotting with the Sadducees. Now Matti and Yudi are both gone."

"Your Highness, if God forbid the earth cracked open and all Jerusalem tumbled in, you would blame yourself," said Miri. "You had nothing to do with these deaths."

I hurtled through the alleys as if I could outrun my remorse. Plump little Miri, on her short legs, trotted to keep up.

All around us, bearded old men and smooth-cheeked boys hastened toward the Temple Mount. Some still adjusted head coverings or knotted girdles around their caftans. In the dark no one could tell the queen from the few other women hurrying toward the Temple.

A strip of sky above the rooftops began to shine silver. How lovely, I thought, to watch the dawn reveal herself. Like a shy bride lowering her chemise. "I wonder how Yannai looks in the high priest's robe," I said.

Miri raised her eyebrows. My veil hid my blush.

We climbed the broad stone steps of the Temple Mount,

slipped through the massive gate and melted into the shadows of the Women's Court. In the innermost courtyard, beyond the Court of the Israelites where the men stood, we could see a bonfire blazing atop the altar.

By torchlight, seven priests led a skittering lamb behind the altar. An angry bleating, then silence. In the hushed gray light, a priest emerged carrying the bloody head of the lamb. My fingers touched the line between my own chin and neck where a knife might sever the jugular. *There has been so much blood, Lord*, I whispered. *If my suspicions led to these deaths, forgive me. You know that I was trying to do what was best for Your people.*

Five priests carried parts of the skinned lamb, slowly, solemnly, up the ramp to the top of the altar. At the summit stood a tall figure in robes and turban the color of the evening sky. Yannai! He cast each piece of the offering into the flames. He poured wine from a huge golden goblet onto the four corners of the altar.

Silver horns trumpeted. Cymbals crashed. As if a wind had swept the courtyard, waves of men and women knelt. I pressed my forehead to the cold stone floor. Longing washed over me. *Please, Lord*, I prayed. *Make Yannai a true priest and a good husband. Let him love me.*

I stood. The sun rising behind the sanctuary sent feathers of pink through pungent clouds of incense. The white robes of Levite singers glowed gold. For a moment I convinced myself that Yannai, silhouetted against the Temple's golden façade, could be all that I had prayed for. *Thank You, Lord!* I exulted as I walked back to the palace through a courtyard bathed in sunshine.

Behind me, I heard Shimon and Yannai talking. Shimon hissed, "How dare you stage a farce on the holiest ground in the world? How dare you defy the Law?"

Yannai snorted. "Whatever the king does is the Law. This priest and prayer nonsense is the farce. I play the part you gave me, Wise Man."

I stifled a chuckle. It was rare that someone had the last word against my brother, Rabbi Shimon ben Shetakh, head of the Sanhedrin.

Shimon stalked into my sitting room, his tunic and gray side-curls flying. "Yannai pitched the breads and meat into the flames as if he were throwing a discus," he said. "When he poured the libation on the corners of the altar, he said, 'Lord, what a waste of good wine!'"

Mocking my brother was one thing. Mocking the Lord was another. During the Days of Awe, this man, my husband-to-be, would have to intercede with the Lord for the sins of all Judea. "How long," said Shimon, "does Yannai think the other priests and the people of Judea will stand for this?"

Chapter 5

Panic washed over me. The night before the wedding, like every other Jewish bride, I had gone to purify myself in the *mikvah*. Step by step I lowered my body into the intimate confines of the pool. I felt a rush of gratitude for this soothing private place. With sudden sharpness, I remembered my father's face: wrinkled, wise, kind. And my mother: stern but reassuring. Neither had lived to see me wed. Neither could help or advise me now. I burst into tears. Was I preparing, for the second time in my life, to marry someone who hated me? The *mikvah* attendant, a portly grayhaired woman, saw the tears and called out, "Your Highness! Are you hurt? Did you stub your toe?"

I ducked my head under the surface and let my emotions pour into the water as if I poured myself into the hands of the Lord. Embraced by the comfort of the waters, I allowed myself to trust that the Lord would guide me.

* * *

"I do not want bloodstains on my wedding gown," I told Miri. Before she helped me put on the gown, she gloved my gnawed fingers.

I peered at my rippled image in the copper mirror. The creamy silk of the gown was lovely. But I was discouraged by what I saw. "I am fifteen years older than Yannai," I said. "I am too tall for a woman, and too weedy. I have a nose like an eagle's beak and I intrude it where it is not wanted. The man I am about to marry thinks I am an old woman."

"That man cannot recognize beauty in anything but horses," said Miri. "You are not weedy; you are regal, like an oak. You are proud, like an eagle. Our people love you. You could walk into the room dressed in sackcloth and everyone would know you were a queen. Why do you want to marry Alexander Janneus? Stable-hands say he is the foulest mouth in the barn."

"He is next in line for the throne," I said. "If the Lord blesses me to conceive in the first few months, I will not have anything further to do with Yannai."

Not true. If Yannai wanted to lie with me, I would open my body like a lily's mouth.

* * *

Head crowned with a virgin's wreath, I sailed on the shoulders of my porters toward the dais and its canopy of pink and white almond blossoms. Chains of fragrant wild roses twined my carrying chair. Caught up in the pageantry of the moment, my heart soared. I imagined Yannai looking tenderly into my eyes. What a hopeful, pitiful fool I was at that moment!

The square in front of the Temple Mount brimmed with men and women craning their necks to see the raised wedding platform. More faces peered from the alleys. His captains led Yannai to the dais. The setting sun blazed on their armor. Young boys, perched on their fathers' shoulders, squinted and shielded their eyes. Women held up the babies in their arms. Maidens in white gowns carpeted Yannai's path with pink and white almond blossoms. Their skirts flared, glowing in the slanting sun like golden chrysanthemums.

Yannai leered at the young women. Some smiled back. They probably thought they had more to gain by flattering a young king than they risked by offending an old queen. Yannai wrinkled his nose at me as if I were an over-ripe fig. Under the arch of saplings, Shimon at my side, I trembled. I was not petite, pretty and plump like these girls. I was tall, flat-chested. My nose was too big. Why would a handsome twenty-two-year-old man like Yannai want to bed a thirty-seven-year-old woman?

I shook off the thought. I can stand as proudly as an oak, I told myself. I held my head high. I wished my father were there, to tell me I was doing the right thing.

"Repeat after me," said Shimon.

"Repeat after me," said Yannai.

Shimon scowled. "You are consecrated to me," he said.

Yannai was silent. "Repeat after me," said Shimon. "You are consecrated to me."

"You are concubined to me," said Yannai. Red mounted in Shimon's face. I could feel the scarlet of my own.

"Consecrated!" said Shimon. "According to the Laws of Moses and Israel."

Yannai pressed his lips together. *How could Yannai be so hateful to me in front of my brother?* I thought. *How will he behave when we're alone?* I thanked the Lord for the raised wedding dais. I prayed that none of the thousands gazing up at us could hear.

"This ceremony will not go forward if you do not say these words," hissed Shimon. "Exactly as I say them."

"Consecrated," barked Yannai. "According-to-the-laws-of-Moses-and-Israel."

"Remove the veil," said Shimon. As Yannai turned back the veil, I forced a facsimile of a proud, gracious smile. Shimon handed Yannai a marble chalice filled with wine. Yannai drained the cup and burped. He offered me the dregs. I pretended to swallow. If there had been any wine in the chalice, I would have choked on it. How could I bear to have a second husband who loathed me? *You must marry Yannai*, I told myself, *or you cannot continue to govern.*

The Temple altar blazed with thanksgiving offerings, peace-offerings, offerings of purification. The air shimmered with the smoke of roasted ox.

Flames danced from the torches surrounding the square. Musicians danced with their own shadows, piping and strumming as they strutted through the crowds. Flower-strewn linen-wrapped tables sagged under silver platters of carved meats. Jugs of wine and oil, and bowls of roasted grains passed from hand to hand. Servants lofted golden trays of grapes, figs, pomegranates and honey-drenched almond pastries.

My head ached.

Midway through the public banquet came a lively chanting of the story of Queen Esther, the Jewish wife of the king of Persia. Esther had saved the Jews of Persia from extermination by the wicked Prince Haman. The story cheered me. Esther's husband was a drunken fool and a womanizer. Yet she was able to act on behalf of her people.

A blare of trumpets. Yannai and I sat side by side in golden thrones nearly buried in flowers. Two tall men in gold-trimmed uniforms strode toward the dais. I held myself erect. The chief steward announced, "To give honor to His Royal Highness King

Alexander Janneus and Her Majesty Queen Salome Alexandra, may we introduce Ananias and Chelcias, generals in the army of Queen Cleopatra III of Egypt. They represent the Jewish community of Alexandria."

Both generals looked more like Greeks than like Jews. General Ananias had a trim gray beard, but no side-curls. His gray hair was cropped as closely as a new-shorn sheep. He unrolled a papyrus scroll. "In celebration of the coronation of King Alexander Janneus and his wedding to Queen Salome Alexandra of Judea, we are honored to present a gift to the Holy Temple from the Jewish community of Alexandria."

A courtier in red silk wheeled forward a cart. He lifted a blue embroidered cloth to reveal a huge golden pitcher and bowl.

General Chelcias stepped forward. He was younger than Ananias, dark-haired, clean-shaven in the Greek style. "We hope you will use the pitcher and bowl in the ceremony of the water-drawing during the harvest holiday," said General Chelcias. "We present them with prayers that you will have a marriage blessed with sons, and a long, peaceful reign, fruitful for all Judea. Though Egypt is our home, Judea is our homeland. We will support you in any way we can."

"Yannai may detest me," I thought, "but Jewish people all over the world recognize me as their queen."

The Jewish community of Rome presented goblets of beautiful blue-green glass. The Jews of Antioch in Syria presented an amphora of the precious purple dye used for royal garments. The Jews of Baghdad presented tapestries; those of Susa, intricately woven red and blue rugs to warm the cold stone floors of the Audience Chamber. How delightful to see the black and white crowds of Jerusalem spiced with the reds, blues and yellows worn by Jews from distant places!

A few neighboring peoples took notice: Aretas, king of the Arabians, sent balm and perfumes from Gilead; the Phoenicians of Tyre sent a fine cedar chest.

I loved the humble gifts from the villages and towns of Judea. Honey from the mountain roses of Carmel. Figs and dates from the oasis at Jericho. Pale golden first-pressed olive oil from Bethlehem. Blush wine from the vineyards of Asochis in Galilee. The vintner who presented the cask was so proud that his round cheeks, circled by a cloud of soft gray hair and beard, were a brighter pink than the wine. "I hope you will come to our beautiful mountains to drink the wine and breathe the clear air with us," he said rapidly. It sounded as if he had rehearsed this line for a week.

I did visit Asochis in little more than a year. By that time the vineyards were ash.

I was especially touched by the gift of two soft wool blankets from the shepherds of my home town, Modi'in. A small boy and an even smaller girl stepped up to give the blankets to Yannai and me. "We know it gets cold here in Jerusalem," said the little girl.

"Our goats have the softest, warmest hair in Judea," said the boy.

"But you have to be careful when you shear 'em," said the girl. "They bite."

Flutes piped, tambourines jangled, revelers danced. The people of Jerusalem would celebrate all night, while stars glittered on the battlements.

Yannai and I entered the palace for the private banquet with invited guests. The gardeners and the head housekeeper had done a lovely job. The inner courtyard was festooned with looping vines, the white table linens adorned with wild roses and pomegranates.

I sat at the head of the women's table, between the wives of Chelcias and Ananias. Both were dressed in different patterns of red and blue silk, with bright silk head scarves. "Contributions from the Alexandrian community do much to sustain the Temple," I said. "We are grateful for your support."

"Your Majesty," sighed Beatrice, wife of Ananias, "we do what we can, when we can. Now that Cleopatra III is in control, we are doing well. She trusts us to handle her business. We did less well under her late husband, Ptolemy VIII. We called him 'Physcon' – bellows – because he was so fat that he wheezed when he talked. Whenever he sensed that Alexandrians were getting sick of his excesses (which were too many and too vile to describe to Your Highness), Physcon would hire thugs to organize riots against the Jews. That would distract the people for awhile. Today we send you money; tomorrow we may ask you for refuge."

I liked Beatrice immediately. Though perhaps a decade older, she was as tall and angular as I was. She too understood that nothing lasts.

Yannai sat at the head of the men's table, between the two Egyptian generals. I hoped they would find common ground talking about war and strategy. Instead, Yannai guzzled wine and brandy like a camel at the trough. His voice got louder and his tone more contentious. The two Alexandrian wives darted glances toward Yannai.

Maybe when Yannai and I are alone, I thought, *the drink will work in my favor.* I had heard that among soldiers, drink often fanned lust. I darted seductive smiles at Yannai, hoping to arouse the glint of desire I'd seen in his eyes when we first met.

I played hostess and queen for as long as I could bear it. Finally I excused myself, pleading illness. Clutching a spray of almond

blossoms in my fist, I walked to our wedding chamber to wait for
Yannai. "My Lady, where is that idiot?" fumed Miri. "He should
be undressing you, not me."

For hours, I paced, gnawing my knuckles and hissing through
clenched teeth. I lay in bed and watched the flapping of drapes and
the flicker of lamplight on the ceiling. Yudi had refused to enter
our marriage chamber. Would my second husband humiliate me
in the same way?

The longing of my body was like a hot wind. My anger and
disappointment could have scalded my new husband. I pawed
the silk sheets into lumps, twisted the corners into ropes. Yannai
finally stumbled in – though not until dawn had sucked darkness
from the sky. He flung open the door, groped his way to bed, and
flopped his weight on top of me. He nearly suffocated me with
the alcohol on his breath. He humped and bumped against me,
blindly, swearing. I had not known what to expect, but certainly
not this. I felt limp and helpless. He picked me up and flung me
to one side, then the other. I scrambled from the bed. I cowered
in a corner of the room. Finally he pinned me, face down, on the
bed. He lifted my buttocks toward him, and, like the animal he
was, entered my womb from behind. I had seen a ram mount ewes
that way when I was a little girl in Modi'in. It hurt so much that I
screamed. He banged away until there was enough blood to satisfy
the most skeptical of the priests inspecting the sheets the next day.

Yannai then vomited over the unbloodied remainder of the
sheets. He wiped his mouth, flopped his head on the mess, and
began snoring loudly. He was sprawled across the bed. There was
no room for me even if I'd had the stomach to stay.

I threw the withered almond blossoms against the wall,
staggered to my old bedroom and wept. I was ashamed. No one,

not even Miri, must know how I had been treated on my wedding night. I wished I could return to the *mikvah* that very moment to wash off the shame. But I had bled. I would have to wait until the end of what would turn out to be a long, long week.

The next afternoon, Yannai shambled into my chamber. I lay with curtains drawn and a cool compress on my forehead. "You really were a virgin, holy Lady," he said. "I did not give you the pleasure a virgin deserves. But tonight ..."

He knelt and kissed my hand. I jerked my hand away from his, as one does when pricked by a thorn. Cautiously I returned my hand to his as one does when reaching for the blossom. Perhaps he was really sorry. Perhaps the next time would be better. I had to find a way to live with this man, or I could not remain queen.

"I am sorry, Yannai," I said. "Because I bled, the Law requires us to remain apart for seven days. You are not even supposed to touch my hand. We will have seven days of feasts to distract you. Maybe after that we can go away by ourselves somewhere."

Yannai's eyebrows knitted together just as they had before every tantrum when he was a child. "Stupid laws," he growled, and stalked out.

Seven nights of wedding feasts multiplied the disaster. Yannai fondled the female servants. He called the oldest man in the Sanhedrin a "used-up she-goat." His favorite soldiers matched him drink for drink. The palace stank of their vomit. "My Lady, get rid of this brute," whispered Miri as she helped me undress at night. "Go into his room while he's passed out and sit on his face."

I shrugged my shoulders and shook my head. Sadness carved a tree of pain between my eyes. Every morning I forced myself awake at dawn, stifled my humiliation, and supervised servants cleaning up broken glasses, wine stains and urine-soaked carpets before the next night's festivities. Every afternoon, I knelt in the palace courtyard beside the ancient leather-faced head gardener, replacing the lavender, rosemary, and dill that had been trampled by the drunken revels of my husband's soldiers. I breathed in the spicy fragrance of the leaves and tried to let the sun bake the bitterness from my body. Each night, while Yannai slept off his drunk, I lay awake for hours in my old bedroom, singing psalms that were mostly sobs. I wondered what my pious father would think now of the cherished daughter he had betrothed to the son of the high priest of Judea.

CHAPTER 6

When the seven days of feasts ended, Yannai demanded that I keep my promise to go away with him. He wanted to show me the fort in Galilee where he grew up. I ask myself now why I agreed to go. The truth is that my handsome husband had awakened my desire. I wanted a real wedding night. Yannai had been sweet and gentle when he apologized. I told myself that the gentle young man, not the monster, was the real Yannai. And I was afraid of what would happen if I said no.

I directed the packing of the four-horse chariot. "As long as I keep him away from strong drink, we should be all right," I told Miri.

She shoved a woven bag full of blankets, dried meats and dried fruits into the luggage space behind the seat. "You think so, My Lady?" she said, with a lift of her eloquent eyebrows.

I wished I could bring Miri. And my guard. If Yannai turned on me, who would defend me? But I had promised that for once, my new husband and I would be alone.

Our carriage clattered over the barren hills. I chewed on my half-healed fingertips, wondering how I would survive this week. Yannai snored.

At the top of a rocky rise, we came to Zippori, a stone fort with a tall octagonal tower. In spite of my worry about being alone with Yannai, I thrilled when he lifted me out of the carriage. While the driver unloaded our supplies at the cottage below, we climbed to the top of the tower. Yannai's former messmates stood at attention and saluted at each turn of the granite stairs. Yannai blushed with pleasure. "Did you see?" he whispered when we got to the top. "All those bastards saluting me. Me, the brat that got kicked out of Jerusalem when he was four years old."

"It makes you feel good to have them show you such respect," I said.

"Damn right. The sergeant was the only one who knew I was the son of the high priest. He warned me that he was supposed to treat me like every other soldier. I was the lowest of the low."

He spat onto the stone floor. "The jokers put lizards in my bedroll and toads under my mess bowl and scorpions in my boots. When anyone was in a bad mood, I got kicked."

"Now you are king," I said.

He grinned. "These fellows are going to drill till their feet fall off. We are going to be invincible. The best army this sorry little kingdom has ever had."

I was as charmed by his bravado as when he was a strutting four-year-old.

We gazed from the top of the watch-tower at rocks and dead bushes.

"I knew that Jerusalem was somewhere past that hill," Yannai said. "I pictured my two older brothers sucking ripe figs while I chewed dry rations."

I had lost my home in the village of Modi'in as suddenly and irrevocably as Yannai had lost his home in Jerusalem. We were two hurt children. Yannai's pain touched my heart. I put my hand on his.

"My mother didn't want me and my father didn't want me," said Yannai. "I never knew why."

I knew why, of course. Yannai had been unmanageable: throwing crockery, punching his nurse-maids, threatening to kill his big brother Yudi. But what four-year-old stops to think when he's angry? I was nineteen when Yannai was sent away. I could not understand – I still cannot understand – High Priest John Hyrcanus sending his four-year-old son into exile. I think he was really getting rid of Judith, his shrew of a wife. I have always blamed Judith for what Yannai became. But now that my own sons are grown, I understand better how difficult it is to raise a son who will become a king.

* * *

Zippori was named for birds. I looked for birds in the pale sky above the fort. I saw only hawks and vultures, wings spread, rising on columns of hot air.

"Wait till you see the waterfall," said Yannai.

He led me toward a house at the bottom of the hill: white-washed stone, nested in green bushes and vines. The tang of balsam tickled my nose. A spring gurgled. Birds whistled, chattered, squawked. "My mother traveled a lot and left servants to take care of my two younger brothers," said Yannai. "I would run down here, splash around, and explore the caves. If my brothers came out, I would say, 'You had better not tell your mother I was here, or next time she goes on a trip, I will kill you.'"

"Your mother would not let you live in her house?" I repeated.

"She brought me to the fort, made a nasty face and said, 'You are going to live here from now on.'"

He spread his tunic on a rock, leaving his chest bare. We sat there, dabbling feet in the water. "I bawled for two days after she left, but I learned pretty quickly that crying or tantrums landed you in the hole with nothing but hard bread and water."

"How terrible!"

He sighed and shrugged. "I asked her why I rotted in the fort while my brothers lived with her. She said she wanted the soldiers to tame me."

"How were they to tame you?"

His lips curved in a tentative smile. "Cleanups. Drills. Sleeping on the ground."

He threw a pebble into the pool. "If I disobeyed orders I was flogged."

I winced. "They flogged a four-year-old?"

He grinned and threw another pebble. "It made me tough. I plan to do the same to my own sons."

"You want to treat your sons as badly as you were treated?"

He stretched those bare muscular arms and chuckled. "It was a great education. Men who fight for a living come from everywhere. Greek, Arabic, Parthian: I can curse or threaten or give orders in almost any language."

Yannai held my hand as we clambered barefoot over moss-covered rocks. I slipped. I strangled on water and clawed frantically at the bottom. Two strong arms scooped me up. As I sucked in air, I remembered my father's arms in Modi'in, pulling me onto his horse and carrying me to safety in Jerusalem.

"Good!" shouted Yannai. "You got your head wet! Now do it again. Take a breath, go under, and look around."

I did. I saw an enchanted world of reed stems, wavering water plants, tiny silver fish, fuzzy green rocks, all punctuated by the bubbles of my own breath. I had been a child of the barren hills. I emerged feeling like a glistening creature of the water. "Teach me to swim," I demanded.

"You are halfway there," said Yannai. "Just put your face in the water, take a look around, and shove your feet against the rocks. Like this."

Following in his wake, I shot across the water and into his arms.

That night, we slept in Judith's house. Opening the front door, Yannai shouted to the sky, "Bitch! Try to keep me out of your house now!"

I grinned at him like a co-conspirator. Judith had made my life miserable, too, when I was a girl. Yannai and I would take our revenge together.

The house, with its white-washed walls, dark carved furniture, and silk couches, was much cooler than the dusty hilltop fort. The driver had unpacked our belongings and supplies in the servants' quarters which, along with an outdoor kitchen, occupied a lean-to at the rear. Yannai led me to his mother's couch, pulled me toward him, kissed my neck. I must have stiffened, afraid of what would come next. Yannai gently stroked my hair, my arms, my breasts. "You do not need to worry," he said. "This time will be much nicer."

This time was exquisite. Softly, slowly, Yannai introduced me to parts of my body I didn't know I had. I stretched lazily and smiled, enjoying the slick of sweat kissing my skin and the delicious sensations buzzing through my body. *Thank You, Lord,* I whispered – too quietly for my husband's ears.

Yannai sprang up and sat on the edge of the bed. "I told the boys down at the barracks that I could make the old queen bee drip honey!" he shouted.

Yannai laughed so hard he had to wipe tears from his eyes.

"How could you talk about me that way in front of a barracks full of rough men?" I demanded.

A minute or so later Yannai was chuckling to himself again.

"Now what is so funny?" I said.

"I just realized that by sticking it to you, I stuck it to the whole damn family. My mother. My father. My two big brothers. They are dead and buried. I am in bed with you. As for your brother, that stuffy snob who thinks he is purer than all the rest of us: he hates me, but he had to make me king. I nailed his sister's precious virginity."

I pulled on my robe and stalked out the door. I would not let him see me cry.

Yannai ran after me. "Shuli! I am sorry!" he said, leaping in front of me and raising his arms to heaven. "I swear to all the gods I did not mean to hurt your feelings. It's just the dumb soldier in me that has to brag."

He folded me in his arms and said, "Let me make it up to you. Us men are like arrows – one shot, we are done. You are like the bow. I can keep you quivering for hours."

He took my hand and led me back to bed.

Afterward, he kissed the sweat from between my breasts, and said, "You are a bonfire in bed, Lady Queen. I don't understand how my brother could have been married to you for twelve years and never touched you."

"We were betrothed as children. Yudi disliked me and put off the marriage as long as he could."

"But not even once – just to try you out?"

I chuckled at the notion of "trying out" a wife.

"Yudi seemed to have no desire for any woman," I said.

"Strange," mumbled Yannai. He pillowed his head on my chest and fell asleep. When he awoke, he burrowed his head in my lap and said, "Hold me, Holy Mama."

My heart filled with such tenderness that tears flowed. Yannai brushed them gently away. He kissed the spot on each cheek where they had been.

The next morning, when I woke, Yannai was sitting naked on the floor, bathed in morning sunshine. He was sharpening his sword and polishing his armor. He sang to himself a song in Parthian. I asked him to translate it. He blushed when he did so. I felt such compassion for my husband. The army had been his only world, the closest thing he had to a home. When feeling happy and comfortable, he did things that reminded him of the best parts of his childhood: polishing his armor and singing bawdy songs.

When he climbed back into bed, I ran my finger along the web of scars punctuating his flesh. "How did you get all these scars?" I asked.

He pointed to a jagged line of raised purple flesh from his shoulder to his groin. "This one I got at Scythopolis, when I was ten. The idiot could not make up his mind whether to go for my heart or my belly, so he missed both. I went for his belly."

"You were fighting when you were ten years old?"

"It was the only way to get respect."

"How did you feel about fighting after getting such a terrible wound?"

"Unbeatable. I've got leather skin and a thick head. As soon as I could stand up again, I practiced my moves until I was the best swordsman in the unit. The best with a javelin. And I could stick on a horse like glue."

I gave him a little smile.

"You think I am bragging?" he said.

"Of course," I said. "You deserve to brag."

* * *

In the afternoon, we scrambled through the bushes near the spring, finding sweet berries. Yannai lifted me onto a sturdy vine and set me swinging. Catching me, kissing me, letting me go again. I realized: never before had anyone behaved tenderly toward Yannai. And never before had someone treated me like a desirable woman. When Yannai touched me – my neck, my cheek, anywhere – my body woke up, as if a butterfly brushed my bare skin.

We paddled again in the pool. Yannai taught me to pull the water toward me as if I were gathering sheaves of wheat. Afterward, we lay on a rock, drying in the sun and caressing one another. "You must be a cousin to the fish," said Yannai. "You wiggle so well."

* * *

The charioteer had left two of the four horses for our use. Yannai cared for them so lovingly: walking to cool them off, wiping their flanks, letting them drink from the stream, talking to them all the while. I was touched. I hoped this meant he would be a good father to our children.

The second afternoon, we rode among the hills. This was the healing I needed: cantering cross-country under a clear and endless sky. The first time I had ridden a horse was the night Father, Shimon and I fled from our little village of Modi'in to Jerusalem. At six, I was almost more thrilled than scared to be thundering across the midnight land, rocking high above the earth, with wind whipping my hair into a banner. I had loved riding ever since.

The dry bushes of Zippori, the little valleys, the outcroppings of stone, reminded me of my childhood in Modi'in. Starlike yellow flowers spangled the moss clinging to clefts in the rock. I recognized the blue flowers of the tough little chicory plant and dug some up to plant in my herb garden in Jerusalem.

A gash in a rock opened into a cave. "We should explore this cave!" I said.

We hobbled the horses by some tall grass and crept into a rocky blackness tucked between boulders. Yannai felt his way first, holding my hand. I was as curious and excited as the six-year-old I had once been. With no strong drink to arouse the demon in him, Yannai was a perfect playmate.

* * *

Yannai pulled at his mustache, scratched his nose, stamped his feet. It was too bad, I thought, that Yannai had to face a social evening among the Sadducee elite before we had a chance to settle back in Jerusalem. And too bad that I had to spend an evening smiling at my enemies when all I wanted was to climb into bed with Yannai.

A servant opened the carved wood-and-bronze door to the home of Diogenes, Judea's ambassador to Rome. Wearing a brocaded toga laced with gold, Diogenes left me at the door and swept Yannai into the room. There were vaulted ceilings and paneled gold-framed walls inset with mosaics of flowers and leaves. More expensive than the cedar walls of the Audience Chamber in the palace. Before I could stop him, Diogenes offered Yannai an engraved golden goblet. "Welcome, King Alexander. I have been saving my best Roman wine for your return. Is it not excellent?"

I wanted to knock the goblet out of Yannai's hand. He took a big gulp and wiped his mouth with his hand. He belched. Now the troubles will start again, I thought.

Diogenes escorted Yannai to the head of a long table. Servants led me to a table populated by wives wearing Greek chitons. Bare arms. Belts underlining the breasts. Even though they'd grown up in Judea, these women seemed unaware that they were violating Judean standards of modesty. Why was I surprised? These were wives of Sadducees. I said, "We are gratified that you honor our marriage in this lovely home."

The silk-clad merchant-priest Phiabi swished forward, reeking of perfume. "Esteemed King Alexander, we have a wedding present for you. A sword of the finest steel – imported from India."

Phiabi's servant presented the sword to Yannai on a silk pillow. Yannai grabbed it. He sliced the air so fiercely the metal whistled.

"And, Your Highness, we would like to present you with a suit of the best bronze armor," said black-browed Hanin. Thanks to his connection to Judith, Hanin had acquired the monopoly on sacred oil for the Temple. He could afford to buy the gaudiest and best of everything. Servants displayed the gleaming, clanking metal.

The barrel-bellied priest Boethus waddled forward in his embroidered gown, purring, "King Alexander, please let me adjust your pillows."

Yannai grimaced. "I am not much of a pillow-sitter," he said.

"King Alexander, I am sure you would rather be in the saddle," said Hanin. "You are the finest horseman I have ever seen."

Yannai smiled. "You like to ride?"

"Your Majesty, Hanin would rather bet on the chariot races in

Syria," said Phiabi. "But now that we have a warrior king, I can think of better uses for chariots."

A servant set before Yannai a silver platter of roasted lamb, encircled by a diadem of grapes and pomegranates. The meat oozed juices. Yannai speared a slice of lamb and tore into it.

"Your Highness, we have all heard about your talent as a soldier," said Diogenes. "We are happy to have you as our general."

"I've been in some pretty good fights," said Yannai, his mouth full of lamb.

"Akko!" shouted Phiabi, waving his knife enthusiastically. "That is the place we should go after! The Phoenicians are completely focused on the sea. They do not know how to fight a land battle. Attack them from the rear, and in a few weeks, we will control the city. Great place for trade. Great place for import and export duties. And a gorgeous harbor. Build a palace on those hills and you could see almost all the way to Rome."

"The Sanhedrin has to approve any plans for war," I objected.

"King Alexander," said Diogenes, "let us retire to my study, so that we can talk strategy without distressing the women."

Miri caught my eye and wrinkled her nose as if she had tasted vinegared wine. My enemies knew that even the queen cannot follow when men go off by themselves. I pasted on a smile while the conversation of the women flapped against my ears like the senseless fluttering of pigeon's wings.

For all his courtly manners, I thought, Diogenes had been a general before he was an ambassador. And from what I had heard, a ruthless and relentless one, slicing off the heads of soldiers who did not leap to follow his orders. Diogenes was from the high-priestly line. Ambitious enough to have planned the deaths of Matti and Yudi. Devious enough to spread a rumor blaming me. But too intelligent to let his hand show. He would let other Sadducees do his work for him.

"This should amuse you," said Yannai on our way back to the palace. "The fat fellow in the fancy shirt wanted to make me a trade."

"Boethus?"

"That is the one. He accuses you of murdering my two older brothers. He said if I would hang you, he would give me his daughter Martha and a whole lot of land and money besides."

My stomach clenched. "You refused his offer?" I said.

"I have seen his daughter," said Yannai. "Looks just like him."

"What did you tell him?"

"I told him it takes a real bitch to murder two men. That's the kind of bitch who can keep him at bay while I am laying siege to Akko."

"Thanks for the compliment," I said.

The word siege was enough to give me nightmares. The Syrian siege of Jerusalem had robbed me of my father when I was not yet seven. The siege of Akko would snatch my husband away in the first delicate months of marriage.

I would not let the Sadducees take Yannai from me. Diogenes had seduced my first husband Yudi to the Sadducee side with all-male banquets featuring fine wines, lute music, soft cushioned couches and long philosophical discussions. Now he was seducing Yannai with soldiery, urging my new husband back to the one arena where he felt confident. I tried my own seduction. I touched him gently and whispered, "How can you go off to war so soon? Our marriage is still in its infancy."

Yannai had drunk just enough to be affable, not mean.

"You show me that you got an infant in there," he said, patting my belly, "and I will come back to meet him."

Two weeks ago, I thought, I wondered how I could rule Judea

without Yannai getting in the way. I have changed my mind. I want him near me. He cannot wait to get away.

"Yannai, many members of the Sanhedrin will be involved in this siege," I said. "It is time to bring back the Pharisee members so there will be a quorum while the military officers are gone."

"You think you should balance out the greed with a little purity, Holy Lady?" teased Yannai. "If that is what you want – anything for my wife the queen."

* * *

Arguments echoed from the massive walls of the Chamber of Hewn Stone. With the return of the Pharisees, the Sanhedrin was almost evenly split. Pharisees and Sadducees glared at each other from the curved benches on either side of the throne. "We will never amount to anything if we do not have a harbor for trade," shouted the merchant-priest Phiabi from the Sadducee side.

Judah son of Tabbai, the vice-president of the Sanhedrin, leaped to his feet on the Pharisee side. "We are a nation of farmers, not soldiers," he said. "And when we are not farming, we should be studying the Law of the Lord."

They went on for hours, one speaker after another standing and shouting. I thought of my father. He never raised his voice, but all the Sanhedrin hushed when he spoke. After the carnage of the Maccabee wars, Father always insisted Jews should never go to war except in self-defense. *If he were here*, I thought, *no one would vote for war.*

Yannai, seated on the throne in their midst, did not bother to look at whoever was talking. He signaled his boredom with the whole discussion. He rolled his eyes, tapped his fingers, stood up to scratch his behind. Finally there was a vote. Pharisees held a slim majority. The vote was against war. I hid a triumphant smile behind my veil.

Yannai stood. "We march for Akko in a month," he announced. He walked out.

My brother Shimon caught up with Yannai at the gate of the Temple Mount. "You cannot do this!" said Shimon. "Only the Sanhedrin can declare war."

"I am glad you enjoyed your discussion," Yannai responded. "But I told you before: I have made a decision. The military officers are with me. The nobles are with me. If half the Sanhedrin, or even all the Sanhedrin, disagrees, I do not care."

Yannai strode toward the stables. "Stop him!" Shimon demanded.

"How?" I said. "He has the army on his side."

I went to my herb garden to cut some chicory leaves for Hannah the cook. "Very good for the digestion, My Lady," said Miri.

"I know," I replied. "My mother used to feed it to the goats to drive out worms."

CHAPTER 7

Leering over the main city gate the next morning was a head impaled on a stake. Miri dragged me out to see. My stomach churned. I recognized the head. It was Yannai's youngest brother Adonijah. I ran back to Yannai's chamber, demanding to know what had happened.

"I got interesting news the other night," he said. "While we were in Zippori, my little brother decided to put his fat rump on the throne. He tried to recruit Ambassador Diogenes and some of the officers of the Jerusalem guard, but they refused. Diogenes thought I should dispose of him before we leave for Akko."

I had freed the two younger brothers from prison when I freed Yannai. I had arranged marriages for them, and they had become part of the priesthood. If Yannai could so casually behead his brother, what would he do if I displeased him?

"What about your other brother?" I asked Yannai.

"Absalom? He wanted no part of this mischief. I told him to take his wife and move to our mother's house in Zippori. I will not kill him unless I see him back in Jerusalem."

Alone in my sitting room, I tried to calm myself with embroidery. I pricked my fingers and tangled the threads. "I am sick," I told Miri. "How could he be so brutal to his own brother?"

"My Lady," said Miri, "the man is an animal."

"What frightens me," I said, "is that Yannai followed Ambassador Diogenes' advice without question. Yannai laughed when that barrel-belly Boethus suggested hanging me. But what will happen when Diogenes accuses me of being involved in some conspiracy? Do you think Yannai will listen?"

"Your Highness, he might," said Miri. "I haven't seen any evidence that he can think for himself."

* * *

I hated to see Yannai leave for Akko, but I did not have time to brood. "I have to prove that the Sadducees killed Yudi," I told Miri. "Or they will invent proof that I did."

"My Lady," said Miri, "tell me what you want me to do."

"Go to the midwife who lives near the Dung Gate. She knows about herbs. And poisons. Find out what herb she recommends for poisoning rats. Then ask if anyone has bought some recently."

I waited on the blue couch, ripping out errant stitches in my embroidery. I had produced enough mistakes to busy myself until Miri got back.

"Your Highness, the midwife recommended three herbs," said Miri when the blue drape had swung closed behind her. "A serving maid came by a few weeks ago to buy one of them – golden-tufted fennel. The midwife told me to dissolve poison fennel in wine, then soak grain in it. The rats eat the grain and crawl away to die."

"Whose maid bought the poison?" I asked.

"My Lady," said Miri, "the midwife did not remember."

Golden-tufted fennel. The name sounded familiar, but I could not remember where I had heard it before.

* * *

I summoned Jason, the man who had been Yudi's valet, to my sitting room. Still dressed in the short Greek-style tunic he had worn when his master was alive, he stood at attention.

"Who visited King Aristobulus on the day he died?" I asked.

The valet looked startled. He blinked rapidly. "Your Highness, Phiabi the Priest came to offer condolences."

"What happened while he was there?"

"Your Highness, I do not know. The priest Phiabi told me the king was very upset, and wanted to talk to him alone. So I stayed away until he left."

"Did Phiabi bring anything with him?"

"Only a skin of wine, Your Highness."

A window opened in my mind. Golden-tufted fennel. "Yudi died spitting blood," I told Miri after the valet had gone. "In Modi'in, when I was about five, one of our goats died spitting blood. My mother showed me a plant with blossoms shaped like tufted golden balls. 'This giant fennel killed our goat,' Mama said. 'It is poison. You must never touch it and you must never let any of our goats eat it.'"

"You think Phiabi poisoned your husband's wine?" said Miri.

"No, I think Ambassador Diogenes, the master of fine wines, concocted the poison. With golden-tufted fennel. But he is too crafty to let his hand show. He probably sent Phiabi to pour the drink."

I anchored my needle in the fabric and stood. "Go to Diogenes' house," I told Miri. "Ask the kitchen-maid if you can borrow something to kill rats."

I dipped the pillowcase I was embroidering into a bowl of

water and scrubbed at a bloodstain. I had pricked myself with my clumsy needle. When Miri got back I still had not succeeded in removing the stain.

Miri held her hand behind her back. "Your Highness," she said, "guess what I have."

"Let me see," I demanded.

She held out a small skin bag. I peered in and held my breath.

"Golden-tufted fennel," I said. "I hope you did not breathe in the dust. Wash your hands. This is a very dangerous herb. Run and get Shimon."

* * *

"Come sit with me," I told Shimon, gesturing to the vacant chair at my worktable. "I have found out," I said, "that the priest Phiabi visited Yudi just before Yudi died. This is the proof we need that the Sadducees were responsible for these deaths."

"Proof?" said Shimon. "I visited you that same day, and you are not dead."

"How did Phiabi know about Matti's death before the announcement at the Temple?"

"Phiabi probably has informants in the palace," said Shimon. "That does not make him guilty of murder."

"Phiabi brought Yudi a skin of wine. Every time Yudi went to a banquet at the home of Phiabi or Diogenes, they made a show of serving him fine wines. Yudi was poisoned. Phiabi had the opportunity to do it."

"Jason, the king's valet, thought King Aristobulus had poisoned himself," said Shimon. "Did anyone see Phiabi put poison in wine and serve it to King Aristobulus?"

"Of course not. I think Ambassador Diogenes poisoned the

wine and gave it to Phiabi."

"That is a very serious accusation," said Shimon, pulling at his side-curl. "I hope you are not making it without proof."

"Not definite proof," I said. "But I have learned that Diogenes keeps golden-tufted fennel in his house to poison rats. Golden-tufted fennel causes the victim to vomit blood, as Yudi did before he died."

"You call that proof?" said Shimon, standing up.

I raised my eyebrows. He sat down again. "When Yannai and I got back from Zippori," I said, "we were invited to a banquet at the ambassador's home. While we were there, Phiabi gave Yannai a sword. Hanin gave Yannai a set of bronze armor. Both were identical to the armor and sword Matti was wearing when he was killed."

Shimon raised his shaggy gray brows and sighed. "When two healthy young men die, there are bound to be rumors and suspicions. You told me you would find proof. What you have told me doesn't come close to proof."

"No, it is not proof. But it is enough to raise questions."

"What do you expect me to do?"

"Start an investigation," I said. "Question them. Question the servants. The people of Judea need to know if they lost their king and general to a Sadducee plot."

"What motive could the Sadducees have for poisoning the king?" said Shimon.

"Conquest. Plunder. Trade. They cannot find enough to rob in poor little Judea. They were disappointed with Yudi because he could not command troops. He was too squeamish. The Sadducees fawned on Matti for months, trying to persuade him to supplant his brother."

"Then why would they trap General Antigonus?" said Shimon.

"Because he refused," I said. "He was too loyal to his brother."

"Why would they want to put Yannai on the throne?"

"He is a talented general," I said, "if nothing else. And he is young. They may have thought they could control him. They had not gotten to know him yet."

I wanted to jerk my brother's gray side-curls as I would the reins of a stubborn donkey. "We have to find out," I said. "If the Sadducees were willing to kill Matti and Yudi, they would be perfectly happy to kill you and me."

"Your marriage has made you light-headed," Shimon said, "and hatred of your enemies has made you reckless. Do not make a fool of yourself talking about murder and treason or you will find yourself accused on equally flimsy evidence. After all, who was closer to King Aristobulus than you?"

* * *

"I told you no good would come of this digging about for evidence," said Shimon.

"What do you mean?" I said.

"Hanin and Phiabi have come to the Court of Twenty-three to charge you with the murder of General Antigonus and King Judah Aristobulus."

I caught my breath. "On what do they base these charges?"

"They say that Jason, valet to King Aristobulus, will serve as witness."

"To what?"

"He will say that you urged General Antigonus to show the king his new bronze armor and steel sword. You said Antigonus was exempt from the ban against weapons."

"Miri goes everywhere with me. She could refute Jason's testimony – if women were allowed to serve as witnesses."

"Jason will also say," Shimon continued, "that you were the only person with King Aristobulus at the moment of his death."

"What did you tell those liars?" I demanded.

"I said that I could not vote on whether to hear the case since you were my sister. But I reminded the other members of the court that they are required to hear capital cases only if there are two witnesses to the actual crime."

"How did the court vote?"

"Pharisees still have a majority on the court. They refused to hear the case unless the accusers can produce two qualified witnesses to each of the crimes."

I could understand Jason's dislike of Yannai. The first time Jason had tried to help Yannai put on his royal robes, Yannai had dismissed the young man from the palace. "Why should I get help from some boy?" Yannai had said. "I can dress myself."

For Jason, dismissal from service in the palace meant no more dressing in silk and no more eating like a royal. But why would he turn on me? Could Phiabi and Hanin really have persuaded Jason to manufacture this monstrous lie?

"I am suffocating in this palace," I told Miri. "Let's go for a ride so I can think."

When we were well away from the palace on the Bethlehem road, I took a deep breath of the clear air. "It's good to be under the Lord's sky," I said, "but the way ahead is no clearer than before. My enemies have failed to unseat me this time. I am sure they will try again."

CHAPTER 8

Silk-robed nobles loitered outside the door of the Audience Chamber, gifts in one hand, petitions in the other. I nodded and walked past them. It gave me a small thrill of pleasure to keep these so-called "friends of the king" waiting while I tended to the affairs of the common people.

"Your Royal Highness," announced Menelaus, the chamberlain, "Seth son of Adam, a shepherd, and his wife Eva wish to approach the throne."

"They may approach," I said.

The shepherd's hair sprang from his body like spines on a hedgehog. Side-locks, eyebrows, beard, even wrists and ankles were bushy as a bear. The wife had missing teeth and a purpled eye. Since women could not bring complaints to the Chamber of Hewn Stone, I had a standing order that female petitioners appear before me.

"Your petition?" I said.

"You wanted to talk," growled Seth, shoving his wife forward. "Now talk."

The wife trembled and hid her face. But I saw the bruises.

"Your Highness," growled Seth, ducking his head, "we came to

Jerusalem to sell lambs. My wife insisted we congratulate you on your marriage."

"Your Majesty, we wish good health and long life to you and the king," lisped his wife through missing teeth. I had to ask her several times to speak more loudly.

"I appreciate your good wishes," I said.

The shepherd turned to leave.

"Stay," I said. "Your wife appears to be injured. I cannot let her go until she tells me how she got hurt."

The woman trembled, cringed, stuttered, and stared at the floor. Finally she raised her head and looked into my eyes.

"Your Highness," she said, "I cannot please my husband. When I serve him dinner, he says it is too early or too late. Or too hot or too cold. If the problem is not dinner, it is our son. One day he says I am too easy on the boy, the next too harsh. If I displease my husband, he whacks me. With his stick or with a fist."

She took a breath, then in a rush: "I would rather starve than go on living like this. Could the queen persuade him to divorce me?"

"Shame your husband in public, will you?" said the shepherd, brandishing his staff. "I'll deal with you later."

I motioned Shimon to the side of the throne. "Can we set her free?" I whispered.

"I detest this man's behavior," he said. "But the Law is clear. Only the husband may initiate divorce."

"A master who injures the eye or the tooth of a slave must set him free," I said.

"The Law makes no such provision for a wife," said my brother.

The Law is what you interpret it to be, I thought. *I can't count on two hands the number of "laws" Pharisees have deduced on the slimmest of evidence from the Holy Torah. Why can't you interpret the Law to show mercy to women?* There was no point in voicing such thoughts. Women had no part in interpreting the Law.

"Talk to the man," I said.

"Seth, my good fellow," said Shimon, "if your wife does not satisfy you, why not send her back to her father and choose a new one who pleases you?"

"Everything would be fine if she would obey me!" The shepherd lunged at his wife, head down, as if he would butt her.

"Papa, no!"

The small son plucked at the father's tunic. The father shoved him aside. "Get behind me, Daniel," said his mother as the shepherd advanced on her again.

"Stand down, man," said Shimon. "Show respect for the court."

I motioned the woman forward and whispered, "Eva, can you flee to your father's house?"

"Your Highness, I did that," said Eva, weeping. "My husband dragged me back. I don't know what he wants from me."

"Summon Hannah to the Audience Chamber," I told Miri.

Hannah, the head cook, entered the chamber wiping her hands on her apron. "My cook needs an assistant," I told the shepherd. "Your wife Eva will serve me here in Jerusalem. When she returns to you, she will be a better cook."

The man shriveled like a dried date. "Please, Your Highness," he said. "Who will care for Daniel?"

"He may stay with his mother."

Tears glinted in the shepherd's eyes. "Your Highness, please! What will I do without her?"

I was startled. "You love your wife?" I said. "Then treat her lovingly. We will send for you when your wife has learned to cook.

And when you, Seth, have learned to control your temper."

I motioned to Hannah. "Take your new assistant, Eva, to the kitchen and show her what she must do," I said. "Arrange beds for her and her son in the servants' quarters."

Hannah took little Daniel's hand and put her arm around Eva's shoulders. "I can give you a poultice for that eye," Hannah said as she guided them toward the servants' wing.

I thought Father would have been proud of me. I whispered to Miri, "This is why I must remain queen. I have the power to keep that brute's staff from his wife's back."

"My Lady," she whispered back, "the only thing that will improve that fellow is a taste of his own staff. But you have done the one other thing that might get his attention. You have emptied his bed."

Halfway to the door of the Audience Chamber, the shepherd turned, growled, and charged at his wife, staff raised. My guards threw him to the floor, wrestled away his staff, and carried him, flailing and cursing, from the palace. I was startled by the look of hatred he shot at me. But a ruler cannot hope to be loved by all her subjects.

I went into the meat kitchen to see how Eva was doing. "I sent her to the trough to wash turnips," said Hannah. "If I leave her alone with a knife she will cut her thumbs off."

I looked for Eva at the trough. "I hope you will be happy in Jerusalem," I said.

Eva flung herself to her knees and kissed the hem of my robe. "Your Majesty," she said, eyes streaming, "I would lay down my life for you."

I was embarrassed. "All you have to do," I said, "is help the cook."

Eva never did learn to cook. I made Eva and her son Daniel my official tasters. Holding her son's hand, she stood eagerly, almost worshipfully, beside me during every meal. She peered and sniffed and sampled each new dish that came steaming from the kitchen. I was quite sure she would not let anyone put poison fennel into a cup of wine, because her son would sip before I did.

In my garden, I planted capers. "The berries should be ripe by the time Yannai gets home," I said. "I'll have Hannah make him a nice spicy dinner."

"Your Highness," said Miri, with her typical raised eyebrow, "do you think that man needs an aphrodisiac?"

I blushed and pressed the earth carefully around the roots of the spiky little plants. "It can't hurt," I said. "But one could plant capers for their own sakes: those lush white blossoms, and the delicate sprays of purple at the center."

"No more beautiful than you, My Lady," said Miri. "But that oaf can't see past the thorns."

CHAPTER 9

My stomach had been churning for weeks.

I looked forward to purifying myself in the *mikvah* pool. I felt far closer to the Lord immersed in those waters than in the pomp of the Temple. "I am longing to go to the *mikvah*," I told Miri one morning. "I want to pray for a son. But I have gone three months without menstrual blood."

"My Lady, I do not want to be impertinent," said Miri, who rarely went a day without being impertinent, "but an average woman – one who didn't have queenly things on her mind – would take that as a symptom."

"A symptom of what?" I said.

Miri grabbed the folds of my gown and billowed it out in front of me. I screamed and blushed. I threw my arms around Miri and spun around the room. Patting my belly, I shouted, "There is a king in here!"

I could not wait to surprise Yannai with news of my pregnancy.

I told Caleb, captain of the Jerusalem guard, that I would be out of the city for a few nights. "Amos!" he said, speaking into the ear of a ruddy-cheeked young fellow. "Saddle three mounts tomorrow at dawn. The queen is going on a private errand. You will be her guard. A *private* errand, so mind you do not go blabbing about it."

The three of us galloped out the gate just as the sky faded from indigo to gray. I was veiled and disguised as a gentlewoman, traveling with my two servants.

The rustle of dry grass reminded me of a baby's soft breathing. The hills curved to the horizon like a baby's soft bottom.

As the walls of Jerusalem disappeared behind the sun-bathed hill, I shouted to Miri, "Can you still keep up with me?"

With just a nudge of my knee, my mare jumped a thorn-bush. Miri vaulted over a jagged outcropping of rocks. I sailed behind her.

"This baby of yours will ride before he walks," predicted Miri. "In the womb, he is already learning."

"Half man and half horse," I said. "Like his father."

Miri was right about many things, but wrong about that. Children – how they grow, who they become – no one can predict. But riding under a sun-bleached sky, far from Jerusalem, it was a joy to imagine riding these hills one day with Yannai and our young son.

* * *

Near sunset we reached Akko. Flecks of mica sparkled in the gray stones of the city walls. Sun flashed on the harbor and on a sea of tents. I saw scantily dressed women. Foreign women, chattering in a dozen tongues.

"Ask them what they are doing here," I told Miri.

"I know what they are doing here," Miri said, "and My Lady, I do not think you want to know."

A heavily rouged woman in a brief yellow top approached Miri. "Tell your mistress to ride away," she said in Greek. "This is a rough place – no place for a gentlewoman."

"Who are you?" I asked.

"We are the king's friends," she said. She paused and added with a smirk, "His very good friends."

I wheeled my horse and galloped back to Jerusalem. Night wind stung my salty cheeks. At the door to the palace, I thrust my horse's reins into the hands of the guard, ran to my bedchamber, threw myself on Miri's shoulder, and sobbed.

* * *

In the fourth month of my pregnancy, I sent for Yannai. He stalked into our bedchamber, growling, "What was so important that you had to call me back to the palace?"

"I am pregnant."

"Good girl!" he shouted. "I knew you could do it!"

He sat on the bed and patted my belly. "There are probably brats from here to Galilee that could call me Papa. But this is the first one I will get to know."

He put his mouth to my belly and shouted, "Are you listening, colt? Better not get too comfortable in there! It's a tough world. As soon as you pop out I'll put you to work."

"What if it is a girl?" I asked.

"He wouldn't dare be a filly," said Yannai. "Not with me for a sire."

"Now that you are home, please stay!" I begged. "I don't want our son to become an orphan before he is born!"

"I smell a trap!" snarled Yannai. "You thought by getting pregnant you could get me to stay in this stinking city."

"How could any woman deal with a man who thinks love is a trap?" I wailed after Yannai left.

"It is a trap," said Miri. "For you."

Yannai did not come back to Jerusalem again until the fall

Holy Days three months later. Another high priest would have spent the morning before the Day of Atonement in penitence and prayer. Yannai was at the stables, drilling the Jerusalem guards. Most of the men left behind in Jerusalem were either too young or too old to be sent to Akko: perhaps a score of cavalry and less than a hundred foot soldiers. Though my belly had swollen like a camel's and my walk had become a waddle, I went to the stables to watch Yannai drill the men. Through a cloud of dust, I saw him standing beside two thirteen-year-olds battling with swords.

"Shield up! Shield up! Save your neck!" shouted Yannai.

As the boy lifted his great round shield, Yannai poked a sword underneath and flipped the shield away. He thrust the sword into the boy's belly. I gasped, until I realized that a charcoal-tipped wooden block blunted each sword-point. "You always got to keep an eye out for someone comin' from the side," grinned Yannai.

He pointed to a smudge of charcoal on the young soldier's tunic. "You're dead, Beni," said Yannai. "Lie flat on the ground and think about that for awhile. But take care no one steps on you."

The cavalrymen were letting their mounts graze at the side of the exercise yard. Yannai vaulted onto his bay mare, Thunder. Lounging loose as a blanket in the saddle, Yannai trotted over to coach the riders. They wheeled and charged, wheeled and charged, until they lined up as neatly as birds on a branch. "Easy on that bit, Yossi," Yannai called to a rabbit-faced boy with protruding teeth. "The way you are hauling at the reins, you are gonna turn that filly's mouth to mush."

Then Yannai set the horsemen and the foot soldiers against each other. The horsemen stooped to aim their lances. The foot soldiers parried and attempted to unseat them. The young fellow named Beni ducked the lance and dove for a knee of the horse.

"Good job!" shouted Yannai. "Now you're thinking like a soldier."

Yannai, I thought, was teaching those boys as if he were their father. This marriage seemed to have a future after all.

Yannai and I walked up the dusty path toward the palace. A voice shouted, "Yossi!"

We turned to see a round-faced young man with pink cheeks and pouting pink lips race his mount toward the rabbit-faced Yossi. It was Amos. He and Yossi were our two couriers. Yossi wheeled and charged head-on. At the last moment, both horsemen swerved, but not before Amos flicked Yossi's leather helmet off his head and into the dust. "Got you, Yossi!" he shouted.

Screeching like a diving duck, the helmetless Yossi wheeled to charge again.

"Yossi! Amos!" called Yannai.

The two boys drew their horses up short and trotted up to Yannai. "I apologize, Your Highness," said Amos, removing his helmet. The tips of his ears burned a deep rose. "I would not have hurt him. We are from the same village. First time we are together on horseback. I could not resist."

"You may look like a puffball, but you are just the type of fellow I want in my army," said Yannai.

"Puffball!" shouted Yossi, reaching sideward to punch his friend's shoulder.

"Rabbit!" shouted Amos, punching back.

Yannai squatted in the dirt. "Jump over me," he said.

"Your Majesty?" Amos quavered, spit leaping from his plump lips. "You said to – to jump over you, My Lord? On our horses?"

"Both of you. At the same time. Right now."

"Idiot!" said Yossi. "Don't you know how to follow orders? The king wants us to jump over him."

The two youngsters trotted to opposite sides of the field. Pikes raised, they charged at each other. Yannai crouched in the middle. Yossi leaned forward. He spurred his horse and bit his lower lip. Amos's tongue stuck out. His face was so red I thought he might faint. Just as the two horsemen came abreast of each other, they leaped over Yannai. Yannai reached up and used his charcoal-tipped sword to slash a black line across each horse's belly. He stood up. "Good job, men!" he shouted. "But never underestimate the man on the ground!"

He grabbed the reins of the two horses. "Make sure you give these two mares a good rub-down before you bathe for the holiday," he said. "They're every bit as human as you are. Probably more so."

The two young fellows waved their pikes in salute. Grinning, they trotted toward the stable.

"You're a good teacher," I told Yannai as we walked. "After the holidays, I hope you will coach me on riding. You ride Thunder as if you were part of her."

"I am," he said.

I took a deep breath. "You would much rather be drilling soldiers than offering sacrifices in the Temple, would you not?"

"Damn right. I see plenty of sacrifices on the battlefield. Those sacrifices at least have a purpose. Not like cutting a varmint's throat and babbling words in a language no one has spoken for a few hundred years."

Another deep breath. I took my husband's hand. "You did not grow up with these prayers and rituals. They do not mean much to you. But to most people in our land they are sacred. It would help your standing with both the priests and the people if you would learn the prayers and show more respect for them."

Yannai drew his hand from mine. "I've tried to learn that meaningless drivel," he said. "How can I remember it? It is meaningless drivel. If the priests are unhappy with the way I do the job, let them find someone else to do it."

"I will get to work on it right away," I said.

* * *

When he crawled into bed after the close of the holiday, Yannai patted the mound of my belly and told me I looked like a cow.

"A cow looks like a cow because it gives birth to a calf," I said. "Do you think babies just appear in the arms of a wetnurse?"

"Sorry, holy mama," he said, kissing my belly. "You are carrying a heavy load. I should appreciate that."

He was so sweet that I took a risk and pleaded, "Please cancel the siege and stay home until our child is born."

"Why should I?" said Yannai. "Nothing I can do to help."

I sat up. "Judea needs you here."

"Why? They have you."

"Our men need to be home farming. Our city walls need to be repaired."

"If you want to lie awake at night worrying about how thick a wall should be, please do so."

"While you are off looking for glory," I said, "I am running the country. Does that bother you?"

Yannai leaped to his feet, purple with rage. "Run the country if you want. But do not *ever* try to run me."

"I was not – "

"I will go where I want to go and do what I want to do."

"I did not mean – "

"If you try to interfere, you'd better start thinking about that afterlife your Pharisees are so sure of."

I stood and faced him. "Afterlife? You are talking about killing me? You would not dare. I made you king."

"You made me king, and you only made yourself queen," said Yannai, giving my shoulder a shove. "That was short-sighted for such a plan-ahead woman. You made me! Ha!"

"I'm sorry! I did not mean – "

Yannai's fists clenched. He bounced on the balls of his feet.

"You and those fool Pharisees of yours. No wonder they invented that stuff about the 'next world.' They have not been able to put a finger on me in this world, so they try to convince me that their God will do it in the next."

"*Their* God? How can you talk like that?"

"Listen, old lady, on the battlefield you hear all kinds of prayers. Cypriots and Egyptians and Syrians and Parthians have forty or fifty gods to pray to. Jews have one. But I've never noticed either them or us getting any special protection from all that praying. Try praying now."

His slap stung my cheek and knocked me off balance. My head hit the doorpost. I spat blood. Yannai strode out the door. Back to his war.

I collapsed on the silk covers like a pile of broken sticks. How had my loving request to my husband provoked this blow? I whimpered, *God Almighty, Merciful Lord, tell me what to do. I cannot stay married to this man. I cannot let him rule alone. Tell me what to do.*

My belly cramped. I pleaded with the baby. "Please stay in there," I wept. "You are not ready – and neither am I."

CHAPTER 10

Morning sun stung my eyes like smoke. I buried my face in the silken covers. I did not want Miri to see the bruises. She did.

"My Lady – your face!" she cried, touching me gently. "What happened?"

I did not answer.

"He hit you!" Miri stomped around the room. "How dare he! You are the queen! Take him to the Sanhedrin! Let him be stoned! Hang him!"

"I wish I could," I mumbled through puffy lips. "King Alexander reminded me that in our land, even the queen is ruled by her husband. It is he who could have me stoned."

"You run this nation," Miri said. "Without you, our land would be in ruins."

"I rule at his whim. If my husband decides he is through with me, I am through."

I turned my head away. My jaw hurt too much to talk more.

Miri came back with cooling cloths and poultices of cabbage leaves (her mother's remedy) to bring down the swelling. Her brows fierce and her cheeks red with tears, she said, "He is evil. Pure evil. You have to get rid of that man."

I looked at the purpled face in the mirror and went back to bed. My mind stewed with revenges. I would take my bruises to the Sanhedrin, and they, outraged, would remove Yannai from the throne. *Really?* I told myself. *You think the Sanhedrin would back the queen in a dispute with the king?*

I will send the Jerusalem guard to ambush Yannai on the way home from Akko, I vowed. Then I pictured Adonijah's severed head lolling above the Jerusalem city wall. If I tried to topple Yannai, within a week the Sadducees would plant my head on the wall and their man on the throne.

I played a game with myself, thinking of wicked ways to do away with my husband. Snake's venom! Dip a message in it, telling him what a fool he is! Yannai cannot read, I reminded myself. Do I really want to kill the man who opens my husband's messages?

Perhaps I could make an accident happen: an arrow from behind, shot by a too-hasty soldier. *If I tried to arrange an accident, what soldier would prefer my command to Yannai's?*

Even if Yannai died in battle, his youngest brother, Absalom, would become king. Absalom already had a wife. I myself had arranged the match to his plump little second cousin, Shoshana.

I scolded myself: *Has this man really brought you so low that you can entertain such thoughts?* Yannai was my husband. He had shared my bed. I was carrying his child. No matter how badly I had been treated, it was sinful to indulge such murderous thoughts. *The Almighty might forgive me the thoughts, but if ever I acted on them, I could not stand before His judgment.*

I had loved Yannai. He had loved me, too. I was sure of it. But Yannai's rage was like a rockslide, reducing thought to rubble. If he *had* loved me, then through a few ill-chosen words, in a matter of minutes, I had lost that love. Sadness and hopelessness enveloped me as if the palace walls had collapsed around me.

I tried to rest. Visions of whippings, burnings, stonings scarred my sleep. As soon as I had made my toilette, I burrowed into the bedclothes again.

*   *   *

At noon, Miri returned. "My Lady," she said, "ten petitioners are waiting in the Audience Chamber."

I remembered coming home with pebbles and thorns embedded in my knees after trying to chase the goat-herds downhill. Mother scolded me for running off and picked thorns from my knee with her needle. Father said, "Scraped knees will never stop my daughter."

I threw off the covers. Through puffy eyelids, I peered at the mirror. My face was swollen, blotched purple and green. "Bring me that ointment made from balsam and Dead Sea mud," I ordered Miri.

As I slathered it on, I told Miri, "Queen Esther lived in a land where the king was absolute. When her people needed her, she figured out a way to get what she wanted from her king."

Like Esther, I would have to plan every word I said to my husband.

I smiled at Miri, cracking the caked-on cosmetic. I squinted at the mirror and pulled a veil over my face. "Yannai does not want to run the country," I said. "He is too lazy and too easily bored. He just needs to believe that whatever I do is his idea. I have been so intimidated by him that I have not been able to think about how to handle him."

*   *   *

After dealing – rather summarily, I am afraid – with the ten waiting petitioners, I sat down to plan my defense against my husband. This would have to be done discreetly. I summoned Caleb, commander of the palace guard, to my sitting room. With a high forehead framed by frizzy hair, an erect stance, and olive-tinted eyes that crinkled at the corners when he smiled, he was an attractive man. "I am concerned that we may be vulnerable while my husband is off at war," I said.

"Your Highness, I am also concerned," said Caleb.

"What do you suggest?" I said.

"Your Majesty, we should build more forts along our borders. We already have a chain of signal towers to tell our priests when the new moon is sighted. Signal flares can also alert us to movement by foreign troops."

"A sensible and thrifty way to bolster our defense," I said. "I would also like to speak to the troops here in Jerusalem and watch them drill."

"My Lady, we would be honored," he said, with the crinkly smile. "When?"

"Tomorrow at this time."

If Caleb had noticed my masque, he gave no sign.

* * *

"I feel safe knowing that the most experienced troops are here in Jerusalem," I told the mostly graying men lined in ranks against the western wall of the city. "I know that you will defend our holy city and our holy Temple."

They cheered.

"I am building new forts along our borders," I announced. "My builders must learn to defend themselves. You will be their teachers. They will drill with you. Treat them as your own sons. I will treat them as mine. Are you with me?"

Jumbled shouts: "Yes, My Lady!"

"Hail to the queen!"

I chuckled at myself. I loved being surrounded by the shouts of men. Walking among them, I took a deep breath, enjoying the smell of their sweat. I felt like a five-year-old girl in Modi'in again, running after the goat-herds. I thought, as I had then: boys – and men – could be obnoxious, but nearly all the things they did were more interesting and exciting than the things women did. There was one crucial difference from those days in Modi'in. I was not a five-year-old, who could be sent home to my mother. I was the one in charge.

* * *

In the darkest hour of night, I sensed something moving in my bedchamber. "Miri?" I said.

"It's me, Holy Lady," said Yannai's voice.

"Don't touch me!" I screamed.

"I came back to say I'm sorry," said Yannai.

"You're sorry?"

Should I call my guards? How dare he sneak into my bedchamber! Would he turn on me again – even kill me?

"I am an idiot," said Yannai. "I was out of my mind."

"I can agree to that."

"You are the queen, not some lousy whore."

"You have noticed?"

"You are the queen and you are my wife, and I had no reason to treat you that way. Will you forgive me?"

"No one in my life has ever hit me," I said.

"I hurt you," Yannai said, and sniffled. "I hurt my wife."

When he was not drinking, Yannai could be so tender. For one week, he had made me happier than I had ever been before. My aching body reproached me at every step, but I hobbled to the clay stove and lit an oil lamp. Gently, my husband touched the purple side of my face. "How could I do that to you?" he said.

Tears glistened in the lamplight – his and mine. "I will never do this to you again," he said. "I swear by all the gods – I mean – I mean – I swear by all that's holy. Never again."

He took my hand, led me to the bed. "Let me share your bed again," he said.

* * *

In the morning, Yannai said, "Will you come with me? I have a gift for you. But it's not here."

"Bring it when you come home next time," I said.

"It can't be moved," he said.

"What is it?" I asked, intrigued.

"You have to see it in the place where it belongs."

Miri jumped backward when Yannai walked out of the bedchamber behind me.

"My Lady?" she said.

Longing and fear warred in my throat so that for a moment I could not speak.

"Please get my chariot," I said. "The king has a gift he wishes to show me."

"Are you sure, My Lady?" said Miri.

"No," I said. "But I am going."

* * *

Yannai's arms circled my waist. I flinched. Then a thrill shot through me as Yannai's strong arms lifted me to the ground.

Telling the driver to wait, Yannai took a firepan from the chariot, lit a torch, and beckoned me to follow him. I remembered that little-boy smile, a mixture of pride and pleading. I had seen it when Yannai was four years old and had a special treasure to show me. I knew how quickly the charm could turn to rage if I refused to come along.

* * *

A dark, humid tunnel. I clung to Yannai's hand. Water trickled down boulders and sloshed into my sandals. Then, ahead of us, I saw shimmering light, delicate vapor. A crystal wall of water.

As we emerged into sunlight, Yannai drew me under a steaming waterfall that tumbled from a hot spring just above the roof of the cave. Our hair and robes were drenched. He kissed me full on the lips. His face gleaming, he nuzzled my belly and kissed me again. For a moment, it was as if we had never left Zippori, never left the magical second week of our marriage. He helped me carefully down the mossy rocks. I floated, my bulging belly suspended in the warm pool at the foot of the spring. As if the pool were a mikvah, I tried to let my anger and fear float away. To let hope flow back into my heart.

Later we stood at the summit, letting sun and breeze dry our clothes, looking over green hills to the shimmering Lake Kinneret, the Sea of Galilee.

Bored by the endless days of siege at Akko, Yannai had made a side trip with part of his force to capture the fortress town of Gadara. With a grand gesture, he pointed toward the shattered walls of the abandoned fort. Splintered olive trees, smashed clay pots, tattered clothing, carcasses of animals littered the hillside below the town. "It was a tough battle, but we got 'em," said Yannai.

"You were very brave," I said. "And so were your men."

After the terrible rift that had almost shattered our marriage, I realized that Yannai needed my approval of the one thing he was good at. I gave him that gift.

* * *

As soon as Yannai left Jerusalem to go back to his troops, I resumed drilling the Jerusalem guard. I believed Yannai truly intended to control his temper. I was not at all sure he could.

In the last splashes of summer sunshine and the damp chill of autumn, with my belly ballooning day by day, I stood on top of the city wall and watched the men march and skirmish. Every day, whether or not my head ached. My soldiers taught my builders to shoot arrows from niches in the city walls. To heave boulders from the parapets. To barricade the gates. I made sure wine, water and sweet grapes were waiting for the men after the drills.

"The drills are going well," I told Miri. "There is a good spirit among the men. Caleb is an excellent commander. If Yannai turns against me, or if Diogenes organizes a Sadducee army, my men will defend me."

I sat down with Caleb and my architect, Philip, a genial, bald Alexandrian Jew, to plan the forts. "Where do we need to bolster our line of defense?"

"Your Highness," said Caleb, "we urgently need a signal tower and fort along the Jordan River, between Jericho and the River Jabbok."

"Put it on the highest mountain you can find," I said. "And

make it impregnable. It should have a view of the Jordan River, the Edomite mountains, and everything in between."

"Your Highness, have you considered the need for a water supply?" said Philip.

"Can we bring water by aqueduct from the Samarian mountains?"

"Yes, Your Highness, I think I can design a workable system. What about storage?"

"Find some caves we can use for cisterns. And Philip?"

"Yes, Your Majesty?"

"Let's quarry and trim the stones close to the villages, so we allow our builders to spend as much time as possible near their homes."

"I'll bring you a design in a few days' time," said Philip, bowing and backing out. I was always amused by the elaborate formality he had learned in the Egyptian court.

"I assume this fort is being built on the king's orders," said Caleb.

"It will be after you remind him of the need for it," I said. "Tell him he should name it Alexandrium as a warning to the Syrians and Samaritans not to venture across our borders."

In Akko, Yannai's battering rams still thundered against the walls. Each time he charged, enemy arrows drove his soldiers back. Yossi, the rabbit-nosed courier with the protruding front teeth, was his usual cocky self. "Your Highness, these idiots from Akko even supply us with arrows," he said when he made his weekly report. "At the end of the day, we just gather up the arrows and shoot 'em back the next day. I figure we need another week before they run out of arrows and we charge in and take over."

Yossi was wrong. The following week he had sad news. Four

soldiers had fallen: one from Bethome, one from Carmel, one from Bethlehem, and one from Ein Kerem. I visited each soldier's family, to deliver the news in person.

In Bethlehem, our carriage squeezed through streets meant only for goats. We stopped at a small stone dwelling. Miri called through the open door, "Queen Shulamit wishes to speak with you."

The woman at the door was young enough to be my daughter, and more pregnant than I. I took her hand. "I am sorry to bring – "

"Don't tell me!" she screamed. "I do not want to hear."

She sank to the dirt floor, sobbing and tearing her clothes.

"I am so sorry," I said.

The young woman rose, wiping a dirty hand across her wet cheek. "Queen Salome, I am sorry for the way I greeted you. I have been dreading this. It is our first, our first – please, I cannot talk now."

She shut the door.

During the ride back, I tried to imagine this young woman's future. How could such a young widow raise an infant alone? Would she return to her father's house or go to her husband's family? Would her husband's family resent having extra mouths to feed? I would send her food and money, but I could not support all the widows who would be left alone at the end of this war. Miri held a mirror while I blotted tears from my cheeks. "It is sad," she whispered. "It is a stupid waste. But it is not your fault."

The chariot lurched over a pot-hole. It is Yannai's fault, I thought. Yannai and the Sadducees. How could anyone think a port on the Great Sea was worth the lives of young men?

In the palace courtyard, I lowered my great bulk beside my

old friend the gardener and nestled three blazing orange calendula into the earth. As if in some small way I could bring life where there was so much death.

"This plant is good for constipation," I told Miri. "A problem for pregnant women."

"Your Highness, I wouldn't know about that," she said. She squeezed my hand. Perhaps Miri knew nothing about the aches and pains of pregnancy. But she knew, and shared, the ache in my heart.

"And you," I whispered to the little foot pressing on my belly from the inside out, "you are new life. At least I can protect you."

By the time I visited Ein Kerem, Bethome, and Carmel, there were more villages on my list. Jolting along the neglected roads from the barren vistas of Jerusalem to the high vineyards of Carmel, my days blurred into a frieze of weeping mothers, stunned wives, stricken and bewildered children.

* * *

Shimon sipped mint tea in my sitting room. "You kept your word," he said. "You got King Alexander to make Pharisees a majority in the Sanhedrin. So that he could ignore us."

"The Sadducees influence Yannai by encouraging him to do what he wants to do."

"His wants lead to disaster."

"I quite agree. I think there may be another way to control Yannai."

"What is that?"

"To persuade all of Judea to turn away from him. To refuse to join his armies or to follow his lead."

"How do you propose to do that?" said Shimon. "He will kill

you if you speak against him.”

"I want you to do it.”

"Thank you," said Shimon.

"Subtly. I want you to establish an academy, to teach young scholars the Law, as Father taught you. We need a new generation of Sages, so committed to the Law that they will not permit Yannai to violate it.”

"I would love to establish an academy," said Shimon. "But not all Jews can become scholars.”

"All Jews can learn the Law," I said. "The graduates of your academy will interpret and teach the Law. Every woodcutter and shepherd must know enough of the Law to follow it.”

"That's a rather ambitious goal," said Shimon.

"The people in the countryside respect the Sages, but the Sages are a tiny minority," I said. "This corrupt alliance of nobles, merchants and priests who call themselves Sadducees can dominate because of their wealth. But not if we win the people to our side. The Sadducees call us Pharisees. Separatists. Let's create a nation of Pharisees.”

"A nation of Pharisees?" said Shimon.

"A nation of families determined to remain separate from the immoral Greek culture around us. Who refuse to fight in Yannai's armies. Who know that the Law of the Lord does not permit the wealthy to drive the common people into poverty. How can Yannai and the Sadducees lead Judea astray if the people's loyalty is to the Law and the Lord?"

* * *

The corvée from the mountain town of Ramathaim arrived at Jerusalem to work on a new aqueduct. The oppressively hot *hamsin* wind stirred tiny cyclones on the dry hills and pasted dust to the roof of one's mouth. Even in the pale gray light before sunrise, half-moons of sweat stained the armpits of each man's tunic. By the time the men stopped work just before noon, wide swaths of sweat plastered their grimy tunics to their backs and chests. Miri and I walked up and down alongside the rows of workers. She wheeled a cart filled with jugs of water. I handed a cupful to a short chunky man. Salty drops of sweat fell into the cup as he raised it to his lips. "You must miss the breezes of your hill country on a day like this," I said.

"Your Majesty, I always miss my home when I am away," he said, wiping his forehead. "But I am proud to build our land."

* * *

The men must have been exhausted, but late that afternoon, they returned to practice warfare: carrying huge rocks to the top of the city wall, and throwing them down onto targets outlined on the dry grass. I saw the same cheerful chunky man, shouldering a boulder that probably weighed more than he did. As he passed it to the shoulder of the man on the step above him, he called out, "Let us show our queen that the men of Ramathaim are the strongest in Judea."

The man on the step above him shouted, "Is that pebble all you can give me? I could lift a mountain."

"What is your name?" I asked the chunky fellow.

"Michael son of Samuel, Your Majesty," he said. "The prophet Samuel was born in our village."

"You are a true son of Samuel," I said.

Michael smiled. "Your Highness," he said, "when I have a son, I will name him Samuel and tell him what the queen said to me before he was born."

When their lessons in war were finished, I led the men, sweaty and dirty as they were, to our banquet room, where Hannah had set up a feast of bread, wine, cheese and grapes. "While you refresh yourselves," I told them, "Rabbi Shimon son of Shetakh, the esteemed head of the Sanhedrin, will teach you about our holy Law."

Shimon stood and pronounced a blessing over the food.

"You men are builders," said Shimon. "Did you know that building is a sacred occupation, its own kind of priesthood?"

The men leaned forward. Shimon had caught their attention. "The aqueduct you are building," he continued, "will bring vitally needed water to our sacred city, Jerusalem. The logs you cut at home in Ramathaim will frame the border forts that provide our defense."

Shimon's voice rang out. "There is a law in our holy teachings that refers especially to builders like you. Whether you build a palace or help your neighbor build his house, you must put a fence around the roof. Why? Women climb to the roof to fetch water from the cisterns, to wash and dry garments, to dry fruit and herbs. Children play at their mothers' feet. When you build, you must think, not only about the appearance of what you build, but of the generations of people who will depend on your work. You are building something that will last long after you are gone. You must teach your sons this law, so that the Law, too, will last for generations after you are gone."

The men bit off hunks of warm bread and grinned at one another. They would return to their village with new pride and a new mission. Shimon flashed me a smile of satisfaction. My brother, who had sometimes doubted me, had truly become my partner. I made sure that my laborers and soldiers received generous rations every day. Shimon fed their souls. I climbed to the roof of the palace at sunset that evening and leaned against the sturdy parapet, surveying my city and feeling my own thrill of pride. I was accomplishing my own mission: I was fortifying both Jerusalem and the faith of my people.

And I, like my sacred city, was no longer defenseless. My blacksmiths shoed horses and forged new weapons, for soldiers in the guard and for the defenders who returned to their villages. Judea's villages were armed with men who had received a cup of water from my hand. Even if Yannai turned against me or the Sadducees tried to overthrow me, I had a core of men who would back their queen.

CHAPTER 11

"I need help with an important decision," I told Shimon. "While Yannai is away, we must have an acting high priest to perform the sacrifices. It should be someone who is genuinely devout. But there is a danger. Whoever holds the post could be in a position to usurp the throne. Do you have any candidates to suggest to the Sanhedrin?"

"I do not trust any of the priests," said Shimon.

"I would be happier if the acting high priest were not one of the Jerusalem clique," I replied. "That crowd shoves, trying to get ahead. I do not trust any of them."

I braced my shoulders as Miri and I walked into the Chamber of Hewn Stone for the meeting with the Sanhedrin. "King Yannai requests," I said, "that the priests in the Sanhedrin choose an acting high priest to serve in the king's absence."

The council voted a recess. The chamber buzzed with clusters of men recruiting votes and offering inducements. Boethus waddled after me. His embroidered tunic looked like an enormous multi-colored pillow. I almost laughed aloud as I faced him, immense belly to immense belly. Mopping his shiny pate and hitching up his sash around the waves of belly that passed for a waist, he cleared his throat. "Your Majesty, my family descends from the high-priestly line. We were first among the families returning from the Exile."

"Yes?"

"You are wise in the ways of the court," he said, smirking. "You could tell your husband that he might avoid a challenge to the Hasmonean dynasty by appointing me as acting high priest."

"I am sure my husband would listen as readily to your advice as he would to mine," I smiled.

"That tub of tallow!" sputtered Miri when Boethus left. "Was he threatening you?"

"A veiled threat," I said. "But there isn't a veil in the kingdom big enough to hide him – or his intentions. He reminded me that the descendants of the Maccabees could be challenged because they aren't from the high-priestly line."

Ambassador Diogenes had returned from Akko for the meeting. He strode into the Audience Chamber reeking authority. "Your Royal Highness," he said, "as a member of the high-priestly line, I consider it my sacred duty to assist His Majesty in the performance of his priestly duties while he is detained in Akko."

"I am sure His Majesty appreciates your devotion to your duty," I said. "He will undoubtedly consider your offer."

The silk-clad merchant Phiabi slithered in as soon as Diogenes had left. "Your Highness," he said, "like my esteemed cousins Boethus and Diogenes, I am of the high priestly line. Because my principal residence is in Jerusalem, I am also – without demeaning the skills of my cousins – especially well-practiced in the priestly arts. And thanks to a modest degree of success in my business, I could make a substantial gift to the Temple treasury."

"Which makes you especially well-qualified," I said.

Phiabi turned to leave. Then he turned back and said, "Your Majesty, I see that you have been drilling the Jerusalem guard."

"I would not want our city to be vulnerable," I said, "while the king is leading the siege in Akko."

"My Lady, you are most foresighted," said Phiabi.

After Phiabi left, I ranted to Miri. "These Sadducees seem to think the only real qualification for high priest is having substantial wealth and the right ancestors. Wisdom, honesty, and piety weigh less than feathers in their scales."

If I did not prevent it, one of my enemies might become the acting high priest.

In addition to the priests who lived in Jerusalem, priests who lived in the villages served in the Temple for a two-week rotation every year. "It is no accident," I told Miri, "that the Maccabee rebellion started in Modi'in. Priests from the villages are much closer to the people."

Each time a village priest came to Jerusalem, I invited him to dine at the palace. Reuben, a priest from Mizpah, seemed to me both sensible and devout. A potter by trade, he was tall and angular, with a long chin and large ears. "He impresses me," I told Miri, "because he brought his wife and two sons to Jerusalem, instead of leaving them in the village. I need to think of an indirect way to suggest his name to Yannai."

Another priest, from another village, understood Yannai better and moved faster than I did. While the factions in the Sanhedrin were still arguing over the appointment, a priest serving a rotation from Kefar Barkai went to Akko and met privately with Yannai. Yannai returned to Jerusalem to announce that Issachar of Kefar Barkai would be acting high priest. As I left the Chamber of Hewn Stone, Shimon trailed me to my sitting room. "Did you know that Issachar bribed the Sadducee priests Phiabi and Boethus to get the post of acting high priest?"

"No, I did not," I said.

"Do you know how much money it took to win all the priests' support?"

"No."

"I suppose you cannot tell me, then, how much he paid directly to Yannai."

My face reddened. "Why would Yannai – "

"Why not?" Shimon interrupted. "It costs money to bring a whorehouse to the battlefield."

CHAPTER 12

Liquid gushed from between my legs. I waddled out of the Chamber of Hewn Stone with as much dignity as a woman the size of a cistern can manage – especially when she's dribbling below. So breathless I could hardly give the order, I sent a messenger to Yannai: "Your son is arriving!"

A house-maid ran for the midwife. Miri helped me into my bedchamber. A fire burned on the hearth. We walked back and forth, back and forth. Pain twisted my gut and bore down on my back. When the pains came, I clutched Miri's hand, steadied myself against the edge of the bed, and squatted over a pillow, as the midwife had taught me. "Your Highness, are you sure you want to use this good silk pillow?" Miri asked.

"Yes!" I screamed. A claw of pain clenched my belly, tightening so that I could not breathe. I thought of all the women who die in childbirth. What if my exhausted womb could not push this baby out? How I wished my mother had been there! She would have known what to do.

The midwife arrived. She checked the space between my thighs and massaged the straining, tearing flesh. "You may leave now," the midwife told Miri.

"You do not know who you are talking to," said Miri. "I have served the queen since I was six years old. Queen Shulamit sat with me when my mother was dying. You can no more pry me away from her than you can cut off her shadow."

"I need her," I gasped. *Miri will not let me die,* I thought.

I felt as if a vulture tore at my innards. When blackness surged over me and I thought I could go no further, Miri squeezed my hand. At last I lay on the bed, and the midwife placed the baby, still slimy and bloody, on my sweaty chest. *Thank you, Lord,* I said, *who makes the barren woman a joyful mother of children.* I traced my finger on the bottom of my child's foot and watched his toes curl. I whispered, "My little Etzi, your fingers and toes are the jewels of Creation ..."

And that is what I ended up calling him – Etzi, baby fingers. Of course, that was not his official name. The name announced at his circumcision and inscribed in the records of the kingdom was Hyrcanus II. I prayed that he would become a wise and courageous ruler, like his grandfather John Hyrcanus. "And not," I thought to myself, "a bloodthirsty fool like his father Yannai."

Now that his "colt" had finally arrived, Yannai took his time about coming home. "Where is he?" I fretted to Miri.

"Your Highness, if I had to wager," she said, "I would bet it has something to do with swords and arrows."

Catapults and siege towers are his toys, I thought. *Yannai cannot bear to leave in the middle of the game.* My husband was so ignorant and so scornful of Jewish law, I feared he would not come home to circumcise his son, as the Lord has commanded, on the eighth day after birth.

Yannai arrived just before sundown on the seventh day. He ran into my sitting room, scooped up the baby (who had been nursing), tossed him in the air and shouted, "Here is the colt! Welcome to the world."

Etzi wrinkled up his face and screamed. "Is that any way to greet your Papa?" said Yannai. "Keep screaming like that, and I will see that you are thrown in the hole and flogged."

I grabbed the baby, put him back at the breast until he soothed, then set him on the couch between us. "Look at his little fingers and toes," I said. "My little Etzi."

"What kind of name is that for a boy?" said Yannai. "If you want to name him after his grandfather, call him John. Make him sound like my son."

"You can call him John," I said. "But I will call him Etzi."

"Are you sure this is my son?" said Yannai. "I see that he has a bunch of little red grapes hanging between his legs. But other than that, he looks nothing like me."

"What do you mean?" I said.

"Look at him. Bald. No mustache. No beard. And waving his hands around like that will get him nowhere on the battlefield."

I laughed and leaned across the baby to give my husband a kiss.

"I am dreading the circumcision," I told Yannai. "I cannot stand the idea that we are going to take this tiny little organ and snip off the foreskin."

"I was not feeling very good about clipping that little thing either," said Yannai. "I could just imagine all these fancy-talking nobles gathering around and making bets on whether I would slip and chop off the whole thing. But I have changed my mind."

I sighed. "The Law of the Lord requires it, so we have to do it."

"Who cares about the so-called Law of the Lord? It is good for the little pisser to start out with some pain. That is why men are tougher than women. When they are eight days old, they find out what life is all about."

* * *

I scheduled the circumcision for early morning. I imagined my mother and father watching proudly from beyond the horizon. Sun buttered the broad windows of the Audience Chamber, polished the reds and blues of the tapestries, gleamed on the gold-trimmed tunics of a room full of notables – and blazed on the knife. I gave my tiny son one last hug, lay him on a white linen cloth on the marble table, and retreated to the adjoining room, peering through the open door with the other women. Shimon, as the godfather, unfastened the baby's swaddling clothes. Etzi shot an arc of urine into the air. Everyone chuckled. Etzi screamed. His face was purple.

Yannai waved the knife and leered. My husband's eyes were red, his face blotched, his head-covering and robe askew. He wheezed alcohol. I ran into the Audience Chamber and tried to take the knife from his hand. Yannai raised the knife threateningly and shoved me away.

"The father must circumcise his son," Shimon said gently. "It is the Law."

One of the women drew me back to the anteroom. I started to cry. Miri held my hand. The women around me murmured sympathetically. One woman whispered, "Your Majesty, it does not really hurt when they are so tiny."

"The knife has not touched the baby yet," said another. "He is just crying because of the cold air hitting his naked body."

I held my breath, praying that Yannai's skill with a knife would overcome his drunkenness. Shimon said the blessing. Yannai did not know it. "Get ready to hurt, you little pisser," shouted Yannai.

He inserted the knife and twisted it to slice off the foreskin. I was astonished at the deftness of the stroke. My child, except for a few drops of blood, was safe. I let go the breath I had been holding. But I did not let go of the anger. How dare Yannai risk the life of his infant son and the scorn of all Judea by coming drunk to the circumcision?

The doctor dabbed the wound with a healing balm. I snatched my screaming son and ran back to my bedchamber. I crawled exhausted onto my couch with the baby at my breast. We both slept for hours.

Miri told me that Yannai did not stay for the feast of circumcision. He rushed out of the Audience Chamber and back to the war. I was relieved. I would not have to try to keep my husband away from the rest of the wine.

* * *

Nights were hard. Etzi clung to wakefulness as if he were standing at the edge of a cliff, holding onto a rope, afraid to let himself drop into the void. I walked him back and forth across my bedchamber. I rocked him, sang to him, and whispered to him. Etzi wailed and flailed, battling this enemy sleep, until I too was inconsolable trying to soothe him. When he finally fell asleep (suddenly, as if sleep dropped over his head like the hood that silences a caged bird), I flopped onto the bed beside him. But I was often too agitated and exhausted to sleep. When I did sleep, I would startle awake, terrified that Etzi might have stopped breathing. I had to cup my fingers on the round baby belly and bring my breathing into harmony with its gentle rise and fall before I could calm myself enough to sleep again. When he woke during the night, I put him to my breast and curled around him,

as close as the earlobe to the ear. Every time I felt the warmth of
my son's body, tears of tenderness and wonder came to my eyes.
This is a new, living being, I whispered. *Born from his father's seed
and my womb. And from Your grace, Lord.*

"Your Highness," said Miri, "I wish I could help you. You are
getting no sleep."

I tried to explain to Miri what satisfaction the Lord gives to
new mothers. "Every time Etzi suckles, I am thirsty enough to
drink a river and hungry enough to eat a goat," I told Miri. "Yet
I feel filled, rather than drained. The tug of my son's lips on my
nipples nurtures me as much as it does him."

* * *

Whether I had slept or not, the daily decisions of governing
fell to me. Grants of land to wounded soldiers. Repair of the
Jerusalem-Bethlehem road (difficult to arrange when most of the
men who should be serving in corvées were with Yannai's troops
in Akko). Miri brought me cool compresses every evening and
every morning for the headache that waxed and waned but never
seemed to go away. Even willow-bark tea ("my mother's secret
remedy," said Miri) did not loosen the iron band that ran from my
forehead to the nape of my neck. "My Lady," said Miri, "forgive
my impertinence, but you cannot lead a kingdom and nurse an
infant. It is too much. You must engage a wet-nurse for the baby."

"No!"

How could I explain? All the wealthy ladies had wet-nurses. But
I had waited so long for this child. I could not be separated from
him. Giving my baby to another woman would be like cutting out
my own liver. Etzi and I were one being. If I could not nurse him,
I myself would wither away.

* * *

I sleepwalked through the next six months. One day I had an appointment in the Audience Chamber with the royal architect, Philip, who dressed in the bright silks fashionable in his native Alexandria. I joked with him that when he retired and returned to his native land, he must leave behind his clothes, so that we could hang them in the Audience Chamber. They would outshine the tapestries. He laughed and unrolled on the marble table two cylinders of papyrus with alternate designs for our new Jordan River fort at Macherus. "In this one, Your Highness," Philip said, "I've sketched in the changes you suggested."

I scanned the two drawings for awhile and said, "So let it be written in the records of the throne."

"Your Majesty," Philip said, startled, "you have not said which design you prefer."

Everyone in the court laughed and forgave these slips. I swaddled baby Etzi in a shawl and carried him everywhere. To the Chamber of Hewn Stone for meetings of the Sanhedrin. To the Audience Chamber when I received visitors and heard petitions. To my conferences with Philip the architect, where I balanced the baby on my hip as I pored over drawings and suggested a few changes here and there. To the site of the aqueduct construction where I sat on a rock, the baby on my lap, to confer with the foreman. To the battlement atop the city wall to review the drilling of my troops. And every single day, to the Temple to thank the Lord for this precious blessing.

When his whimper told me that the baby needed to nurse, I excused myself from whatever meeting I was attending and went into an adjoining room. The world narrowed itself to my breast and my child. I have never again felt as fulfilled as with that tiny mouth nibbling at my breast and that soft warm baby skin touching my own.

* * *

Each day at sunrise I stood atop our eastern wall, realizing how vulnerable we were. I strained to look for signal flares from the chain of towers leading to the border forts. How long would it be before Syria took advantage of the king's absence and attacked? Villages were hungry, the priests corrupt and the queen perpetually exhausted. Yet all Jerusalem beamed on the baby and me, like a whole city of uncles and aunts.

Finally, the nights of wailing stopped. I caught up on my sleep. Baby Etzi learned to laugh: laughs that shook his round belly and his fat little chin. I could not resist leaving the Chamber of Hewn Stone from time to time to go into a private room and tickle the skin of Etzi's tiny feet. My favorite game was making noisy kisses on his belly-button. He would laugh until his face turned red and the tears came.

But Etzi was a sickly child. Often he vomited as soon as he had nursed. When he started eating solid food, painful rashes inflamed his little bottom. His nose, red as a grape, dripped as steadily as a water clock. Sometimes he gasped for breath. His face, fingers, and feet turned gray. I blew into his mouth, praying frantically that his color would return and he would survive. These attacks terrified Etzi. Afterward, he clung to me for hours as if his life lay in my hands.

CHAPTER 13

●

A forest of masts filled the harbor at Akko. The crown prince of
Egypt, Ptolemy IX Philometor, whose people called him Lathyros
(Chickpea), had come to aid Akko. He brought ten thousand
cavalry and eighty thousand Cypriot mercenaries. The nearby
port of Gaza also sent cavalry. Yannai signed a truce with Lathyros
and marched back to Jerusalem. Lathyros – treacherous as always
– bombarded his former allies in Akko and Gaza.

I welcomed the returning Judean troops at the main Jerusalem
gate. The ramparts were crowded with women and children
craning for a sight of their men. I invited Yannai to my sitting
room to tell me about the battle. I had a pot of hot mint tea
waiting for him, and some surprise news.

As soon as I had heard that Lathyros had landed at Akko, I
had sent messages to Cleopatra's Jewish generals, Chelcias and
Ananias. They replied that Cleopatra would help us. She hated
her oldest son. She would not allow Lathyros a foothold on the
Phoenician coast. I thought Yannai would be pleased at my quick
thinking.

"Idiot!" he said. "Do not stick that pointed nose of yours into
matters you know nothing about."

I had resolved not to get into a fight with my husband. But as soon as he spoke, I exploded. "We were in no danger from Akko or Lathyros when you left on this stupid adventure. Now we are."

Yannai's face reddened. He leaned forward as if he wanted to hit me.

"Akko and Gaza will fall to Lathyros any day," I said. "Do you think he will just turn around and go back to Cyprus? Judea will be next."

Yannai's arm arched over his head. His tea-cup shattered against the false window with its painted garden. He stalked out.

* * *

My message to the Egyptian generals had a consequence I had not anticipated. Lathyros was enraged to learn that I had arranged an alliance with Cleopatra while he was signing a truce with Yannai. He launched his full force against Judea. First to feel his fury was the Galilean city of Asochis.

Yossi the courier, who had stopped to visit a cousin in Asochis, raced to the palace to inform Yannai and me of the attack. The Egyptian prince Lathyros must have learned a few things about Jews. He attacked on the Sabbath, when no one would be in the fields to raise the alarm.

The Jews of Asochis were relaxing in their homes. Catapults hurled boulders from a nearby hill. Ten sturdy stone houses collapsed in ten minutes. "My cousin and I ran out of his house," said Yossi. "You could hear people screaming from under piles of rubble. You could see a leg here, the back of a head there. We worked in teams, lifting off the big stones, with the screams getting weaker and weaker."

I had heard screams like that when I was a little girl. Boulders from Syrian catapults crushed random buildings in besieged Jerusalem. The randomness was terrifying: never knowing which house would crumple next. Flaming arrows scorched the rooftops. Along with other children, I had helped to smother the flames with rags soaked in our dwindling water supply.

"The men of Asochis had only a few weapons," said Yossi. "They were slinging stones, sticks and bricks."

"My people are so brave," I said, weeping.

"Yes, My Lady," said Yossi. "Brave but almost defenseless. There were thousands of armored Cypriot soldiers. They galloped down the hill and through the streets and trampled the defenders like insects. I saw a man pinned through the navel to the door he was trying to defend – like a harpooned fish. A man on foot grabbed for a horse's bridle. The Cypriot soldier raised his sword and split the poor fellow from the crown of the head to the gullet."

"And the women and children?" I hardly dared ask.

"Trussed like fowl and raped – both girls and boys, as young as six or seven."

"Did none of the people of Asochis survive?"

"I heard the Cypriots brag that they killed four thousand. And captured ten thousand as slaves."

I remembered the plump gray-haired Asochis vintner so proud of his wedding wine. The Cypriot soldiers probably thought he was too old for the relative mercy of slavery. I felt as if I had lost a favorite uncle.

I berated myself. Did I know for certain that Lathyros intended to attack Jerusalem? My father had always warned about the danger of alliances. If I had not asked for help from Cleopatra III, Ptolemy Lathyros might simply have gone home.

Of course, if Yannai had not attacked Akko, none of this would have happened. We were two blunderers. And our people suffered.

I sent Yossi to give his report to Yannai, who as usual was at the stables. Yannai stormed into my sitting room. "This is your fault, bitch. If you had not sent a letter to your so-called friends, we would not be in this mess."

"We can sort out the blame later," I replied. "Lathryos's men have bronze armor. Our men have only oxhide. We have neither money nor time to get complete sets of armor. We will have to empty our treasury to buy bronze shields for our men."

* * *

"You will slice through these Cypriot idiots like a knife through cheese," Yannai reassured the troops massed in front of the main city gate. I was not so optimistic. Yannai had only three hundred soldiers on horse. According to the reports I had received, Lathryos had ten thousand cavalry, and five times as many footsoldiers as Yannai. Were we sending our men to slaughter? We have to do something, I told myself. I kept quiet about my doubts. The men cheered, waved their swords and their shiny new shields, and marched off in a crisp, eager file.

Yannai's soldiers were waiting when Lathryos's army crossed the Jordan River at Saphot. The front ranks of the two armies crashed, bronze on bronze. Yannai had faced difficult odds before. He was confident of his position on the river-bank. He would pour arrows on the Cypriots in midstream and drive them back into the river.

* * *

This time a different courier brought the news: Yossi's friend, the round-faced "puffball" Amos. "They rode right over us," wept Amos, wiping his muddy, sweaty cheeks with the back of his hand. "Our men were fearless. They rode straight up to the enemy to plunge a javelin into the horse's neck so it would topple and kill the rider. Some of our fellows managed to gallop past a Cypriot soldier, turn 'round in the saddle, and slice off his head from behind. But those Cypriots kept comin' and comin.' There was just too many of 'em."

How vividly I remembered our men cheering and glittering as they marched out the Jerusalem gate! I choked, picturing enemy horses trampling those shiny shields and lithe bodies into the mud. "How many did we lose?" I asked.

"At least three thousand men and all but fifty horses," Amos said in a rush of words. His puffy pink lips trembled and I thought he might break down. "Those Cypriots were chopping our men's arms and heads as if they were trimming trees," he said. "Their cavalry rolled over us like a plow with a thousand blades."

"Usually your friend Yossi is the courier," I said, with a feeling of dread.

Amos threw himself at my feet and buried his face in his arms. All I saw were the crimson crescents of his ears. "He was my friend – my best friend. One of those filthy pigs stabbed him in the belly. His guts spilled out like sausages. I sent my lance through that pig's neck. It went in under the chin and came out the back. But for Yossi, there was nothing – nothing I could do."

"No more," I said. "I can't bear to hear this."

I squeezed Etzi so tightly to my chest that he wailed.

"What happened to King Alexander?" I said.

"I don't know. My own horse was cut down. I was able to grab the reins of another, and I came to report to you."

"How long do we have before the Egyptian prince attacks Jerusalem?"

"It depends on how many villages he wants to destroy on his way here."

CHAPTER 14

Ptolemy Lathyros and his Cypriot mercenaries chewed up the villages of northern Judea.

Yannai returned to Jerusalem with the remnant of his army. As soon as he dismounted, I rushed toward him, relieved to see him unscathed. He turned his back and stalked away.

Finally, Cleopatra's fleet chased her son back to Cyprus. Cleopatra then ordered her own troops to conquer Akko.

A message from General Ananias: "Cleopatra's vizier is urging her to take Jerusalem. I warned her that if she tried, General Chelcias and I and Jews all over the world will rise up to protect our sacred city."

I was grateful to Ananias. No doubt he had risked his life by giving that advice. But for the moment at least, he had managed to change Cleopatra's mind.

"We have to talk," I told Yannai, "whether you want to or not. I have a message from Cleopatra."

"So?"

"She wants to make a peace treaty with us. You should gift her a good bit of silver, or she might find Jerusalem too tempting a target to pass by."

"I thought she was your friend," said Yannai.

"This is the way of friendship among queens," I said.

We traveled to Akko in our gold-trimmed carriage (the most expensive we had), followed by Ambassador Diogenes and fifty men on horseback.

The Egyptian queen met us at the quay. Thousands of her soldiers, mounted and on foot, surrounded the walls of Akko and kept watch from its battlements. Sun flashed on the metal of their crested helmets, shields and cuirasses. There was an answering flash of sun on the sea. We seemed to have stepped into the middle of a vast mosaic. Our guard of fifty mounted soldiers in their oxhide armor looked no more significant on the beach before the city wall than the small, dark button at the center of a vast, golden flower.

Two hundred courtiers in dizzying patterns of red, green and yellow silk bowed to the ground as Cleopatra's chief steward, in red silk, announced "the Empress of Heaven and Earth." Surrounded by soldiers in blazing bronze, Cleopatra's carriage, gilded from top to bottom, rolled toward us. Its horses were swathed in gold livery. The gold traces of the carriage were shaped like serpents striking, with fiery, ruby eyes and tongues. Cleopatra stepped from the carriage onto the bare back of a slave. The chief steward assisted her to the ground. Two more bare-backed slaves unrolled a crimson carpet before her as she stepped to the earth. Drums thrummed. Lances, metal vests and greaves clanked as her soldiers marched before, beside and behind her.

A wreath of gold laurel leaves perched atop the swaying curls of Cleopatra's dense, black wig. She was short and pudgy, with round rouged cheeks and three chins, but she walked with as much confidence as the goddess she pretended to be. The belt of her gold-bordered, purple chiton underlined her breasts, swollen and jiggling like a goat's dugs before milking. With bangles covering her bare, hairy arms, loops of silver and gold around the folds of her neck, and earrings made of golden coins, she jingled as she walked. Her eyes glittered shrewdly under emerald-painted lids.

Neither Yannai nor I knew how to greet her. While we hesitated, Cleopatra stepped up and put a hand on the baby's curls. "I see you have a new little one," she said in Greek.

"Yes," I said, smiling. "He goes with me everywhere."

"Drown him," said Cleopatra. "Take my word for it. The older they get, the more trouble they are. I had to bring an army and a navy to chase my oldest back to where he belongs."

There have been very few times in my life when I could find no words to respond. This was one. I flushed and took a step backward.

"I am jesting," Cleopatra said. "Grandchildren are a pleasure, and there is only one way to get them."

"Then I should let my son grow to manhood?" I said.

"Long enough to sire your grandson," she said. "Then ship him as far away from you as possible. If you want to keep your throne, that is."

"I will keep your advice in mind," I said. "Meanwhile, we would like to present you with a gift to thank you for your assistance on our behalf."

Two of our soldiers brought a chest piled with a thousand silver talents. "You are most gracious," said Cleopatra, raising her eyebrows and slightly tipping her head.

Two of her courtiers brought out a gilded table containing the papyrus scroll of the peace treaty. Cleopatra's chief steward read it aloud in Greek. Ambassador Diogenes read it in Aramaic. Cleopatra and Yannai affixed their seals.

Cleopatra's servants set up a red-silk tent and laid out a feast: meats, breads, cakes, fruits, wines. Yannai immediately mumbled something about needing to supervise his soldiers. Cleopatra and I were alone except for baby Etzi.

What a dilemma! Cleopatra's food was not kosher. Besides, I had not brought Eva the taster. "Today is a fast day for me," I said apologetically. "But I am grateful for the opportunity to talk with you. You have been most kind to the Jewish residents of Alexandria."

"I depend on your people," said Cleopatra. "They can read and write and calculate, and they are not under the thumb of the Egyptian priests."

I leaned forward. "Under the thumb of the priests?" I repeated.

"If I did not send my own representatives to supervise the harvests," said Cleopatra, "none of our taxes would find their way to Alexandria. The priests would keep everything."

"It's a problem," I nodded. If Cleopatra had figured out some ways to counter the greed of the priests, it would be worth having a longer conversation.

"The people in Upper Egypt do not realize how much money it takes to maintain a beautiful city like Alexandria," said Cleopatra. "The Temples, the fountains, the harbor, the parks, the guards, the gymnasia, the library. We have the greatest library in the world – at least one copy of every book ever written."

"And you pay for all this by taxing the harvests?" I said.

"Hardly!" said Cleopatra. "We tax the grain when it is harvested, and again when it is milled, and again when it is made into bread. Every bale and jug must have a royal tax stamp. If the stamp is missing – my supervisors are well armed. And of course we select the best of the pigs. We have different stamps for imports and exports. Nothing moves in or out of the city of Alexandria without a stamp. Because your people are so helpful with the business of the harbor, we may be able to offer you a special rate on Egyptian wheat. It is the best in the world."

"Perhaps you would be interested in trading for olive oil from our groves?"

"My dear, it is time you brought your Judea into modern times. We do not barter. We deal in coins. We tax every sale by every vendor, large or small. At the harbor and in the marketplace. You cannot trade with a silver talent that is half the weight of a man. Do you have a mint?"

"Thank you for that suggestion. Do you pay your soldiers in coin?"

"Of course not. How would we pay for our wine and olive oil and our silks and perfumes, our Italian glass and marble? We pay our soldiers with land. They retire to an estate in Upper Egypt where they are too happy and too busy to think about revolt."

We were silent for a moment, while Cleopatra concentrated on the cakes.

"I hope you were not offended by my remark about drowning your son," said Cleopatra.

"I knew you were just joking," I said.

Cleopatra cleared her throat. "Your son is no danger to you now. But I treat my children and my treasures the way I treat my soldiers. Spread them out – one on this island, one on that – so they cannot join forces against you. And keep the children and the treasures on different islands."

This was rather chilling advice. I hugged Etzi a little closer.

Cleopatra's courtiers advanced with a sedan chair. Cleopatra had received a message. While his mother was besieging Akko, her son Lathyros had reprovisioned at Cyprus and sailed on to attack Alexandria. Lathyros was named Ptolemy Philometor – Mother-loving. But there was plainly no love lost on either side.

"We will meet again," said Cleopatra as her servants lifted her back into her carriage.

"As friends and allies," I said.

"Of course," she said.

She leaned out the door of the coach. "I like you Jews," she said. "You're clever."

Her troops spurred their horses into the holds of her ships, ready to sail for Egypt.

"The rings on her little finger probably cost more than all the gold basins in the Temple," Yannai whispered as the procession of courtiers in their shimmering silks followed Cleopatra's coach to the Egyptian camp.

I would have liked to visit the beautiful city of Alexandria, and to talk further with Cleopatra. But within a year, she was dead – murdered, not by Ptolemy Lathyros, the son she hated (though reportedly he had tried to arrange her assassination, and she had tried to arrange his), but by Ptolemy Alexander, the son she preferred.

* * *

On the way back to Jerusalem, I stopped at Asochis. Where the town had stood was a black field of tumbled buildings and rubble. Not a person remained. Not even a goat. Nothing left of the vineyards but charred sticks pointing at the sky. I wrapped Etzi in a blanket, his face toward my shoulder. I was glad that he was too young to understand what we were seeing. Miri squeezed my hand. I put the baby into her arms. I knelt, sifted the sooty earth through my fingers, and said a prayer for the gray-haired vintner.

*   *   *

Yannai strode into my sitting room while I was seated at the table rereading the terms of our treaty with Cleopatra.

"Next time, old lady, leave the fighting to me and stick to your cisterns," he said. "You think you are some kind of diplomat? Thanks to you, half of Judea is charcoal. I have lost an army's worth of good men, and we are under some kind of obligation to that fat, little bitch with all the gold jewelry."

"I made a serious mistake," I replied.

"The lady admits a mistake! I lived to see the day!"

Grinning, he sat on the couch, leaned back, folded his arms.

"We should meet with Ambassador Diogenes," I continued.

"You are trying to make friends with my good friend Diogenes? Be careful not to get too friendly. You can be replaced."

"We need to think more about our foreign policy. Ambassador Diogenes can – "

"I can tell you what Diogenes will say because he has already said it to me. He says we have an opportunity right now. The royals in Syria and Egypt are busy killing each other. Rome is tied up with a slave revolt and pirates raiding its ships on the Great Sea. Now is our chance!"

"Our chance for what?"

"Our chance to make Judea a respected nation instead of a pitiful byway. To recapture the lands we held under King Solomon. You remember Solomon? That wise, old lecher you always quote to me?"

I leaned forward in my chair. I said, "What would it mean to recapture the lands that Solomon held?"

Yannai counted off on his fingers. "Solomon conquered the Philistines, Edomites, Moabites, Ammonites, and Hittites. He controlled the ports of Gaza, Jaffa, and Dor on the eastern shore of the Great Sea and an equal amount of land east of the Jordan River. In other words, everything from the Euphrates to the Red Sea. I aim to get it all back."

I buried my head in my hands for a moment. "You are dreaming," I said. "We have just suffered a terrible defeat, and you are dreaming of conquest."

"Cleopatra will not be back. You heard her: she has enough trouble with her own sons."

I sipped my mint tea and mustered my reasons. "We are Jews. We are different from other nations. Why would we want those foreign lands?"

"Defensible borders, my dear Shulamit. Surely you, the great strategist, realize that Judea is so tiny we can be trampled like a bug."

"Just what we need," I said. "Foreigners corrupting the morals of Judea."

"Judea's morals need a little corrupting. This place is the capital of boredom."

I paced the sitting room. "If we did manage to conquer these lands, there would be constant rebellions."

"I'll make 'em all convert to Judaism or go into exile. That should satisfy you."

"What kind of Jews would they be if they convert only to escape exile?"

"If they are as good Jews as I am, that's good enough."

"God forbid."

"If they are as good Jews as you are," said Yannai, "I could not stand it."

"Thank you."

"You are welcome."

I stood in front of Yannai. "Let us be practical. We laid siege to Akko and ended up being invaded ourselves."

"Thanks to you."

"Our army has been decimated."

Now Yannai was pacing, too, puffing with excitement as he worked out his plan. "We can strike some weaker city. Gaza is next on my list. We need a port on the Great Sea. Lathyros bombarded Gaza. All we have to do is walk in. We will make them regret that they sent troops to help Akko."

"As you said, half our land is charcoal. Our people will not stand for another war."

"When our troops ride back with gold and silver piled in our wagons," Yannai replied, "the people will cheer."

He smirked. "And you, for the second time in your life, will have to admit I am right."

"Yannai, please – "

Yannai sat on the couch. He gestured to me to sit on the chair. "I have decided on a plan," he said. "You have already made one big mistake. It would be a much bigger mistake to argue against me."

His brows bunched with a threatening look that was becoming too familiar. I was silent.

"We leave the day after the Sabbath," Yannai said. "Right now, I have a meeting with my captains."

He stood, stretched, and strode out.

I did not see Yannai for the rest of the week. He came into my sitting room to say good-bye just as I picked up our crying baby to comfort him. "Let him bawl," said Yannai. "What are you going to do – ride with him into battle to wipe his bottom?"

"If you are not going to remain in Jerusalem to raise your son," I said, "do not criticize the way I do it."

Yannai spat on the camel-hair carpet and walked out.

* * *

The Gazans – to no one's surprise – did not simply open their gates to our troops. Yannai set up his goatskin tents and catapults and began a siege.

In nightmares and daydreams, I relived the Syrian siege of Jerusalem when I was not quite seven. I remembered sheltering in shadows from the merciless sun. Waiting to sip my water ration until my tongue felt thick as wool. I could taste the stale, moldy pita doled out once a day in stingy shards. I remembered Father trying to lead the women and children out of Jerusalem's gate and back to their home villages. Only to be trapped without food or water in the barren valley when the Syrian king changed his mind and refused to let them pass. I remembered crows swooping down to peck at Father's withered body.

* * *

I summoned Caleb. "Do we have enough manpower to defend Judea while Yannai is laying siege to Gaza?" I asked him.

"I am concerned, Your Highness," said Caleb. "I told the king that we did not have enough soldiers to conduct this siege and ensure the safety of Judea. But I do not seem to have the king's ear."

"You know who has his ear?" I said. "The four Sadducee leaders:

Diogenes, Phiabi, Boethus and Hanin. Phiabi, being a merchant and trader, was especially insistent that we need a port."

Caleb stared at the false window for a few minutes, as if he could see beyond the painted garden. "If it pleases Your Majesty, I have four recommendations. First, more troops in the border forts in case of attack from Syria, Egypt or Arabia. Second, contacts in the villages, in case of rebellion. I will watch your builders as they train with my men. When I find an intelligent and trustworthy man, I will send him to you."

"Very good," I said. "We can send messages back and forth to the villages when we deliver building supplies. Your other recommendations?"

"I would suggest, My Lady, that you appoint Amos as your personal courier. He can remain with the troops in Gaza and report to you on your husband's movements. Amos is admirably loyal to you."

"I will do that," I said. "What is your fourth recommendation?"

"Your Majesty," said Caleb, "we have remained safe from Syria for the last three decades for only one reason. The Syrian princes have been too busy fighting each other to attack Judea. Can you apply the same principle to the Sadducees? If you can encourage them to fight among themselves, they may be too distracted to undermine you."

I laughed out loud. "You are a wonderful strategist," I said. "I am blessed to have your help." Then I looked into his eyes. "You understand," I said, "that neither the king nor any of your soldiers must know about this conversation."

"Of course, Your Highness," said Caleb, looking back into mine. "I am honored to have your confidence."

* * *

I read through the schedule of village corvées. The men from Ramathaim would be coming in two weeks. When they arrived, I summoned Michael, the short chunky mountain man, to the Audience Chamber. "You are a fine worker and a skilled fighter," I said. "I am sure if I need your help, you will give it. I need to hear from you regularly, regarding the mood of the people in your district."

"With pleasure, Your Highness," he said. "If you would be so gracious, I have a petition for you."

"Of course," I said. "What is the problem?"

"I would like to marry a girl from my village. A lovely, hard-working girl. Makes a delicious pot of lentils. I am a woodcutter and she is the daughter of a woodcutter. Her father has no money for a dowry. I have no money for a bride-price. Her family would accept my offer, but the headman of our village says that without a marriage settlement, we cannot marry."

I turned to Shimon, who as always was seated at my side. "Is the marriage settlement required by the Law?" I asked him.

"There must be at least a token," he said. "But a token is sufficient. A few coins. Let the couple marry now and set aside some amount, month by month, so that if God forbid something happens to her husband the wife will have means to survive."

Shimon sat at the marble table and quickly wrote a note for Michael to give to the headman of Ramathaim. "Thank you, Rabbi Shimon," said Michael. He bent and kissed my brother's hand. "You have given me my heart's desire."

I congratulated myself. I had personal connections to men in Ramathaim, Beth Zur, Ein Kerem, Lod. I could count on Amos, "the Puffball," to report to me on the actions of Yannai's army. It was a start.

I had a hard time thinking about Caleb's final recommendation. Three of the four leading Sadducees had approached me about the appointment as acting high priest. There was good potential for rivalry. I would never have suggested any of them for the job of high priest. What could I do to set them firmly against one another?

My guard told me that Amos was unsaddling his horse and would soon bring me important news from Gaza. Phiabi happened to be in the Audience Chamber requesting that guards be provided (at the crown's expense) for his caravans. "I expect to hear any moment now about the surrender of Gaza," I said. "You must be pleased. You have long been urging the king to acquire a harbor."

"Indeed, Your Highness," said Phiabi. "That has been one of my fondest dreams."

I thought back to my conversation with Cleopatra and had a sudden inspiration. Why not co-opt Phiabi by appointing him as harbormaster, with the task of exacting duties on imports and exports? Those taxes, unlike the tithes for the Temple and the poor, could be reserved for the maintenance of the court, the army, and the city of Jerusalem. Harbor tariffs would take a slice from the profits of foreign merchants. But Yannai would no longer have to rob our poor farmers and shepherds to supply food for his soldiers. I was not happy to give Phiabi an opportunity to pilfer the harbor tariffs. But he would have an incentive to be loyal to me rather than to the Sadducee party. I broached the idea to Phiabi.

"Your Highness, this is indeed a wise decision," said Phiabi, bowing out backward. "I promise: within three days I will bring you a plan."

* * *

Amos burst into the Audience Chamber, reeking of smoke. Traces of tears streaked his round cheeks. "Your Highness, may I speak with you privately?" he said.

In my sitting room, Amos told me the full story of the Gaza truce. Yannai's army – mostly mercenaries with a handful of Jewish officers – had marched through the gates of Gaza peacefully, as promised, and ordered the citizens to turn over their weapons. That evening, a drunken Yannai shouted, "How many of our boys did these barbarians kill? They deserve to be punished. And we deserve to be rewarded!"

Yannai's mercenaries grabbed statues and gold, raped girls and women, and torched the Senate building. With all the Gazan senators trapped inside.

I remembered the surrender of Jerusalem when I was seven. The victorious Syrian king rode in with horsemen and elephants to sign a treaty. He gathered up the mounds of silver tribute, bound his hostages, and rode away. What if instead he had turned his soldiers loose to rape young girls like me? What if he had burned the Holy Temple with all the priests inside?

Yannai came home from Gaza grinning. He expected congratulations from an admiring wife. He came to our bedchamber, sweaty and blood-stained, without even bathing. I blocked the door, screaming, "How could you make a treaty and break it? Have you no honor?"

"You are a queen, and it shocks you to hear about someone breaking a treaty?" said Yannai, placing his hands on both sides of the doorframe. "Have you been living in a cave all your life? Listen, Holy Lady, these Gazans lashed at us for months. With poisoned arrows, like snakes. My comrades laid down their lives to capture that city. Who should I reward? My comrades or my enemies?"

"Comrades!" I snapped. "Those foreign soldiers-for-hire who signed up to fight with you because you paid them well? If you stop paying them, they will desert you in a minute and go to any king who pays them better."

"So? I would do the same. But let me tell you. When you are out there, if your soldiers are not your comrades, you are dead. Money goes only so far, and after that, loyalty is the only reason a man risks his life for his commander."

I retorted, "I hope you can find a good source of money, because what would keep soldiers loyal to a man like you, I do not know."

Yannai lunged at me. But I was ready. I stepped adroitly into the bedchamber and barred the door. What did I hope to accomplish? A hundred times since that day I have wished I had shut my mouth.

CHAPTER 15

Within days, Yannai returned vinegar for vinegar. He moved his "comrades" and his full entourage of camp followers into the palace. "How dare that man insult our queen by turning the palace of Judea into a brothel!" said Miri. "Your Majesty, you should hire one of those whores to cut off his 'implement' before it falls off from overuse."

I did not trust myself to reply.

As promised, in three days Phiabi brought me a suggested list of tariffs, a plan for a harbor office where they would be levied, and even designs for a tax stamp and several denominations of coins, with images of the seven-branched menorah, the cornucopia, the palm tree, and the pomegranate.

"Phiabi may be greedy," I told Miri later. "But he is efficient and capable."

"Your Majesty," said Miri, "I am sure he is thinking of the coins that will tumble into his lap if you appoint him as harbor-master."

I had told Phiabi I would consult with my husband and let him know when he could proceed. Both Phiabi and I knew what that meant: we could do no more about the harbor plan until Yannai was sober. Who knew how long that would take?

The great rooms, littered with smashed crystal and torn drapes, stank of vomit and piss. As I walked down the broad main staircase one day, a naked soldier and his naked woman tumbled past me, almost knocking me over. They were so drunk they felt no pain. They sprawled on their backs at the bottom of the stairs, showing their nakedness to the world. I worried that they had been killed by the fall. But after a few minutes, they fumbled toward each other, attempting to couple right there. In front of their queen and everyone in the palace. They giggled and flailed about as my guards dragged them away.

I had to stop this. I tried to think what Father would do. I could not bear to imagine his knowing about such depravity in the palace.

Maybe if I apologized to Yannai for insulting him, if I were truly abject and contrite, he would forgive me and we could start over. I entered the banquet hall with its curved sconces and beveled red-cedar ceiling. Wine puddled the pattern of light and dark woods on the inlaid head table. Seated there, seven very drunk women with painted eyes and gauzy wraps leaned on an equally drunk Yannai. He had flung open his robe, showing his hairy private parts. On one of his knees lounged a woman whose gown had slipped off her shoulder to expose one breast. Yannai turned to me, growling, "Bitch, where is our dinner?"

I was afraid if I tried to speak or move I would start crying.

A woman clad in yellow gauze slurred to her friend in blue, "King Yannai should not talk to his wife that way. She is the queen."

"He cares no more for her than for the lowest scullery," laughed the blue-draped woman.

"Do not fool yourself. She is still the queen to him. And to him, you and I are as alike as lentils."

"But he certainly has an enormous appetite for lentils!"

Yannai stood, dumping the bare-breasted whore on the floor. "You think your hole is so great?" he shouted, leaning into my face. "There are better holes all over Judea."

He turned his back to me, lifted his robe, and waggled his bare rear end.

"Your Majesty, you can still do it," said Miri when I gave her the short version of my encounter with Yannai. "You can still hire some whore to suffocate him. To sit on his face."

* * *

Judah son of Tabbai, the vice-president of the Sanhedrin, told Yannai that members of the Sanhedrin were concerned about the presence of heathen women in the palace. Yannai said, "Would you rather I bring in more Jewish whores?"

Shimon berated me: "How can you permit these abominations in the palace?"

"You men decreed that a woman must bow to her husband's wishes," I said. "Do you expect me to have any influence on the man?"

When I walked into the Chamber of Hewn Stone, Yannai, slouching on his throne, bellowed, "Get that bitch out of here."

Both Sadducees and Pharisees were silent, gaping. Ambassador Diogenes stood, suppressing a grin. *He will say that a woman should not be in the chamber,* I thought. He sees that Yannai hates me, and he will make up some excuse for Yannai to hang me.

Ambassador Diogenes surprised me. "Perhaps we should recess the Sanhedrin for today," he said. "We all need to rest."

I realized: my husband's drunken savagery might be my best protection from the Sadducees. With Yannai on the throne, Judea needed me. But who would protect me from the man himself?

Sitting on the edge of my silken couch, I prayed, *Almighty, what should I do?*

The first step was suddenly clear. Because Etzi was a sickly child, I must have another son. A queen is nothing if she is neither a wife nor a mother, I told myself. Being a wife requires a husband. Being a mother requires only a child. If I were pregnant, Yannai might hesitate to kill me until his second child was born. And even Yannai must realize that Judeans would disapprove of killing a pregnant woman or a nursing mother.

That night, Yannai, sprawled asleep at the table, got up to piss. I was waiting for him. "I am sorry I spoke harshly to you," I whispered, running my fingers over his sensitive spots. "I was so worried about you, so lonely without you, that I was half-crazy. You are my first, my only, my true love."

That very night, I conceived our second son. "At least from having all these camp followers around, I have picked up some good techniques," I thought with chilly satisfaction when I realized I was pregnant again.

This second child was conceived in deceit. I thought of it as an "it," rather than a "he." Having Etzi in my womb felt like completion. This new creature felt like a parasite, sucking away my energy and joy. I worried that my fury at my husband had twisted this fetus's soul. I prayed: *Almighty, please help me to love this child. Unequal love can poison.* I felt hopeless. Even the Almighty had loved Abel more than Cain.

* * *

The heavier and more awkward I got, the more I tried to ignore this alien being growing inside me. I concentrated on my work.

One day Etzi climbed on the blue couch next to me and tried to push my great mass of belly out of the way. "No room for Etzi," he sniffed.

I gathered him onto my lap as best I could and snuggled my cheek to his. "There will always be room for Etzi," I reassured him.

Neither Etzi nor I could put off the soon-approaching day when we would have to make room for one more.

* * *

Tobit came into the world red-faced and squalling, his little fists and feet striking furiously at the air. Yannai snatched the newborn from my arms. "He is already a fighter!" said Yannai. "This one is mine!"

I named the baby Aristobulus II – Tobit – hoping he might be as gentle, honest and conscientious as my first husband. (Yudi seemed a much better man to me – and a much better king – now that I had someone to compare him with.)

Tobit's birth brought a brief truce in the war of wills between Yannai and me. In the early morning dimness, Yannai and I lay on the bed together, the oil lamp flickering our shadows against the wall, the new baby sleeping snugly between us. In the afternoon, when all Jerusalem rested, we sprawled on the silk bedcovers, bathing our naked bodies in the stream of sunlight. Yannai tickled the baby. Then he tickled me. I giggled. He put his nose to the baby's nose, and then to my nose. He kissed my still-swollen belly. *Maybe this marriage is possible after all,* I thought. Love flowed from my heart, a gentle wave, washing over my baby and my husband, drawing the three of us together. Cupping one hand to protect the baby's blood-crusted umbilical, Yannai put his lips on Tobit's belly and sputtered a silly sound. "Like a duck squawking," I said.

"Like a horse fart," said Yannai.

Miri, always so tactful, was careful not to bring Etzi to my chamber except when Yannai was out of the room and Tobit was sleeping.

For eight days – until Tobit's circumcision – Yannai and I lingered quietly together, admiring our tiny, beautiful child. I managed to keep Yannai away from strong drink until after he had circumcised the baby. Then came the feast.

* * *

"Nice," said Yannai, sniffing the roast lamb and the sprays of balsam in the banquet room. He surveyed the linen-covered tables, the bowls of dates and almonds, the trays of meat and fish, the shimmering crowd of silk-garbed guests, and seemed content. I dreaded this feast of circumcision. For seven days, Yannai had been sober, even loving. Now he would drink, and anything could happen.

At first, the wine just made him jolly and a bit argumentative. When I commented on the excellence of the lamb, Yannai insisted that goat was better. "Whatever you say," I agreed.

"You're just saying that," said Yannai. "You like lamb because it has no flavor – like everything else about this court. I like goat because it's tough; even when it's roasted, it kicks back."

"Whatever you say," I repeated.

"We should take a vote of the Sanhedrin," said Yannai, his voice rising.

"Why not just call in the acting high priest and ask him?" I suggested. "He eats from the meat of the sacrifices just as we do."

How could I have made such a stupid suggestion? Yannai loathed the acting high priest. Issachar of Kefar Barkai would raise one eyebrow haughtily and turn his head away if another priest spoke to him without using his full title. He veiled his hands in silk while performing the sacrifices, as if his hands were too pure to be sullied by blood. When Issachar heard Yannai's question, he dismissed it with a flick of his white-gloved hand. "It is obvious," said the acting high priest. "If goat were better, it would be brought as the daily offering."

Yannai thumped the table with his fist. "Look at the way he flicks his wrist at us," he growled. "'Obviously,' he has no respect for royalty."

He turned to the guard standing beside him. "Take this man," he said, grabbing Issachar's sleeve, "and cut off his impudent right hand."

"Yannai!" I protested. "You asked for his opinion."

"His opinion was wrong," said Yannai.

The guard took Issachar's elbow and hurried the white-faced priest out of the room. Fortunately, the guests at the long banquet tables were too busy conversing to realize what was going on.

When the guests left, I paced from wall to wall of my sitting room, too agitated to sleep. I have got to prevent Yannai from drinking, I thought. Drinking, he thumps the table and chops off the hands of anyone who disagrees with him. Sober, he tickles the baby and caresses my breast. Yannai could be so brutal, but when he had time to think about what he'd done, he was contrite. *When he wakes up tomorrow and realizes what he has done,* I told myself, *I will talk to him about his drinking and why it has to stop.*

* * *

The next afternoon, when Yannai finally woke after his all-night drunk, I approached him in the now-deserted banquet hall.

I hoped the swaddled baby sleeping on my shoulder would soften him enough to listen to me. I hesitated, unnerved by the sour-sweet smell of alcohol that breathed from Yannai's pores. I was struggling for the right words when Yannai turned to his guard and barked, "Bring me the hand of that idiot."

"We did not know, sir, that you wanted it preserved," quaked the guard, turning pale.

Yannai ignored me. He glared at the door in stony silence until the guard returned with the hand: grayish, bloody, with gristle and shattered bone sticking out from the stump. Yannai was sober enough to spot a problem. "This is a left hand, not the right hand. Bring the executioner! And bring Issachar!"

Issachar stood before us in the expanse of the dark-paneled banquet hall. He reminded me of the dried stem of a weed in a winter garden. His face was gray, the stump of his left wrist wrapped in blood-soaked bandages. "Your Majesty," he begged. "Is it not enough that I am blemished and banished from the priest-hood? I must be able to eat, and to earn a living when I return to my village."

"Is it not enough that you insulted my taste, but you also have to insult my intelligence?" snarled Yannai. "I know your kind: you bribed him to cut off the left hand instead of the right, did you not?"

Issachar said nothing.

"Did you not?" roared Yannai.

"No, Your Majesty," said Issachar, trembling.

"And now you lie about it."

"No, My Lord."

"As for you – " He turned to the executioner. "Do you want me to believe you do not know the difference between left and right?"

"Your Highness, perhaps the instructions were not clear," mumbled the executioner.

"Liar. You took that bribe. Guard, bring out a chopping block."

Issachar and the executioner trembled. To the executioner, Yannai said, "Do you know the difference between a hand and a head?"

"Yes, my Lord."

"Then cut off his other hand."

"Now? Here?"

"Here and now, where I can see it."

I clutched the baby and shut my eyes. I heard the thunk of the axe. I sobbed. I got up to leave, averting my eyes from the blood splattered over the table. Yannai said, "Issachar. When you go back to your village, tell the people this is what happens to the hand that extends a bribe. And as for you," he said to the executioner, "do you know what happens to the hand that accepts the bribe?"

"Your Majesty," faltered the executioner, "must I lose my hand also?"

"No. You will lose your head. Guard, take him away. Save the head for my inspection, or your own will roll."

Racing back to my bedchamber, I clutched the baby to my chest so tightly that he squalled. Miri, wheeling Etzi in his wagon, hurried after me, her face white. I did not trust myself to speak.

I sent a message to Shimon. "Find me a plausible candidate for acting high priest. Immediately."

* * *

Birth had ripped my private parts and seared my belly. Every time I turned in bed, I cried out. Every time I relieved myself, my belly clenched and fire flared in my loins.

Too exhausted to venture out of bed, I nursed my new baby and wept. I hated myself for this passivity, but I felt as heavy as wet sand. Like sand, I had no spine. If I tried to move, I would crumble.

CHAPTER 16

By the time I recovered, Yannai had sold the high priesthood again. That sneak Phiabi had hacked out his path to power without my help.

"Phiabi is a great fellow," said Yannai. "His son Ishmael is going to try out for the acting high priest's job – says he can make the sacrifices a lot more interesting. Phiabi is going to donate new supplies and equipment to replace what we lost in the battle with Lathyros."

A tryout for the job of acting high priest? "My husband doesn't know the difference between worship and stagecraft," I railed to Miri.

I pleaded illness and did not attend. Afterward, Yannai told me, "You missed a good show. The man is quite a dresser. His mother made him a silk tunic worth a small fortune. So many jewels stitched into that thing I am surprised he can stand up. It will definitely brighten up the boredom of the daily sacrifices."

Ishmael's two grown sons – Phiabi's grandsons – became Temple treasurers. Yannai saw no contradiction between punishing his last acting high priest for bribery and accepting a bribe from the new one. Defying the Law of the Lord was no sin, but woe to the man who disregarded Yannai's whims.

I had had such hopes for our marriage during the seven days before Tobit's circumcision. Now it took all my will to maintain a civil face when Yannai spoke to me. I was relieved when he galloped out the gate for another military campaign.

Within weeks, messengers from ten different villages crowded the Audience Chamber. Beards and side-curls bobbed in agitation. "You must help us," said a tall gaunt man, bent over his walking stick. "The sons of Ishmael do not collect tithes, they commit robbery. They take three times the usual tithe. We will starve."

"If we refuse to pay, they beat us with clubs and sticks," said a small man. He hopped from foot to foot like a bird, illustrating his words with flailing hands.

"When they know we have nothing to give, they beat us anyway," said a man with sunken cheeks and sad eyebrows.

The messengers waited in the anteroom, telling each other stories in loud, excited voices. I paced before my throne. Was there anything I could do about this corruption? I am ashamed to say it, but I was afraid. Ishmael was Yannai's choice for high priest. I had seen what happened to people who opposed Yannai's choices. But I had to do something.

"I am outraged by what is happening," I told the messengers when I summoned them back into the Audience Chamber. "It will not continue."

The only solution, I thought, was to wrest the treasury from the Sadducee priests. Without enraging Yannai.

"I have to find a way to disqualify Ishmael as high priest and his sons as treasurers," I told Miri.

"My Lady," said Miri, "you thought Phiabi delivered poisoned wine to King Aristobulus. If you could prove that Phiabi was the culprit, would that disqualify his son?"

"It might," I said, "but I would have to find a witness. Two witnesses."

"What about King Aristobulus's valet Jason?" said Miri. "Except for you, he was the last person to see King Aristobulus alive."

Hanin and Phiabi had tried to persuade Jason to testify to a lie. Could I persuade him to testify to the truth?

"How can we find Jason?" I said. "It has been years since he worked here."

"Your Highness, I am only guessing," said Miri, "But I may know how to find him."

* * *

"My Lady," said Miri, "you'll have to sit down before I tell you the news."

"Did you find Jason?" I asked.

"I did," said Miri. "Guess who he works for!"

"Phiabi?" I said.

"Not only Phiabi, but also Diogenes."

"Did you speak to him?"

"He wasn't at either place. Do you know where he was?"

"How could I possibly guess?" I said.

"He was on the way back from Akko."

"Akko? What was he doing there?"

"My Lady, Phiabi and Diogenes have business interests in Akko. And Antioch. And Jaffa. They'll be starting in Gaza soon. It seems the boundaries between nations are no problem for them. Jason is their private courier."

"I am amazed at your skill, Miri, in digging out information. How did you learn all this?"

Miri dimpled and blushed. "In my free hours, I make friends with various stable-hands. They gossip even more than the kitchen maids."

"You are even more valuable to me in your free time," I said, "than when you are by my side. I will have to give you more free time."

"Your Majesty," said Miri, "do you know what else I discovered?"

"I'm beyond guessing."

"Before he became valet to King Aristobulus, Jason was a courier for Hanin, the oil merchant. He delivered messages between Hanin and Judith, King Alexander's mother."

I remembered: Judith was Hanin's cousin. Judith had persuaded High Priest John Hyrcanus to give Hanin the monopoly on sacred oil for the Temple lamps. "Remember how Judith suddenly appeared, claiming to be regent," Miri said, "when High Priest John Hyrcanus was in his final days? Jason was the courier who summoned her. And here is something interesting: when Lord Hyrcanus died and King Aristobulus came to the throne, Hanin recommended Jason as the king's valet. What do you make of all that?"

I sighed. "I do not know what to think," I said. "Clearly, Jason has access to a lot of information. He may have been a spy for the Sadducee leaders. He may even have poisoned King Aristobulus. One thing is certain: we will never get Jason to give information against the Sadducees who supply his bread. If we want to take the Temple treasury back from the Sadducees, we will have to find another way."

"Your Highness," said Miri, "I'm wondering why Jason did not go back to Hanin's household when King Alexander dismissed him from royal service."

"Maybe Hanin and Diogenes wanted to spy on Phiabi," I said. "Perhaps Phiabi did not know that he was carrying poisoned wine."

"Perhaps," said Miri.

"I have been assuming that the four leading Sadducees act as a group," I said. "But Diogenes and Phiabi and Boethus all competed for the post of high priest. Perhaps Hanin uses Jason to spy on the other three."

"Perhaps," said Miri.

"Perhaps," I said. We both burst out laughing.

"We sound like a pair of bandits planning to rob a caravan," I said.

"Your Majesty," said Miri, "to catch a bandit, you have to think like a bandit."

* * *

"I want you to be my eyes and ears," I told Miri. "Take as much time away from the palace as you need. Bring me any information you can glean. In any case, I have depended too much on you to care for my boys. I want to spend as much time as I can alone with them while they are young."

Tobit walked early – at ten months. He was tireless. When we walked in the public square, he ran. If I brought him to the Audience Chamber, he zoomed back and forth, buzzing like a fly. If confined to the nursery, he climbed onto chairs and jumped off. Always he had to catch up with or do better than his brother. When Etzi climbed on a bed, Tobit climbed from the bed to the windowsill. More than once I had to grab my younger son to prevent him from jumping from the window into the courtyard.

When Tobit was two and Etzi four, Yannai gave the boys

wooden swords. Tobit loved his sword and took it to bed at night. In the morning, he whipped it out from under the cover. He whooped. He galloped toward Etzi. He whacked his brother on the leg. Etzi did not parry the blow. He howled and ran to me, cheeks red, eyes and nose streaming.

I clenched my fists. "Tobit! Stay away from your brother!" I yelled. "Etzi! Stand up for yourself!"

How could two boys from the same womb be so different? One early spring day, when Etzi was five and Tobit three, we strolled through Jerusalem's narrow stone alleys, peering into the market stalls. Etzi clung to my hand, venturing from my side only once to run his hand along a length of woolen cloth. Tobit, quick as a lizard, darted from the wool merchant's stall to the spice stall, swooping and bouncing. I couldn't help smiling. Tobit was as lithe and lively as his father. I wished Etzi had some of Tobit's energy.

Tobit shouted, "Raisins! I want raisins!" and "Almonds! Mama, I am starving!"

"Hold out your hands," offered the vendor of dried fruit. He filled Tobit's cupped hands. I smiled and paid the vendor.

Along the top of the low stone wall bounding the main city square, Tobit teetered, one foot in front of the other. At three, he already had his father's daring. Etzi scattered handfuls of grain for the pigeons.

As we left the square, barefoot women in ragged dresses and kerchiefs shooed the pigeons away. They swept up the remaining grain that Etzi had scattered, and toasted it on a rock before a small fire.

"Our storehouses should have enough grain to feed the poor," I told Miri when we got back to the palace. "Why are women begging and scavenging in Jerusalem? I will not let Yannai feed his soldiers from widows' bread."

Patched-together tents sprouted outside the city wall, crowded with husbandless women and their unruly children. Rasping coughs echoed among the tents. What protection could these rags give from the chilly rains of a Jerusalem winter? At least ten tiny bodies were buried outside the city walls: children who had succumbed to the winter cold.

I opened the storehouses and ordered my workers to load carts with grain and dried fruit. Yannai would be furious if his requisitions were not filled, but I would deal with that when he found out. Miri and I took Etzi and Tobit and distributed food in the tent city. Ragged women and children swooped toward us like pigeons descending on a pile of garbage.

* * *

The next day, clouds shrouded Jerusalem. Miri tried to amuse the boys in the nursery. I sat at the work table in my sitting room just outside the nursery, talking with Isaiah, stoop-shouldered master of the Jerusalem storehouses.

"Your Majesty," Isaiah said, "next year will be the Sabbatical year, when the Lord commands us to let the fields lie fallow. Many people have fled the villages to come to Jerusalem. We will need to requisition more food this year from the farmers and shepherds."

"I do not see how we can ask the country people to give more," I said. "They are already pleading for relief. We dare not provoke more people into giving up farming and coming to the city to seek work."

Sadducee leaders traveled from village to village, blaming the famine on me.

It was nearly time for the Feast of Mordechai, which would

require a great public banquet. Hannah the cook, square-chinned and ruddy, brought honey pastries for my approval, stuffed with dried figs and chopped almonds. I winced when I thought of the families who did not have bread.

I strolled into the nursery to offer pastries to my sons. Tobit grabbed Etzi's. "Would you make him give it back?" I asked Miri.

I tried to ignore Tobit's taunts and Etzi's screams but found it hard to concentrate.

My next meeting was with Little David, my red-headed chief mason. "Families are sleeping in the city squares with no shelter but their cloaks," I said. "At least once a week I hear of a child who has died from the chill. We must extend the city walls and build housing for the newcomers."

Little David, who got his name from his great girth, pointed a rust-haired forearm out the window. "There is high ground on the north side, Your Highness. We could – "

We were interrupted by a screech from Etzi and a shout from Miri. "Stop this! Tobit! Into that corner! And Etzi! You over there! Not a word from either of you until the changing of the guards."

"I will pace out the dimensions and give you an estimate," said David.

"We have to get agreement from the Great Sanhedrin to expand the walls of Jerusalem," I said, "but the need is so obvious that I do not think there will be a problem."

"Mine!" shrieked Etzi.

"Put that down!" shouted Miri. "Tobit! Etzi! Both of you."

Little David raised his eyebrows, shrugged and grinned. "Boys," he said.

But not my boys, I thought. *If my workers hear their princes shouting and fighting, what will they think of their queen?*

A great weariness pressed on my shoulders. With screams, taunts and sobs echoing in my ears, everything I had to do, from budgeting for bricks to giving a menu to the cook, seemed like a burden too great to bear.

I can cobble together a truce in Akko, I thought. *Surely I can teach my sons to be civil to each other.*

CHAPTER 17

Messengers trekked to every village, to summon the seventy-one members of the Great Sanhedrin. If I could not persuade them to meet immediately after the Fast of Esther and the Feast of Mordechai, those men who were still in the villages would become involved in spring planting. We would lose the spring building season and might be unable to finish the new wall by next winter.

I fretted for the two weeks it took the elders to assemble. Decorously veiled and accompanied by Captain Caleb and Miri, I toured the tent city with the first five councilors to arrive. We ducked lines of laundry, circled around screaming eight- and nine-year-olds pounding each other with dirty fists, and glanced into ragged shelters. Women and children huddled listlessly under piles of rags, trying to insulate themselves from the chill of early spring. As we left the camp, we passed a woman and five small children lying on the ground close to the path. The woman scrambled to her feet. She jerked the arms of the two oldest, forcing them to stand. They hung their heads, shy and sullen, wavering on their feet. "Show respect," snapped the woman. "This is our queen."

"Hungry, Mama," wailed the smallest child, clinging to her leg.

"These are elders who have traveled to Jerusalem for a meeting of the Great Sanhedrin," I said. "Will you show them where you sleep?"

The woman pointed to the ground. "Your Majesty, we got no tent," said the woman. "We sleep right here."

I brought the elders and this one family into the palace. Hannah the cook served them bowls of lentil soup. One of the elders said the blessing of thanks for bread. The woman and her children tore at their pita like jackals. While the elders blew on spoons of hot soup, the woman and her children picked up their bowls and drained them in a gulp. The woman knelt to kiss the hem of my robe. "The Lord protect you," she said.

"And you also," I said.

After my guard had returned the family to the tent city, I spoke to the elders. "Ten children from the tent city died from chill this winter," I said. "I will find places for each member of this sacred council to sleep tonight. Before you fall asleep, think about how you will persuade the Council of Seventy-One to expand the city walls. We must build new housing for these wretched women and their children before next winter. Where can a Jew turn for shelter, if not to Jerusalem?"

At the first meeting of the Great Sanhedrin, David the mason presented his drawing of the new wall and the new apartments. The five elders made impassioned speeches. Those who may have been opposed were too ashamed, I think, to vote against the plan. I felt a small thrill of triumph. David and his workers began laying the first row of stones the next day.

* * *

After the meeting of the Great Sanhedrin, I summoned Ambassador Diogenes.

"You must persuade the king to stop engaging in wars of conquest," I said. "Our land is on the path to ruin because of the expense of supplying his armies."

"Your Highness," replied Diogenes, "with all due respect, in the fullness of time, our land will benefit from your husband's conquests. The ports he has secured will increase our trade, and the conquered peoples provide fertile fields and plunder."

"Who benefits from the ports and fields and plunder?" I retorted. "Only the merchants and landowners who already have more than their share."

"We are surrounded by hostile lands," said Diogenes. "By expanding our borders, the king keeps all Judea safer from foreign invasions."

"But my husband says he means to keep fighting until he has taken all the lands once occupied by Solomon," I said.

"He is a talented soldier," said Diogenes. "I think he will do it."

* * *

Yannai arrived in Jerusalem on a rare visit, eager to play with his sons. "John! Wrestle with your Papa!" said Yannai, slapping Etzi on the cheek.

Etzi was startled and scared. He tried to run away but tripped. Yannai grabbed him by the arm, sneering. "Those sandals not enough to protect your precious little toes? Maybe you need boots. Or are your feet too delicate?"

Yannai treated Tobit the same way, but Tobit loved it. He pummeled his father with his fists. Yannai roared with laughter. Yannai got on his knees to "fight" with Tobit. When Tobit landed a blow on Yannai's nose, Yannai shouted, "Punch me! See if you can knock me over! Go for blood!"

When Yannai left the room, Tobit trotted at his father's heels.

The next day, Yannai and I, with our retinue of guards, took the boys for a walk in the city. Tobit broke through the line of guards and scrambled onto a stone wall, shouting, "Papa! Watch me jump!"

In the stables, he called out, "Papa! Put me up on the horse! Watch me ride!"

At the dinner table, he slopped his cup of watered wine onto his upper lip and shouted, "Look, Papa! I have a mustache! Like you!"

I couldn't help smiling. Tobit was so eager, so charming, so like the best parts of Yannai. If only he had not inherited Yannai's temper.

* * *

Construction on the new wall had gone slowly. "I am sorry," said Little David, my chief mason. "It is almost impossible to retain enough laborers for the village corvées. As soon as I assemble a crew, the king drafts them for his next battle."

After David had gone, I fumed to Miri, "What kind of ruler robs his people of food and shelter, his villages of their men?"

"Most rulers," said Miri. "Except you."

As much as I worried about the famine, the tent city, and the continuing waves of refugees, I worried almost as much about the daily battles between my sons.

One day when he was nearly five, Tobit shouted, "Etzi! Wrestle!"

He twisted his brother's arm, and smacked Etzi so hard that my oldest son fled from the nursery with a bloody nose.

Before I could stop myself, I did something I regretted. My hand shot out and slapped Tobit on the face. He fell backward onto his bed, his nose dripping red on the blue silk. I did not realize it then, but with that blow, drawing blood from Tobit, I had crossed a boundary. It would be impossible to get back to neutral ground.

Tobit leaped to his feet and tried to hit back, but I held him at arm's length. He twisted furiously and managed to land a hard kick on my knee. I winced. It was like being kicked by four-year-old Yannai. How had Tobit turned out so similar to the father he hardly ever saw?

"You hate me!" Tobit screamed, smearing the crimson dribbling from his nose.

"I'm sorry. I did not mean to do that," I said, reaching for a cloth to stanch the scarlet trickle. He pushed me away.

"You hate me!"

"Your father smacks you, and you seem to like it."

Again he wiped away blood. "Papa is teaching me to fight. You hit me because you hate me."

I sat on the stone floor so that my eyes were level with Tobit's. "I hit you because you hurt your brother."

"You hate me. If you loved me, you would let me hit back."

I stifled a chuckle. Tobit must have inherited his reasoning ability from his father. "Why do you go out of your way to bother your brother?" I asked Tobit.

"Etzi is a baby," said Tobit, sniffing up blood and spitting it on the floor. "All I have to do is stare at him and he starts to cry."

"He cries because you hurt him."

Tobit turned away. "You always believe him and not me. I know I am going to get in trouble whether I hurt him or not, so I might as well hurt him."

"Why do you want to hurt him?"

He turned to glare at me. "Because you love him and you don't love me."

The worst thing a child could say to his mother – and the hardest to refute. "Why do you say that?" I asked.

"Anything Etzi wants you give him. Anything I want, you say no."

I touched Tobit's shoulder. He pushed away my hand. Such guilt I felt! Tobit was a treasure: quick-witted and adventurous. He would be a fine leader some day. But how could I make him feel loved when I constantly had to punish him to prevent him from becoming his father?

"Etzi asked for a pigeon in a cage," I said. "You asked for a knife. A bird in a cage won't hurt anything. A knife will."

"Papa will give me a knife. He likes a boy who can fight."

* * *

Etzi named his new bird Feathery. I bought Feathery from a pigeon vendor near the Temple. The man's pigeons were bred to be sacrificed at the Temple by worshippers who could not afford a lamb or goat. To attract customers, the vendor had taught his birds to do tricks: to balance on a finger, fetch sticks, tap on the bar of the cage to get food.

The vendor (Etzi called him the Bird Man) supplied Etzi with a cage made of bent and interlaced reeds. Etzi spent hours training that bird. He would lay out a tidbit of grain, to coax the bird along, and then another. It followed him like a puppy. Such patience my eldest son had! Such concentration. He will be a good priest, I told myself.

"Your Majesty," said Miri, wrinkling her nose, "the nursery smells of bird dung." I watched the bird tap-tapping behind Etzi. Its head jerked forward like a nodding old beggar woman hurrying after a likely source of alms. I shrugged. I could live with the mess.

Etzi had developed his own pastime instead of simply reacting to his brother.

* * *

Etzi, with Feathery perched on his shoulder, was cleaning out the bird's cage. Tobit, bored, whacked Etzi's rear with the wooden sword. Feathery flew out the window. Tobit snatched Feathery's cage and threw it out the window. I was busy trying to deal with the food shortages. I had no patience for such nonsense. Etzi ran out the door to recapture his bird. Tobit rushed after his brother, brandishing the sword. I grabbed the sword and tried to break it over my knee. That failing, I used it to whack Tobit on his behind. And again on the back of his leg. And again. My arm worked up and down like the lever on a pump. I was so angry my breath came in gasps. Six red welts, leaking blood. "You – will – never – do – this – again!" I shouted.

But I knew Tobit would do this, or something like it, again. And I was afraid I would beat him again.

I was furious at myself, and furious at my son. Tobit was a little boy, but I felt as helpless to control him as to control his father.

That night was a sleepless one. I had beaten my son. How could I have done such a thing? I was less competent at the everyday discipline of children than the humblest peasant woman. Other parents spanked their children. But my own parents had never hit me in the six precious years I had lived with them. I was as much a brute as Seth, the husband of my official taster, Eva. It was clear that Seth – who had pleaded with me not to take his wife – had loved Eva, as I loved Tobit. Yet he beat her so badly that she ran to the court for mercy. What kind of love is so easily outmatched by fury?

How could I rule my kingdom if I could not rule my sons? How could I mother my sons if I could not rule myself?

I considered turning the boys over to Miri. But she was my confidante, my sounding board, my spy. I needed her for other, important work. I thought of Cleopatra's advice: send them to different islands. I gave up and engaged a nursemaid for each of the boys. I furnished two identical whitewashed nurseries on opposite sides of the palace. "Keep them apart," I instructed the nursemaids. "Do not let their paths cross."

* * *

"I'm going to take Tobit back with me," announced Yannai on his next visit home. "To the battlefield?" I objected. "He's only five years old."

"So? I was four when my father sent me to live with soldiers."

"But he didn't send you to a place where there was fighting. It's too dangerous."

"Danger makes men," said Yannai.

"Who will take care of him while you are in battle?"

"I have friends in camp."

"Your whores? You cannot expose him to those 'friends.' What morals will they teach him?"

"He's better off with immoral tarts than with a hypocrite who preaches peace and gives her son a bloody nose and six whacks with a wooden sword."

Tobit must have shown Yannai his bruises. I was ashamed.

After a week, I rode to Yannai's camp to bring Tobit back. Arriving at the camp in late afternoon, I found Tobit bare-chested, his cheeks and shins and blackened feet smeared with dust and sweat. He was sitting on the lap of a whore in a blonde wig. She popped almonds into Tobit's mouth while she cuddled him on her lap. I was sickened. "Let him go right now!" I ordered.

"Why?" she said. "He likes it."

"I have come to take you home," I told Tobit.

"No!" he shouted. "I want to stay here."

Yannai appeared, his face below the visor crusted with sweaty dust. He peeled off his oxhide armor, grabbed a wooden sword, and shouted, "Tobit! Put up your guard!"

Yannai dropped to his knees, parrying and thrusting, and roaring with delight when his son managed to touch his belly with the wooden sword. Tobit's black curls danced. He thrust with his sword, blocked with his small round shield. His eyes shone.

"I am glad Tobit has had a taste of your life here," I said. "I have come to take him home."

"I want to stay with Papa!" shouted Tobit.

"What does he eat?" I asked Yannai.

Tobit reached into a sack and pulled out a handful of dried salted goat meat and chunks of stale bread.

"Where do you sleep?" I persisted.

Tobit dug a heel into the ground. "In the dirt. Like the other soldiers."

"I am not going to let you take him home and turn him into mush like the other one," said Yannai. "He is flogged when he disobeys. He learns to live tough and to stay alert. That is the way to build a leader."

Yannai seemed to have forgotten the misery of his own childhood. Or maybe not. He was giving his second son something he had never had: a father.

I tried to hug Tobit but he twisted away. I realized, *If I let him stay, I will lose my son.*

With a flash of pain, I remembered his infancy, when the sun warmed his bare bottom as he lay on the bed between Yannai and me. But what could I do? My second son no longer wanted me for a mother.

"We will try it your way," I told Yannai.

"Maybe it is for the best," I told Miri as we rode back to Jerusalem.

"Your Majesty," said Miri, "he will learn to behave like his father. Is that what you want?"

"He was behaving like Yannai even when he never saw his father," I said. "Maybe it is in the blood."

* * *

When Yannai and Tobit returned to Jerusalem for the Days of Awe, Tobit was riding a horse. Erect and grinning, his black curls streaming like a horse's mane, he held the reins in one hand and seemed perfectly at ease, even though his suntanned legs barely stretched the width of the horse's broad back.

I hate to admit it, but I was relieved to have Tobit away so much. Of course I missed his bubbly energy. But when Tobit was with his father, I did not have to worry that my sons would kill each other before either reached manhood. Now – too late – I realize that letting Tobit go with his father was the worst mistake of my life, even worse than marrying Yannai.

CHAPTER 18

Yannai swayed and lurched as he entered the Holy of Holies, the innermost chamber of the Temple. On our most sacred fast day, in the most sacred place in the world, Yannai was drunk. In front of all the people and the priests. In front of his own sons. In front of the Lord God. Had he not even a shred of fear of the Almighty? On this day every year, all Israel stood to receive the judgment of the Almighty. On this day, the Lord held in his hand, not only the life of his high priest, but the lives of all the Jewish people. I prayed that the Lord would not punish all Judea for Yannai's sins.

When three stars had appeared and the fast day ended, Yannai, lounging on the arm of another soused soldier, stumbled into the banquet room to resume his orgy. A drunken soldier ripped off the dress of a serving woman. He shoved her onto the table and tried to violate her right there. Her husband, a tall, muscular, quarrelsome man, was also serving that night. He grabbed the soldier's sword, sliced him through the gut, and fled. Within twenty paces Yannai's soldiers wrestled the slave to the ground. In the morning, Shimon sent Yannai a message: "Your slave has killed a man. You must appear in court."

To my surprise, Yannai went to the Chamber of Hewn Stone and sat on the golden throne there. I sat on a bench off to the side, clenching my fists in fear of what would happen next.

Shimon said, "Stand on your feet, King Yannai, because I have witnesses who will testify against you."

"You have witnesses who will testify against me?" said Yannai.

"I have witnesses who will lop off your head."

"What demon has possessed my brother?" I thought. "Doesn't he know what sort of man Yannai is?"

Hastily, I called out, "Isn't it true that cases involving capital crimes must be voted on unanimously by the full Sanhedrin?"

Yannai understood the point.

"You have forgotten your place, esteemed head of the Sanhedrin," said Yannai. "I don't have to testify just because you say so."

Ambassador Diogenes spoke. "Your Majesties, as always, are correct," he said. "A king may neither judge nor be judged."

"I call for a vote," shouted the acting high priest, Ishmael son of Phiabi. "Stand if you wish to require the king to testify."

Shimon stood. He was the only one. The other Pharisees kept their eyes on the floor. The Sadducees clapped. Shimon's face flamed as he left the chamber.

What was Shimon thinking? I wondered. Did he think that even the Sadducees were so alienated by Yannai's behavior that they would throw him out?

I hurried to catch up with my brother. "Shimon," I whispered urgently. "Leave the city. Hide. Immediately."

* * *

Sukkot, the harvest festival, began four days later. With the cares of the harvest over, and the last warmth of summer glowing on the hills, Sukkot was always a joyous holiday. Farmers preparing to plant their winter wheat swarmed to the city to witness the prayer for rain.

The hills outside the city gate bristled with makeshift shelters of branches and leaves. Autumn sun lit walls and towers with a honey color. Pilgrims jostled in Jerusalem's alleys shouting greeting to friends and relatives. They thronged the Temple court, waving branches of rustling palm, spicy myrtle and willow. Bright yellow citrons wafted fragrance.

On the second day of the festival, Shimon's students from the Jerusalem academy crowded the first row of spectators in the Court of Israelites. Boys perched on walls, hoping to glimpse the high priest pouring the water libation. I was pleased and proud to see the scores of young men who were learning from Shimon.

Crowds lined the path from the pool of Siloam, where the priests would dip out the water. Flutes trilled. Levites chanted. Hands clapped in rhythm and cheers echoed as two priests hoisted the golden jug up the hill, over the bridge and through the Water Gate into the Temple Court. A long blast from a silver horn. People hushed. Yannai, standing at the top of the altar, high above the crowd, raised the golden jug toward the sky. But instead of pouring the water libation onto the four corners of the altar, Yannai lowered the jug, and with a mocking smile, poured water over one bare foot, then the other. He scrubbed his toes with his sash. I was furious. The crowd hissed. Shimon's students pelted Yannai with citrons. Thousands of citrons flew through the air as others followed their example. The yellow fruit smashed on the sides of the altar, the pungent smell strong in one's nostrils. Watching the rain of yellow missiles, I felt as Lot's wife must have felt when she looked back at Sodom. A world was about to be destroyed.

Immediately, Yannai's foreign guards – though foreigners were forbidden to enter the gates of the Temple Mount – rushed in from the side gates and sliced through the crowds. Shimon's students were the first to be cut down. A young man with a wisp of brown mustache and beard screamed, clutching hands to his blood-soaked belly. A boy of thirteen called, "Mama!" as he stumbled blindly, his face running blood. A boy no older than ten had been slashed like a carved roast of lamb, from neck to groin, his bloody tunic flapping away on two sides from his bony ribs.

Scrambling to escape the Temple Court, men skidded on sticky patches of blood. Women shoved, holding babies aloft as if fleeing a flood. In the midst of the mob, some people had fallen, their faces crushed under rushing feet. Choking on the stench of blood, trying to close my ears to the screams, I grabbed my sons by the arms. Miri and I dragged them to the palace. Behind me, I could hear Yannai's guards clattering down the steps of the Temple Mount, chasing Pharisees. A guard with a list pointed out targets. Fury and grief were gall in my mouth. Yannai's mockery of the water libation had been a deliberate provocation. He had mowed down his opponents when they least expected it – during the most joyous and carefree holiday of the year.

Pharisees and their followers had come to Jerusalem from all over Judea for the harvest festival. Yannai and his mounted mercenaries sped after the fleeing Pharisees. Who knows how many unarmed people died that day? I prayed that the remaining Pharisees would find good hiding places in the barren hills outside Jerusalem. They could not outrun Yannai's cavalry. Weeping men lugged bodies from the Temple steps to the burial ground outside the city gates. Dazed women searched among the corpses for their men. There were no words I could say to comfort them. I took a shovel and worked beside them, digging the burial pits. Instead of a holiday parade, the evening torches lit a mourning procession. Like a necklace of death, the trench stretched nearly the length of the city wall.

Somber men and women stood in separate lines to receive the sprinkled water that would remove our corpse uncleanness. I mounted the wall and spoke to them by torchlight. "Except for the priests, nearly every man and woman in Jerusalem has touched death today. It would take more water than there is in all Jerusalem to wash the grime of the grave from our faces, hands and hearts. Tomorrow, together, we will scrub away the blood that has polluted our holy Temple. And tomorrow, together, we will prepare to defend our holy city. Those who have desecrated it cannot be permitted to shed more blood within these gates."

I did not speak about the blood that would be shed in the villages loyal to the Pharisees. It would be as much as I could do to keep Yannai from re-entering Jerusalem.

When I got back to the palace, Miri told me that Tobit had run to the stable to say good-bye to his father. She had run after him. She'd arrived in time to see him gallop off with the soldiers, riding high on his father's saddle, his face alight with the joy of the chase.

* * *

At midnight, Miri, carrying a lit taper, called me to the Audience Chamber. Five of Yannai's Jewish officers, grim-faced, waited silently as I mounted the throne. Caleb, his shadow large on the wall, spoke for them. "King Yannai is a demon," he said. "Give the command, and we will drive him over the cliffs and destroy him."

I knew he was right. But how could I give this order?

"You're talking about civil war," I said. "The Sadducees will support Yannai. How can I send Jews to fight Jews?"

"King Alexander is a Jew fighting Jews," said Caleb. "Even if he denies being one of us. The Maccabees were Jews fighting Jews. If they hadn't fought the Jewish Hellenizers, the Law of the Lord would be forgotten by now and we'd all have become Greeks."

"Come back in an hour," I said, "and I'll give you my answer."

I tried to pray, but I didn't know what to pray for. "Give me strength, Lord," I said. "Give me wisdom. Tell me what is right."

What would Father have done? For an hour, I paced, waiting for the way to become clear. Caleb returned. I did not know what I would say until I opened my mouth.

"I don't think we are strong enough to defeat King Alexander on the battlefield," I said. "Plan to defend Jerusalem if we are attacked, but do not attack the king."

Caleb looked as if he wanted to argue with me. A small grimace tugged at a corner of his lips. He sealed his mouth. The Jewish officers left.

* * *

A scream. It was two hours after midnight. I jumped to my feet. Etzi was running down the stone hall of the palace in his bare feet, howling. He dodged the guards who sprang into the corridor. I tried to get in front of him. His open eyes stared blankly. He veered around me, seeming to see my form but not to recognize me. I finally caught him. He struggled and slapped. One of the guards picked him up. Etzi twisted and bit. The frantic flailing slackened as the guard carried the sobbing boy back to his bedchamber. By the time Etzi was placed on the silk coverlet, he had lapsed back into sleep. I curled up beside him and held him.

In the morning, I asked Etzi what had frightened him. "Demons," he said.

"Tell me about them," I said.

"I can't!" he screamed. "Don't make me!"

Miri and I spent the day in the women's court of the Temple, on our hands and knees, beside the women of the city, scrubbing bloodstains from the stones. How else could I let them know that I shared their anger and their grief? Cleaning the men's court would take longer. There were so few men left in the city.

The priests had erected high wooden barricades around the altar to prevent survivors from attacking them during the worship service. *You need not worry,* I wanted to say. *Unlike Yannai, I and all the people of Judea would never think of spilling blood on the Temple Mount.* When the Temple courts had been cleaned and whitewashed, the priests held a rededication ceremony. But the Temple was tainted, for me and for all Judea. I still came to the prayers, but the only prayer that came to my lips was, *"Pour out Your indignation, Lord ... Avenge the blood of Your servants."*

After the rededication, I spoke to the people in the square outside the Temple Mount. "Men and women of Jerusalem," I said, "we have a new task. Most women, I know, have never fit an arrow to a bow, but you will learn, both to make arrows and to shoot them. Caleb, captain of the Jerusalem guard, and his men will teach you. Together, we will prepare to defend our city."

No one asked, as Caleb had, why I didn't order the troops to hunt my husband down. It was, in those days, still unthinkable for a Jewish woman – even a Jewish queen – to turn against her husband.

* * *

Etzi's night terrors with their screams and frantic blind running continued. Etzi was eight years old. His priestly training was supposed to begin right after the holiday. He refused to enter the Temple Mount. "You will be the high priest someday," I said. "You have to learn what to do."

He shook his head stubbornly. He retreated to his dove-cote, where he was training Feathery II. I didn't insist. I could understand his reluctance. We had both seen too much blood.

* * *

I rode out to Yannai's camp to bring Tobit back. Tobit ran up to meet me.

"We smoked 'em out," he said, thrusting out a proud little chest and a soot-smeared chin. "It's good Etzi didn't come with us, 'cause he's scared of fire."

Leagues away from Jerusalem, Tobit was still trying to outdo his big brother.

"What do you mean, smoked them out?" I said.

"We caught some Pharisees hiding in a cave. Some teachers and some boys. Papa said it would be stupid to go into the dark. They'd have the 'vantage. We built a fire at the entrance. I throwed leaves on it. We waved the smoke into the cave. The boys runned out. Our archers shot 'em. Like flushing partridges from the brush, Papa said."

I winced and felt like weeping. Tobit did not seem to realize that the boys in the cave were human beings, living souls. I could imagine them choking and terrified. Pierced and bleeding. I could imagine the parents who loved and mourned them. But to Tobit

– as to his father Yannai – it was just sport.

Tobit was already launched on another story. "Papa says fire is the best weapon when you want to punish a whole village. At Beth El we set fire to the fields and threw torches onto the roofs. It was so bright: like we made the sun come out at night. You had to hide your eyes. And the flames sounded – whoosh! Like wind."

"Surely Papa didn't let you near the fire," I said.

"Yes, he did!" shouted Tobit. "I'm big! He let me throw a torch into a stack of grain! People ran out of their houses screaming. Papa's soldiers rounded up their goats. We roasted them on spits and had a great feast! Papa said that'll teach the people what happens when you go against the king. People need a strong man to lead them. Papa said I have to remember that when I'm king some day."

Yannai was wrapping a bandage around the left hind ankle of his beloved mare. Sneezing from the dust and hay and horse-flesh, I stared down at him. "What are you teaching our son?" I demanded. "To set fires? To execute unarmed boys? To steal flocks from his subjects?"

"I'm teaching him to love battle," said Yannai. "Something every king needs to know. Something you can never teach him."

"I'm taking him back to Jerusalem. I won't have him learning to be a brute like you."

Yannai stood, wiped his forehead, and leaned forward across his mare's dusty flank. "Try to stop me," he said, "and you'll find out what a brute I can be."

Chapter 19

❧

Yannai – thank God – was bored. With so many of the Pharisees dead or in exile, he interrupted his raids on the villages to briefly pursue his other favorite sport – conquering or driving out the peoples on our borders. Judea got a brief reprieve. I was able to travel to the villages. Patches of winter wheat that hadn't been looted or burned stood neglected in the fields. I persuaded the women and children to come out of hiding. My workers helped them cultivate the brambled fields. Scant bushels of winter wheat and last year's wrinkled dried fruit began to appear in the market. We were even able to resume building the extension of the city wall, though with women and old men carrying stones of modest size, the wall grew slowly.

The women of the tent city seemed transformed by the opportunity to work. Gone were the shrill carping voices and the petty disputes over whose miserable shelter went where. When a young woman in a smudged apron struggled with a heavy stone, an older woman came up to her saying, "Here, let me help you."

Before they began to carry the stone, the younger woman asked, "Do you have a firm grip?"

The older responded, "I'm ready. Watch your toes now. There's all sorts of sharp rocks on the path here."

No longer were they helpless and ashamed, unable to provide for their children.

The young boys and girls helped, too – taking care of babies and bringing pebbles and mud to fill the cracks in the rock. There were no more fist-fights. The old men showed youngsters where to put pebbles. They seemed rejuvenated by the chance to make a difference.

I took a quiet satisfaction in knowing that we were building with the rubble from the Akra, the Syrian citadel that had violated the sacred space of Jerusalem until High Priest Simon tore it down.

As the sun climbed, the women's hair straggled from their head coverings and sweat glistened on their foreheads. The spirit among the women was very different from the good-natured boasting and competition of the men who worked on my corvées. The women, and the children too, shone with eagerness, determination and pride. Tired as we all were, I shared their pride. Each evening when the work was done, the women and children gathered at the wall. "When I look at what you have accomplished," I told them, "my hope is renewed. Thank your neighbor. She is building your future, as you are building hers."

"Hail to the queen," they shouted back.

* * *

After months of nightmares, Etzi slept through the night for one whole week. I wanted to celebrate that bit of progress. Etzi and I strolled among the market stalls with Hannah the cook, picking out fruits for the Sabbath table. A vendor held out a dried fig. "Still very tasty," he said.

At Etzi's side, a boy appeared, bony, bare and gray as a sapling in winter. He had a ragged scrap of brown cloth tied around his waist like the last dead leaf. "Give me!" he begged, in a crow's voice.

Etzi cowered and clung to me. The boy snatched the fig and ran. His bare feet were so cracked and dry they left patches of blood on the stone floor of the alley. The vendor leapt after him, but I grabbed the man's sleeve. "Let him go," I said. "I'll pay for the fruit. This shipment should have been tithed and the tenth part given to the poor. Come to the Audience Chamber this afternoon to explain why this hasn't been done."

"Your Highness, the other merchants and I have paid our tithes," said the vendor. "Why haven't the priests distributed them?"

That night, Etzi ran through the palace again, screaming and blind. I sent a message to Yannai's younger brother Absalom, still living in the cottage in Zippori. "I would like my son John Hyrcanus II to board with you for a month or so. He suffers from night terrors and needs to be out of Jerusalem for awhile."

Absalom had two daughters, one Etzi's age and one two years younger. It would do Etzi good to have playmates who didn't equate playing with fighting.

* * *

The stone tower of the fort seemed to stand at attention as our carriage labored up the long hill. Zippori! The horses turned, abruptly, toward the left. We heard the sibilant cries of hundreds of birds before we glimpsed the bouquet of dense green peeking from a cleft in the rocks. My ears filled with the whoosh of tumbling waters, my nostrils with the tang of trees, my heart with the pain of the honeymoon lost.

Our driver helped us down, Etzi clutching Feathery's cage to his chest. I hadn't seen Absalom in nearly ten years. He opened the door himself and folded Etzi into a big hug. Etzi shrank away, embracing his bird-cage as if he feared it would be crushed. "Don't worry," said Absalom. "I don't eat boys or birds. Only lamb and pita. And those I'll share with you."

He winked at his wife, Shoshana. They seemed content. I had chosen well when I betrothed Absalom to this round, soft-bosomed woman.

Absalom was still the mild young man I remembered. He was compact and solid as a donkey, with rosy cheeks and high curved eyebrows signaling affability, innocence and surprise. The curly hair had given way to a shiny bald dome. I remembered another curly head, frozen in a ghastly grin. When Absalom rode away from Jerusalem, his brother Adonijah's skull was still impaled on a spike above the city wall.

At the dinner table, Absalom covered Etzi's hand with his own. "You're going to be with us for a month," he said. "So tell us what you want to do while you're here."

"I don't know," mumbled Etzi, withdrawing his hand.

"What do you like to do in Jerusalem?"

"I like to play with my bird."

"Does the bird have a name?"

"Feathery II."

"I see. Named after Feathery I, I'll wager."

Etzi nodded.

"Zippori is the Garden of Eden for birds," said Absalom. "Your cousins will show you around. You can choose a place for your bird to live."

"Look!" said Absalom's elder daughter, Abigail. She and her little sister, Michal, parted the bushes. A cloud of twittering birds rose from the greenery. Straight ahead was the waterfall. Beside it, the ledge. I remembered Yannai spreading his tunic for me to sit on. Tossing pebbles into the pool as we talked. Holding my hand as we waded on the slippery stones. I remembered swinging on those thick, twisted vines.

"Feathery II can have his own private bath," said Absalom. "And if he isn't too shy, you can swim with him."

Etzi laughed – a small, tentative sound.

"And if the girls are properly dressed, they can swim with you too."

The two girls, standing behind their father, giggled. The eight-year-old, Abigail, was a plump, soft and feminine version of Absalom. A round, laughing face and eyes flecked with amber. The six-year-old, Michal, raven-haired and quick as a black-bird, seemed to dance even when standing still.

"In Zippori," said Absalom, "birds don't have to live in cages."

Etzi's lip trembled. "But if he's not in a cage, he might fly away."

"You can build him a dove-cote. You're going to play with your cousins. He should have a chance to bring a few of his cousins here too."

Abigail fetched the carpenter, Adam. He brought tools and wood.

"How many pigeons are we building for?" asked Adam.

Etzi shrugged. The carpenter settled on his haunches and drew with a stick in the mud beside the pool. "If you're thinking of ten or so for starters, we can build it like this. That way we can add on when you're ready to take in more."

Shoshana whispered to her husband. "We'll leave the four of

you to do the building," said Absalom. "We adults aren't as quick as you. We haven't finished our lunch."

Etzi glanced quickly at me, his lip trembling and his cheek twitching. "I'll be just inside the door," I said.

Adam took Etzi's shoulder and turned him away from me. He pointed to the diagram and asked, "Do you think we should make a rounded roof, like Feathery's cage?"

"He'd like that," said Etzi. "It would make him feel at home."

"Let's take a look at Feathery's cage," said Adam, "and figure out how it is made."

"It's easy!" said Michal, plunging her arm and face into the pool. She emerged dripping, holding several reeds torn out by the roots. "We can use these. As long as they're soaking wet, you can bend them into any shape you want."

Adam cut a swatch of reeds for each of the three children. "Dunk them in the pool to soak," he said. "But be sure to weigh them down with stones so they don't all float away."

Absalom, Shoshana and I tiptoed away while the three children bent over the pool, giggling and grabbing at drifting reeds.

"Thank you for treating my son with such kindness," I said when we were back at the table. "He has become so fearful. He needs this respite."

Shoshana smiled. "He is welcome to stay with us as long as he wishes," she said. "Jerusalem these days is no place to bring up a child."

"It's been so many years since I've seen you," I said. "How do you feel about your life here?"

"It's quiet," said Absalom. "I like that."

"Do you miss Jerusalem?"

"Never. This is my home."

"Here," said Shoshana, "there is nothing to fear. We can be ourselves."

"It's been years since I've seen this place," I said. "It's as beautiful as I remembered."

"My brother Adonijah was a fool," Absalom said. "I told him to stay away from politics. It's a fatal disease. It killed our mother, our grandfather, and two of our brothers. But he'd caught the infection – just like our mother – and there was nothing I could say to stop him."

I was tempted to defend politics – the only way to accomplish the most important things. But I could understand how Absalom felt.

"Yannai had no love for your mother," I said. "Tell me what it was like to live with her."

"I gather you had no love for her either."

"It was mutual," I said. "If I hadn't imprisoned her, she would have chopped me up like so much ground lamb."

"That's a bit of an overstatement," protested Absalom.

"Not much."

"I can't tell you what it was like to live with her," said Absalom, "because she was hardly ever here."

"Where did she go?"

"She visited her cousins – priests in the districts and military officers in the forts. She'd stay away for months."

"I understand that a messenger traveled regularly between Judith and several of the priests in Jerusalem," I said. "She was probably building alliances, hoping to start a rebellion. Or to take over the throne if your father were killed in battle."

Absalom shrugged. "You may be right. I was just a youngster at the time and didn't understand. Besides, as I told you, politics upsets my stomach."

"What was it like to have Yannai for a brother?"

"Without intending disrespect, Your Highness, that is a question I would rather not answer."

Shoshana peeked out the window at the children absorbed in building the dove-cote. "Etzi is settling in," she reported.

"Maybe he would be less upset if I left quietly," I said, "without saying good-bye."

I started to cry.

Shoshana put her hand on my shoulder. "In the short time I've been with Etzi," she said, "he seems rather quiet, like my husband. Politics may upset Etzi's stomach too. Perhaps, like Absalom, he was not meant to live in Jerusalem."

She may be right, I thought, with a stab of sadness and dread. I shoved the thought away.

"It's impossible for him to live anywhere else," I said. "He will be king."

Etzi seemed to have less trouble parting with me than I did with him. At the last moment, he ran indoors with an amusing request. He wanted me to send the Bird Man to Zippori with a family of carrier pigeons. "That way Feathery II will have company and I can send you letters, Mother!" he said. This seemed to me a harmless frivolity. I had heard of carrier pigeons, but I doubted any bird could find its way from Zippori to Jerusalem over the dry hills, all pocked with identical rocks, dry brush, and knobby-kneed goats.

* * *

The palace seemed empty, with Yannai and Tobit chasing Pharisees, Shimon in hiding and Etzi in Zippori. I found it hard to sleep. I even missed Etzi's nightly bouts of screaming. Three weeks later, the Bird Man arrived at the Audience Chamber with a trembling pink-and-blue-feathered pigeon perched on his wrist. I excused myself from the waiting petitioners and hastened to my sitting room. As I removed the fragment of papyrus tied to the bird's leg, I trembled a bit myself. "It's nest-building time for the wild birds," said the brief note in Etzi's scrawled calligraphy. "Abigail has been showing me the nests."

I smiled. Taking Etzi to Zippori was one of the few things I had done right. I missed cuddling Etzi when he had trouble sleeping, but it was better for him to be in a place where he didn't have that trouble.

Later that summer there were other messages: "Michal fell out of a tree and broke her arm." "Abigail is teaching me to swim."

I pictured Etzi paddling in the pool and remembered Yannai teaching me to swim. Seeing the effectiveness of the carrier pigeons, I ordered the Bird Man to set up a dove-cote in each village. He trained my village contacts – Michael, Yoel and the others – to send messages. I thanked the Lord that Shimon, in his brief sessions with them, had managed to teach them the rudiments of reading and writing. But none of the news was good. Jerusalem, as well as the towns and villages from Gaza to Galilee, simmered under a hot sun, a merciless drought, and the shortage of manpower caused by Yannai's endless wars. "Bad news," I told Miri, as I unscrolled the latest message. "I have to find a way to send emergency food supplies, or the news will surely get worse."

* * *

The copper sun hid behind a scorched haze, the cobbles hot enough to singe one's feet. In the central square of Jerusalem, sweaty young men in white tunics shifted and rumbled like storm clouds. An old man with twitching white brows harangued them, shaking his walking stick. "I was younger than you when Judah Maccabee led us against the Syrians," the old man shouted. "I threw rocks until I learned to make a bow. Where are the young men to defend us today? This so-called king, this Yannai, is worse than the Syrian King Antiochus who polluted our Temple."

"You're right!" yelled someone in the crowd.

"He's an apostate!" yelled the old man.

"A pagan!" shouted someone.

"He desecrates the robe of the high priest!" shouted another voice.

"We must rise up!" shouted the old man. "Follow the example of the Maccabees! Climb the battlements and shoot the demon down when he rides up to the city gate."

"Yes!" shouted a volley of voices.

I was standing with Miri in the shadow where the alley emptied into the square. One of the youths at the front of the crowd glanced toward me. He grabbed the old man's sleeve. Looking nervously in my direction, several young men hustled the old man away.

The crowd hushed and dispersed. I imagined I could hear them whisper to one another: "Is the queen our ally or our enemy?"

"I can't force the rain to fall," I told Miri, "or the crops to grow. But I can at least open the storage sheds and send seed grain to villages where crops have failed."

"What will the king do if you ignore his orders for rations?" said Miri.

"I won't have to deal with him," I said, "until he comes back to Jerusalem."

I couldn't force the rain to fall, but I sent my masons to hollow out new rock cisterns. When I could spare them, I sent laborers to help the villagers dig new wells where old ones had run dry.

No point in working in the palace garden. The flowers and herbs I had planted had shriveled into dry sticks.

"And if the rain still doesn't come?" said Miri.

"We'll continue," I said, "to pray."

CHAPTER 20

"He's not dead!" Tobit screamed, his cheeks raw from scraped-off tears. "You should have let me go after him!"

Amos the courier dismounted and staggered toward me. His face burned red as a rooster's crest. Blood streaked his tunic. "Ambush!" he gasped. "Arabs. East of the Jordan."

"The king?" I blurted.

"Can't find his body. Tried. Cliff's too steep."

"His body?" I choked. "What happened?"

"Aretas. Charged us with mounted camels. The king's horse reared and fell backward over the cliff."

Aretas, canny king of the Arabians, had given us perfumes and ointments of Gilead for a wedding present, and had supplied Yannai with horses for years. But Aretas's bandits raided our villages for food and goats. Yannai had decided he must be stopped.

* * *

Captain Beni led Tobit's horse toward the stables. When he saw me, my son vaulted from his horse, turned his back on me and pulled the sweaty beast into the stall where Yannai usually kept his bay mare. Instead of grooming the horse, Tobit flung himself on the straw in the corner, sobbing and swatting furiously at my hand when I tried to touch him. Beni bent over the boy. He tried to pull Tobit to his feet. Tobit shook him off and curled into a tighter ball. Beni touched the boy gently on the shoulder and spoke softly.

"I believe you," said Beni. "I saw something moving in the bushes at the bottom of the cliff. I'm going back. You guard the stall till I bring your Papa home."

Beni put a blanket over Tobit and walked with Amos, Miri and me up the hill toward the palace.

"You'll get yourself killed," Amos told Beni. "That canyon is a sea of boulders." He gestured at the blood on his tunic. "I got scraped and scratched from my knees to my nose when I tried to go after him. If you try to climb down, you'll start an avalanche."

"I'll have someone stand on the cliff and lower me by rope," Beni said. "I'll search till I find something. Either a living king or a half-eaten carcass with the royal crest on its shield."

"I'll be the man on the cliff," said Amos. "Every fool needs a friend."

* * *

I didn't know what to hope for. Yannai had brought chaos to Judea. But if he died, the chaos could collapse into anarchy. In my heart, too, there was anarchy. There was not an inch of my body that had escaped the bruising of Yannai's mockery. Yet when I thought of Yannai in pain or dying, I felt as anguished as if I were watching the torture of my own helpless child. Though I still throbbed with fury at his treatment of me, those sunlit days in Zippori and Gadara had unleashed a longing in me that could only be satisfied by Yannai's touch. My heart was like a seed that has lain dormant. Once you water it, you can't order it not to grow.

* * *

It was my job to prevent the tumult that might follow Yannai's death. As soon as Beni and Amos returned with Yannai's body, we would need an emergency meeting of the Sanhedrin to name the king's successor. They should name Etzi, Yannai's eldest son, as king, and me as regent. But unless I moved quickly, Diogenes and his allies would put their own man on the throne. And find some excuse to get rid of Etzi and me.

* * *

Past midnight. The clay lamp in my sitting room flickered on two men emerging from the dark of the corridor – Beni and Amos. The half-naked body of my husband, covered with blackened blood and massive purple blotches, sprawled on a pallet. A bone protruded from a leg snapped at an inhuman angle. An arm hung slackly, flapping like the rein of a riderless horse. In spite of everything, I had loved this man. I moaned softly and wept. There was an answering moan from the body on the pallet. Yannai lived.

I wrung the hands of Beni and Amos. I wanted to thank them, but grief, relief and dread so warred in me that I couldn't speak.

I summoned the doctor. In the half-light of the lamp, the doctor stitched and splinted Yannai's broken leg; re-set the dislocated shoulder; extracted splinters, thorns and grit from the wounds that covered Yannai's body; and squirted skinfuls of brandy over the poor bloody flesh. He applied an ointment of balm and cumin and wrapped linen bandages around Yannai's legs, arms, torso and head. Each time the doctor touched him, sweat started afresh on my husband's forehead. Each time the doctor moved a limb, Yannai winced. He locked his jaw to choke any further moans. I wept at his pain and his courage. After the doctor left, I bathed Yannai's face with a damp cloth. Brandy breathed from his pores. "Call the Sanhedrin," Yannai groaned. "Now."

"But it's the middle of the night," I said.

"By morning I may be dead," he said.

I tried to be as gentle as possible while helping him put on a fresh tunic. Beni and Amos, waiting in the corridor with the pallet, carried him carefully through the silent street to the wide door of the Chamber of Hewn Stone. The shadows of swaying robes flowed through the lamplight as murmuring nobles and priests took their places on the benches. A voice growled, "A pity. If they'd brought back a body, we might have had a chance …"

Yannai scowled and flushed. Sweating from the effort, he pulled himself to a sitting position. "I'm going to walk in," he insisted, "and stare those bastards in the face."

Leaning heavily on Amos and Beni and biting his lip with each slow step, he let them drag him to his seat at the center of the semicircle of benches.

"Brethren," he said hoarsely, "I was wrong to bring foreign soldiers and foreign whores into our holy city. I admit it before you and before the Almighty. The Almighty has seen fit to spare me. Will you do the same? Tell me what I must do to win back your favor and the favor of the people."

Among the faces gleaming white in the dim room, there was not a single Pharisee. Yannai's Sadducee allies refused to answer. After a long silence, Diogenes spoke. "If you are truly sorry, you will leave Judea. Then we might win back the respect of the people."

The Sadducees filed out. No one looked at Yannai. But they

had spared his life.

Beni and Amos carried Yannai out of the chamber. As the two men lowered their king onto the pallet, we heard a small voice and saw a tear-stained face. Tobit had been listening outside the Chamber door. "Papa," he said. "Why do they hate you?"

* * *

It was nearly dawn when I went to bed. I had slept for barely an hour when Miri shook my shoulder. "Syrian and Pharisee troops are massed at the border," said the messenger waiting in the Audience Chamber. Dust clotted the sweat on his face.

The remaining Pharisees had allied themselves with Demetrius, a Syrian prince, to depose Yannai. I sent for Commander Caleb. "How could Judeans plot with a Syrian prince to overthrow the king of their own land?"

"Because Judea cannot tolerate another year of Yannai's rule," said Caleb. "You are our queen. Join the Pharisee side. We will follow you. Lead us."

"We can't surrender to Syrian rule," I said. "Everything we have built since the war of the Maccabees will be destroyed."

"The Syrian prince will leave here in a week," Caleb said. "He's got trouble at home. He has four brothers, all battling each other for the Syrian throne. It won't take him long to realize that he has more to lose in Syria than to gain in Judea."

"Isn't there some way we can prevent this war?" I said.

"The king is badly injured," said Caleb. "No one would be surprised if he died before morning."

I had trusted Caleb completely since he first took command of the Jerusalem guard. Could I count on his support if I continued to protect Yannai? "I can't speak to you now," I said. "Let me think."

What would Father have done? I had no idea. I buried my face in my hands and prayed. *Lord, what should I do? Yannai is destroying Your land. Making a mockery of Your Temple. But how can I kill my husband? How can I ally with a Syrian prince against Judea?*

I was furious with the Pharisees. They claimed to love the Lord more than their own lives. Yet they had opened the gates of His land to pagans. Was my brother Shimon part of this betrayal?

I sent for Caleb.

"I cannot submit Judea to the rule of idol-worshippers," I said. "Will you stand by me, or will you, also, desert me?"

Caleb's face turned stony. "I will not defy my queen," he said. His back was stiff as he wheeled and marched out.

The Egyptian prince Ptolemy Lathyros, and his Cypriot mercenaries, had sailed back to join the Syrian offensive. The odds against us were overwhelming. The rebel Pharisees had recruited to their cause nearly all my trusted Jewish officers except Caleb, Amos and Beni. To defend Judea, I would have to fight alongside the hated King Yannai, his foreign mercenaries, and a band of unscrupulous Sadducees.

"Yannai's only allies," I told Miri, "are corrupt men who covet power. They might well shoot their king from behind."

"Good," said Miri. "Let them kill each other off."

Even Miri did not dare to tell me I was fighting on the wrong side. But I knew that's what she thought. Was I right? Was I wrong? I feared the Lord too much to kill my husband. But perhaps I could have driven Yannai into exile. And saved the lives of many Judeans.

I had to try to prevent this war. Diogenes had been a commander of troops before he had become an ambassador. I sent for him. I felt as if pebbles rattled against the backs of my sleepless eyes.

"It seems we have become allies," I told Diogenes. "You are a diplomat. You must stop this war."

"No diplomat can talk sense to a poisoned arrow," said Diogenes, "after it has left the bow."

I turned so that he would not see my tears.

"Summon the Sadducee commanders. Yannai will muster his mercenaries. We will not let the Syrians near Jerusalem."

"What orders do you want me to give the men?" said Diogenes, as if he were used to taking orders from me.

"Our spy says Demetrius plans to camp tonight near Shekhem. We will march there today, and tomorrow at dawn we will drive the Syrians from our land."

Diogenes' face remained immobile, except for a glint of excitement in those steel-gray eyes. "Is Yannai well enough to fight?" he asked.

"He's not dead," I replied, "if that's what you mean."

I couldn't help admiring Yannai as he galloped off at the head of the troops. Brownish blotches of blood leaked through the cloths bandaging his legs, arms and head. With one leg in a splint and one arm in a sling, every jolt must have hurt him terribly. Regardless of all the hateful things he had done, when Yannai was in pain, I felt an echoing pain in my own body. Despite my attempts to separate myself from him, my body – and my soul, too – were tied to my husband.

Tobit ran screaming after his father's horse, demanding to go along. At the city gate, Miri and I lifted my son by the armpits. He squirmed like a lizard, trying to escape. We dragged him – kicking, howling, and trying to bite – back to the palace. I had engaged a tutor to stay with him. To restrain him if he attempted to leave again. I was too despairing and too angry to have any sympathy for my son. "Papa needs your horse," I said. "If I hear that you've tried to get out of Jerusalem, even when Papa comes back you will never ride that horse again."

* * *

"I have to make one more attempt to stop this war," I told Miri.

"You heard the ambassador," she said. "Can you stop an arrow after it has left the bow? Or a rapist after he's – "

She glanced at my scowling face and stopped in midsentence. For once, Miri's wit had gone too far.

"Tell Amos to meet me at the stable," I said.

To carry out my plan, I would have to arrive at the battlefield by nightfall. Leaving Caleb and his men to defend Jerusalem, I slipped on a black gown, saddled my horse, and with Amos close behind, galloped after Yannai's troops.

Dust had choked the sunset into gray submission. We stopped in a small copse of trees at the edge of the wheat field that would be trampled to mud in the next day's battle. The Syrian and Egyptian troops had pitched their tents on a hill barnacled with gray rocks. The oily smell of roasted meat rose on the smoke of their campfires. The dusk made everything dreamlike. Off to the left the white tunics of Pharisees moved in the dimness like grazing sheep, their campfires giving off the toasty smell of puffed grains. In the shadows of the valley, Yannai's troops staked their horses to munch in the wheat field and called directions to one another as they set up camp. I gnawed my fingernails and waited for night.

Darkness was complete except for the red embers of cooking fires speckling hill and valley. Amos and I crept toward the Pharisee camp. We heard the mournful chanting of evening prayers. I prayed steadily as we moved forward, "Lord, turn the hearts of my brother's men."

Amos whistled. A Pharisee peered into the darkness. Amos stepped forward and said, "Stand. I bring a message from the queen."

The men sitting around the campfire scrambled to their feet. They pulled daggers from their belts. I stepped into the firelight. The Pharisees knelt.

"Come home," I said. "All Jews are brothers. There should never be bloodshed between us."

I recognized Betzalel, the weaver and dyer who had made the drapes for my sitting room. He was a red-faced man with a broad flat face and fingers that seemed too thick for the fineness of the fabrics he made. He was a Pharisee member of the Sanhedrin. "Your Highness!" he said. "We will gladly follow you."

He pointed toward Yannai's camp. "We will never again follow him."

"How can you follow a Syrian prince against a Jewish king?" I said. "After all the blood our fathers bled to buy our freedom?"

"If there were a Jewish king, we would follow him," said Betzalel. "But there is none."

"He's more pagan than the pagans," said a gaunt man silhouetted by the dying embers.

"Why does the Lord let him live?" came a voice from the far side of the fire.

"Only because we haven't had the courage to drive him out," said Betzalel. "Until now."

Amos and I went from campfire to campfire. Not one Pharisee volunteered to switch sides. When we got back to the wooded copse on Yannai's side of the battlefield, Amos went to report to

Beni. Yannai poked his head out of his tent and snarled, "What is that bitch doing here?"

I gritted my teeth. I refused to react.

"I hope you had better luck than that Syrian bastard did," said Yannai. "He sent eight morons with bags of gold and silver, trying to buy off my soldiers for his army. You may call my guys money-hungry mercenaries, but they'd rather fight behind a real soldier than a pompous ass like the Syrian prince. Not one of my men flipped."

"We're equally unsuccessful," I said. "Not one Pharisee came back to our side."

"Too bad for them. After tomorrow the farmers will use them for manure."

Brave words. Yannai's foot soldiers were outnumbered at least three to one. As for horsemen, Yannai led fewer than a hundred. The Syrians and Egyptians had three thousand.

Yannai was right about one thing: his foreign soldiers were loyal to him. When the two forces met, Yannai's outnumbered mercenaries fought like cougars. But even cougars can be crushed by Syrian elephants. Corpses from both sides littered the battlefield. Severed arms, gory necks without heads. I picked my way among them, trying to find any wounded who might still be alive. Black flies sucked at oozing wounds, drank from eyes and lips. Soldier-enemies embraced in death, impaled on each other's swords. Its rider crushed under the saddle, one horse lay on its back, legs jutting into the air like an overturned table. A few horses stepped gingerly over the corpses of men and mounts, sniffing at the hacked bodies, searching for their masters. Was there anyone left alive?

I wept, directing my men where to bury the Judean dead. Far off, on the other side of the battlefield, a man moved toward me. I recognized him: the royal dye-master, Betzalel. He knelt before me, his face in his hands. "We were wrong to fight alongside a Syrian king against our own people," he said. "We've told the Syrian prince that if he advances any farther into Judea, he'll have to fight us. We can't fight on Yannai's side, but we won't fight against him."

"The king is alive?" I said.

"Like an incubus, he reappears in the dark of night. They say he's fled to the mountains. We're going home."

"And my brother?"

"Hiding in the caves with a small group of men."

Bitterness strangled me. I could not speak. "Why," I wanted to scream, "didn't you halt your attack last night, while this field was covered with wheat instead of blood?"

I wondered: were the Pharisees skilled enough to stop the Syrians they'd invited to invade?

Fortunately, Caleb's prediction was correct. While the Syrian prince, Demetrius, had been advancing on Judea, his rival brothers had taken over the territories Demetrius controlled. Having lost all his supporters in Judea, Demetrius returned to Syria to plunge into the war among the contenders for the throne. The Egyptian prince, Ptolemy Lathyros, sailed off to deal with a revolt in Upper Egypt. "Finally," I told Miri, "our people have realized the insanity of this war."

"You underestimate," she said, "the stubbornness of men."

* * *

The Pharisees miscalculated. Instead of returning home, they attacked Yannai and his Sadducee soldiers in the king's mountain retreat. Without the backing of Syrian horsemen and professional soldiers, the Pharisees – mere scribes, farmers and shepherds –

crumbled before the Sadducees, who were military officers from military families. "Yannai's archers were shooting downhill," Amos reported. "The Pharisees are not very good archers, and they were shooting with the sun in their eyes. The Pharisees didn't even have armor. They were massacred. There must have been at least a thousand bloody white tunics scattered on the rocks."

Diogenes and Hanin and their sons marched eight hundred Pharisees to Jerusalem in chains, whipping their backs as if they were donkeys. I watched the Pharisees stagger through the city gates. *Under all that sophistication,* I thought, *Diogenes is as much a brute as Yannai.* Betzalel was the last in line. The whip had carved bloody slashes in the back of his tunic. "Water," moaned Betzalel. "We've walked three days without water."

I sent a servant with water. Hanin's whip drove my servant away. I thanked the Lord that my brother Shimon was in hiding.

* * *

Noon. The sun glared overhead. No shadow fell. The Pharisees stewed in the heat of the main square, tottering from thirst. On a shaded palace balcony overlooking the square, Yannai joked with his bare-breasted concubines. Slaves brought trays of cakes, figs, pomegranate juice and wine.

On a balcony across from Yannai and his women, I waited. Yannai's guards dragged into the square another shuffling line of prisoners: the Pharisees' wives and children. Shackles bound their hands and ankles. They twisted to left and right, trying to shield themselves from mocking eyes.

"Here's a toast to the righteous Pharisees," said Yannai, gulping a tumbler of strong drink. He leaned over the balcony, screaming, "You self-righteous pigs looked down on me. Well, now you have to look up. You think you can put me on trial? You think there's a Lord of Justice? Tell him to swoop down and rescue you. Otherwise, I'll be the Lord of Justice."

Guards hoisted the Pharisees one by one with a crane and fastened them by their chains to high poles. They hung by their wrists. They coughed, finding it hard to breathe. Every movement pulled shoulders from their sockets and brought a wince of pain. Their families wept. At a motion from Yannai and a command from Diogenes, the soldiers unsheathed their swords. Yannai screamed, "You don't approve of my girls? Well, here's what I think of your bitches."

While the Pharisee men hung there, watching, soldiers cut the throats of every woman and child. Blood soaked the women's clothes and splattered their bare feet. Blood from the mothers poured on the heads of the children. I saw a young woman, bleeding from the throat, drop the infant she was holding head first onto the stone plaza. The baby's head hit the stones with a cracking sound. As she fell, the young woman knocked over the four-year-old girl clinging to her skirt. From under her mother's body, the little girl screamed until a soldier cut the girl's throat. I retched. I forced myself to stay. To be a witness. Yannai and his whores drank toast after toast to the spectacle.

Betzalel kicked and twisted when his wife and small son were slaughtered. His wrists bled where he'd pulled against the shackles. His body dangled where his armbones had separated from the joints.

The eight hundred Pharisee leaders had died of thirst by the midnight watch. I gave orders to remove and bury all the bodies. Centuries-old tradition said that no corpse could remain overnight in Jerusalem. Yannai countermanded my order. His soldiers prevented my workers from entering the square. In the slanting sunlight the next morning, eight hundred dead Sages on poles cast shadows over the grisly corpses of their wives and children. The bodies had become so swollen and blackened in the heat that I couldn't tell Betzalel from any of the other Pharisees. My first husband, Yudi, had worried that a single dead body might taint the sacred city.

I warned the few Pharisees remaining in the villages: "Hide in the caves, or flee the country. Yannai will try to kill you all!"

Yannai saddled up a horse for Tobit and rode off to hunt down the surviving Pharisees.

I went to the Temple every morning, touched my forehead to the cool stone floor, tried to merge my soul into the chanting. I was too ashamed to pray. How could I have loved this man Yannai? I'd felt sorry for the rejected little boy, attracted by the handsome young man. Despite all the excuses I'd clung to, I had to see Yannai for what he was: a bloodthirsty, sadistic tyrant. I went to purify myself in the *mikvah* pool. I felt as if I'd never again be clean. The water on my breasts, the tears on my cheeks, reminded me of innocent bodies, bathed in blood.

Lord, you commanded us not to kill, I prayed. *Why do you let Yannai do it over and over?*

CHAPTER 21

"You know why we came back, don't you?" Tobit said. "Papa is too drunk to stay on a horse."

Tobit was nearly thirteen – pimpled, skinny, and surly. He had grown almost as tall as I was. "I know you always looked up to your father," I began, hoping he would hear the sympathy in my voice. Tobit walked out of the room. My heart ached for my youngest son. He had cut himself off from me. Now, with his image of his father shattered, he must have felt entirely alone.

* * *

Quietly, without truces or reconciliation, the civil war ended. It had devoured thousands of Jewish lives. When I got word that Yannai was returning, I sent him a message to garrison his troops outside Jerusalem, to lessen the risk that the people of the city would rise against him. If possible, I hoped to avoid a confrontation between my troops and his. When he agreed, I told the men and women who had guarded the walls of Jerusalem so loyally for six years that they could be excused from their shifts. To my surprise, no one tried to assassinate Yannai or to prevent him from returning to Jerusalem. I sent messages to Shimon and the surviving Pharisees to come back to Jerusalem. None did.

Whores and drunken soldiers repopulated the palace, their lewd shouts penetrating even to my sitting room.

I had entered the change of life. I was hot, I was cold. I wept with no reason. I couldn't sleep. Yannai and his whores were unbearable. Repulsive.

Writhing in my damp, tangled bedclothes, I prayed, *Please let me sleep, Lord. I won't be able to deal with Yannai if I don't get some sleep. Let me not lie here, remembering the thousand hurts he's inflicted, the obscenities and blasphemies, the thousands he's killed or tortured, the thousands he's sent to die because war is his sport. I'm afraid, Lord. I don't know what words will leap from my mouth when I see this toothed Leviathan, this flopping, gobbling, slobbering excuse for a man.*

I asked Tobit to dine privately with me in my sitting room. He refused. Every time I entered a room where he was sitting, he stood and walked out. "He should show more respect," said Miri. "The respect any son owes to his mother. The respect every subject owes his queen."

"I know why he is so hostile to me," I said. "There's something I never told you. When he was about five years old, I beat Tobit. Six whacks with a wooden sword. He's never forgiven me. I've never forgiven myself."

"Don't make excuses for your son's rudeness," said Miri. "Parents are supposed to hit their children. It's part of teaching them. I think you didn't hit that boy enough. Didn't King Solomon say, 'Spare the rod, spoil the child?'"

"Solomon had a thousand wives," I said. "What did he know about child-rearing?"

According to Miri, Tobit spent most of his time in the stables or riding the roads leading out of the city. The day before his coming-of-age ceremony, Tobit appeared in my sitting room. "I don't want you at my coming-of-age," he said. "If you're there, I won't do it."

I stayed away. After the ceremony, Tobit stopped in my sitting room long enough to say, "I'm a man now. I don't have to listen to you ever again."

That hurt. I tried to tell myself that this was just Tobit's way of asserting his manhood. But I kept picturing the bloody wounds on a little boy's leg.

* * *

My sons – separated since childhood – were together again. When Etzi spoke, Tobit echoed him, in a prissy, whining voice. When they walked a corridor of the palace, Tobit "accidentally" shoved Etzi against the wall. In strength, though not in wisdom, both my sons had become adults. Capable of killing one another.

I followed Tobit to the stall where he was grooming his horse. "Why do you bully your brother?" I asked.

"You can't change people," he snorted. "Some are born to take, others to be used."

"You think your brother lets himself be used?" I asked.

"Yes, and the servants in the palace let themselves be used. And so do you."

"I? I let myself be used?" I blurted.

"By Father and by the Pharisees."

"No one dictates to me. I do what I think is right."

"Father is a drunk. If you hadn't run the country while Father fought and caroused, the people would have assassinated him long ago. Do you think he would have lasted all this time without you to protect him?"

I didn't know what to say.

"Father won't last long," Tobit said. "And he is going to make me king when he dies."

Before I could stop myself, I blurted, "Not if I can help it."

I felt like the blind old patriarch Isaac learning that he'd been duped into giving his inheritance to the wrong son. But in my family, neither son was the right son. *Etzi is too timid,* I thought, *but Tobit is too hard.*

I walked away, motioning Miri to follow. "Sometimes I feel like roasting that boy alive," I said.

"Pluck him first," said Miri. "I hate the smell of burning feathers."

"Unfortunately, Tobit is right," I said. "Etzi is ineffectual. He can't possibly rule Judea. Tobit is capable, aggressive – he might make a good leader. But young as he is, he's already cynical and ruthless. He has no fear of the Lord. After the destruction caused by Yannai, Judea can't stand another such leader."

"There's only one solution," said Miri. "You'll have to live forever."

CHAPTER 22

Every day since Etzi had returned to Jerusalem, I had prayed for him. *Please, Lord*, I said. *He is a sweet young man. Help him develop the confidence, the decisiveness, he will need to lead Your people.* When he offered sacrifices, Etzi looked as if he wanted to apologize for throwing meat and bread into the altar flames.

* * *

There were no more formal banquets, no receptions for visiting dignitaries. Yannai drank with his concubines in the formal dining rooms. I did not want to risk another war by trying to expel my husband's whores from Jerusalem. I told myself that Yannai's drinking would kill him soon enough. I just had to survive until that happened.

Philip and I designed a lovely colonnaded winter palace at the oasis in Jericho. Architecture was the only Greek art not in absolute violation of the Lord's Law. I pored over the drawings, changing gateways and porticos and the designs of the mosaic floors. I spent weeks riding out to supervise the building. When the work was finally complete, I stayed in my Jericho retreat for weeks at a time, swimming in the tiled pools, building an irrigation system, and planting row upon row of fragrant balsams. *Some day*, I thought, *healing balms will be made from the sap of these trees.* I walked round and round my estate, loving every inch of it. Finally I had built something that my husband had not destroyed.

When I was in Jerusalem, I tried to shut my ears to the constant disputes between my sons. I built a second palace in Jericho, identical to the first, so that they wouldn't fight over which of them should inherit it after I was dead.

Rain came. Dust turned into mud. Food, shelter, and men to work the land were still in short supply, but Judea enjoyed an uneasy peace. I sent the men I could spare to repair aqueducts and rebuild roads. Yannai was too drunk to notice or care what I did. For nine years, Judea limped along, timidly blossoming. I toured the forts I had built, the villages my men had repaired, the replanted fields, and thanked the Lord for permitting me to preside over the healing of His land.

Nine years. Enough time that Yannai and I could have made peace in our marriage if he had been willing to leave his whores, to sit across the table from me and share my bed. Instead I heaved a sigh of relief every time Yannai and his camp followers left Judea for yet another skirmish abroad.

* * *

Etzi surprised me with an uncharacteristically bold request. "I miss Abigail," he said. "I want to marry her. Would you speak to Uncle Absalom for me?"

I was delighted. At twenty-four, Etzi was finally becoming a man.

"I think your son is a fine man," Absalom said when I spoke to him and Shoshana. "I wish he and Abigail could live in Zippori instead of Jerusalem. I hate to send my daughter to that swamp of a city."

As soon as Tobit heard about the betrothal, he demanded that I arrange a marriage for him with Abigail's younger sister Michal. At twenty-two he was still trying to compete in every sphere with his older brother. "Michal is a wild-cat," commented Etzi. "A perfect match for Tobit."

Some mothers have mixed emotions when marrying off their children. I was happy to get my sons away from each other. Let them have someone new to fight with. My laborers built two houses for my sons on opposite sides of Jerusalem. Having two weddings to plan had an unexpected benefit. I had less time to agonize about my own marriage.

When Etzi advanced to the wedding dais, I felt a surge of affection and hope. His face shining, he turned back Abigail's veil and looked into her eyes. *This girl will be good for him*, I thought. *She is sensible. She encourages him. He will become a man.*

As the two sipped wine from the wedding cup, throngs cheered.

At Tobit's wedding I was in turmoil. Michal was a striking girl, with ebony hair and a lithe, slender body. They were a good match, and I was happy for them. Tobit was clearly proud of his bride and she of him. But all during the wedding banquet, Michal averted her eyes from me, talking busily to the woman on her left. *Has Tobit already poisoned her against me?* I thought.

* * *

Both daughters-in-law became pregnant within the first year. Becoming a grandmother was a landmark in my life. It meant almost as much to me as becoming a mother. *The descendants of the Maccabees will continue to lead Judea*, I told myself. *Regardless*

216 QUEEN OF THE JEWS

of which son seizes power, there is hope for the grandsons.

Hearing of the pregnancies, I remembered my father. How often I wished my sons had known my father! With his example, they might have turned out differently.

Yannai was bored again. He saw no reason to remain in Jerusalem for the births of his grandchildren. He mustered troops for another expedition.

Michal gave birth first, to twins. She and Tobit named the boy Alexander, after Yannai, which was quite appropriate. The girl they called Miriam. An intentional slight – not naming the girl after me.

Abigail gave birth to a girl, whom she and Etzi named Alexandra – a name, she explained, intended to honor both Yannai and me.

* * *

Tobit did not march on Yannai's new expedition. He said he had responsibilities in Jerusalem. I suspected my younger son had schemes as well as responsibilities. I instructed Daniel, my kitchen boy and taster, to follow Tobit. Daniel had lived in the palace since I'd rescued his mother Eva from her brute of a husband, the shepherd Seth. Daniel had grown into a big, squarely built young man, like his father, but not so hairy, and with a much better disposition. Daniel was married now, with a son. A young man walking with a small boy should not make my son suspicious.

"We followed Tobit for three days," Daniel reported. "On the first day he went to the home of Diogenes, on the second day to the home of Boethus, and on the third day to Hanin. I'm afraid if I follow him any more, he'll start to notice."

"That's enough," I told Daniel. "You've confirmed my own suspicions."

* * *

"Your Highness, I'm getting reports that worry me," said Caleb, commander of the Jerusalem guard. He was still erect though the frizzy hair was now gray and the forehead lined. "Prince Aristobulus has been in Damascus," said Caleb.

"Doing what?"

"Hiring mercenaries and buying weapons. Did you send him to do that?"

"No. Where is he getting the money?"

"Where do you think?"

"Diogenes, Boethus and Hanin?"

"And Ishmael son of Phiabi. I have no proof, but that would be my guess."

"Put the guard on alert."

"Your Highness, if your son is hiring mercenaries and you did not send him to do that, you had better hire some mercenaries yourself."

CHAPTER 23

"The king is very sick," said Amos, still flushed after his gallop. "Dying, I'm afraid. Can't get out of bed. He's calling for you. And for Prince Tobit."

"I have urgent business elsewhere," said Tobit.

"What is more urgent than your dying father?" I asked.

He strode off without a reply.

"I will be needed here, Mother," said Etzi. "If Father dies, God forbid, I will have to act as high priest."

You don't want to get anywhere near a battlefield, I thought – and immediately scolded myself for such disloyal thoughts.

I summoned Miri and set out in my chariot for the fortress of Ragaba, where Yannai was in the fourth month of a siege. Shimon came as representative of the Sanhedrin. I would have to trust Commander Caleb to defend against any surprise attack from Tobit. I planned to stay at Yannai's side until he recovered or died. Alone in the chariot with Miri, I put my face in my hands, leaned against her shoulder, and cried.

* * *

I peered into the musty dimness of Yannai's tent. His skin was yellow, his nose red, his face puffy and webbed with red and purple blood vessels. His hands trembled. His fingers were contorted. Even the fingernails twisted. My heart flinched to see my husband sobbing in fear and pain.

"Shuli? Is that you?" Yannai wailed. "Gimme my sword. Gotta kill 'em. They're eating me!"

"They're eating you, Yannai?" I asked.

"Giant insects. Chewing on my skin. Oh! Help! Everything hurts!"

His legs, yellow, thin, protruded from under the cover, twitching as if attached to strings. There were patches of scaly purple skin. Mushy bruises, oozing pus.

"Look at me!" he shouted, throwing off the covers and opening his robe. "I'm turning into a woman! I've got boobs! And a belly! And I can't get it up any more. The sexiest whore in camp can sit on my butt naked, and I don't feel a thing!"

I covered him up. He was so lewd and pathetic that I could hardly suppress both my laughter and my tears.

"There are no giant insects," I said. "It's the drink that's killing you. Sick as you are, I can still smell alcohol on your breath."

I didn't mention the other stenches – of urine, vomit, and decaying, pus-ridden sores.

"Save me! You're the Holy Mama!" Yannai cried.

"You can save yourself," I said. "Stop drinking and repent for the evil you've done."

"Repent? Sorry? Sorry. Sorry. Sorry," he babbled. He shook like a dry leaf in the wind. "I am sorry, sorry, sorry. I treated you like a snake, Holy Mama. Sorry, sorry, sorry for the way I treated you."

"I'm worried about our sons," I said. "They may kill each other even before you are buried."

"What should I do, Holy Mama? Save me!"

"You should make me regent and turn over the government to me," I said. "I will restore the Law. Maybe for a few years at least I can stave off war between our sons."

"I'll do it! Will that save me?"

"Nothing will save you from dying, Yannai. But you may save your soul from the suffering of Gehenna."

"What's going to happen to my body?" snuffled Yannai. "The people will tear it to pieces and hang it from trees for the birds to peck."

"You must reconcile with the Pharisees. They can make sure you have an honorable burial."

"The Pharisees? Your self-righteous brother and his friends."

"Yes. Whatever you may think of them, they are the only ones who can protect you from the anger of the people."

"I'll do it, Holy Mama," he whimpered. "I'm sorry."

It took twenty-seven years of Yannai on the throne to prepare my brother Shimon for what he was about to do. Shimon and I had discussed the plan before we came to Yannai's camp. Shimon entered Yannai's tent with a parchment he had readied. I called in Yannai's two top commanders: two witnesses who would be considered impartial both by Yannai's supporters (if there were any left) and his opponents. Regardless of how much they hated Yannai, some Judeans would fight my plan.

"Shimon," I said, "Yannai is too weak to write, but he will tell you his wishes."

Silence. "Do you remember what you decided?" I prodded Yannai. "About the regency? That your sons are not mature enough to rule?"

"Yes, that's what I decided. That's what I decided. That my sons are not mature enough to rule when I die."

He breathed heavily and lapsed into silence. I was afraid he would die before he could complete the thought. "Who will be regent, Yannai?" I prodded him.

"You will be regent, Holy Lady. Queen Shulamit will be regent."

"And what will happen to the Pharisees, whom you persecuted?" I persisted.

"I'm sorry, sorry, sorry."

"So the Pharisees may return to the Sanhedrin?" I clarified.

"Yes, be good to the Pharisees."

"You were wrong to persecute them?"

"I was wrong, wrong, wrong. And if you don't turn my body over to them, the people will rip me limb from limb."

"You will let the Pharisees decide what should be done with your body?"

"Yes. Hang it on a tree or bury it in the ground. They decide."

I handed Yannai a quill pen and the parchment Shimon had brought with us. Yannai made his mark on it.

"I will pray for you to the Almighty, who forgives sin," I said.

"Thank you, Holy Mama," Yannai said, hugging his head to my waist.

Shimon moved as if to speak. I signaled him to be silent. I motioned Shimon and the commanders – and even Miri – to go away. They quietly left the tent.

I sat on the bed. Yannai put his head on my lap and cried softly. I cried too, seeing this mighty tree of a man rot and fall. "Everything hurts, Shuli," he moaned. "Sorry, sorry, sorry, sorry."

Eventually he slept.

* * *

Five people were with Yannai when he died: Shimon, Miri and I and Yannai's two top commanders, Beni and Naftali. I remembered Beni as a young recruit. Yannai had flipped away Beni's shield and "killed" him with a charcoal-tipped sword. Now Beni carried himself proudly, a man of authority. Years of living in the open had carved deep grooves at the corners of his mouth and stained his cheeks the color of oxhide. When Yannai drew his last shuddering breath, Beni sobbed. "I know he drunk himself to death, Queen Shulamit, and he was a mean drunk. But he was a soldier's soldier. I'll miss him."

It had not occurred to me that Yannai's soldiers could love him. "What made you love him so much?" I asked.

"He was the bravest, toughest man I ever met. He never sent us no-place that he wouldn't go himself. He was always with us – leading us – not up on some hilltop looking down."

"You admired that."

"If he saw you doing a good job, he'd promote you, whether you come from a military family or not. You can hear, Queen Shulamit, that I'm no good at speaking but I'm a good fighter. He taught me everything I know."

"You were very close to him, weren't you?"

"He heard that I didn't have no mother or father, and he took me under his wing. He treated me like a son, even more than Prince Tobit sometimes. I'll never forget him."

* * *

I didn't want to demoralize the troops. "I am your commander now," I told Yannai's captains. "Tell the men that Yannai is sick. I will be in charge until he is better."

Captains Beni and Naftali knelt and swore allegiance to me. "You're his widow, Queen Shulamit," said Beni. "I'll follow you."

* * *

Breathing in the goaty smell of my goat-hide tent, I studied a sketch of the besieged fortress. "Your Highness," said Miri, "two soldiers beg to speak with you."

The soldiers were carrying a third who had been hit in the gut with an arrow.

"If we take out the arrow, Your Highness, he will bleed to death," said one of his mates. "But if we leave it in, the wound will become infected and he will die of fever. What should we do?"

I had never had to make such a decision. I looked at Miri. Her mother's home remedies would not solve this problem. "Is there a healer nearby?" I asked.

"Only a nomad woman, Your Highness," one of the soldiers said.

"Bring her to me," I ordered.

The woman was swathed in black. A veil of gold coins covered all but her eyes.

"Do you know how to stop the bleeding of a wound such as this?" I asked.

"I have a mixture of mud and herbs that may work," the woman said.

"Prepare it," I said, holding out more gold coins to add to the veil.

The soldier bellowed in agony when his mates pulled out the arrow, but the mudpack worked to stop the bleeding. By the next night, however, he was burning with fever. I gritted my teeth and tried to deafen my ears to the poor fellow's shrieks so I could think about what to do. He screamed all night until he died.

It was time to stop this senseless waste of lives. I summoned the commanders. "How has the fort managed to hold out all this time? They must have a source of water."

"Yes, My Lady," said Beni.

"Attack the fort tomorrow. Break down the gate. Find the source of water and surround it. If necessary, poison it. It's time to finish this."

I heard my own voice as if it were a stranger's. Where had my voice gained such authority? Then I understood. I was now truly the queen.

* * *

The gate splintered. Lances and swords raised, my troops swarmed in.

At a signal from Captain Beni, my porters carried my chair through the shattered gate. Our soldiers herded the bound captives toward me – bony, gray-faced, some crawling on hands and knees.

"What should we do now?" asked Captain Naftali. "We would bring them back as slaves but they are too weak to walk to Jerusalem."

Those captives who wished to do so were permitted to fall on an upturned sword. My soldiers dispatched the rest. There was blood everywhere. I felt sick. I did not weep.

On the way out of the gate after the executions, I saw the body of a young Judean soldier who had been killed in the first assault on the enemy gate. An ax had split the young man's skull. Bloody flesh pulled away from white bone. A white-and-gray porridge of brains spattered the ground. Yet on his cheek lay only the fuzzy beginnings of a first beard. "Bury him," I told a Judean soldier. "We will come back with wagons and bring the Jewish soldiers home for a proper burial."

One body, in a wooden box, came back with the troops. Yannai's reign was over. I vowed that as long as I lived, not one more Judean soldier would die on foreign soil.

BOOK
TWO

CHAPTER 1

64th year of the Hasmonean dynasty (76 BCE)

Caleb, commander of the Jerusalem guard, stood at attention. "King Alexander Janneus is dead," I said. "No one knows yet except you, my brother Rabbi Shimon, and the two battlefield commanders. Tell the priests to prepare to anoint my oldest son Hyrcanus II as high priest."

"Further orders for me, Your Highness?"

"The Jerusalem guards should encircle the city. As soon as my younger son, Aristobulus II, hears of his father's death, he will come to the palace with his troops and attempt to take over. But he cannot be permitted to do so."

"The kingship will pass to your older son, Hyrcanus II, I assume."

"King Alexander named my son Hyrcanus high priest. He bequeathed leadership of the kingdom to me."

"King Alexander bequeathed the kingdom to you?" echoed Caleb, and paused. "A very wise decision."

"Just before the king died," I said, "in front of his commanders and Rabbi Shimon son of Shetakh, head of the Sanhedrin, King

Alexander signed a document naming me as regent and returning the Pharisees to the Sanhedrin. Here is the signed document. Can you help me enforce it?"

Caleb scanned the agreement. "Very good, My Lady. With your permission, may I give you some advice?"

"I rely on your judgment."

"Don't tell your sons about this plan until just before the anointing ceremony. When they learn of it, you should have at least ten trusted officials in the room. I will station some of the Jerusalem guard outside the room. With the rest, we will surround and disarm Aristobulus's troops."

* * *

Tobit and Etzi shuffled through the blue drapes into my sitting room. I invited them to sit in two hard chairs facing my blue couch. The ten guards on either side of the couch stood at attention, swords drawn. "I have sad news," I told them. "During this recent campaign, your father perished."

Neither son asked about the circumstances of their father's death. "And now?" asked Tobit.

"Before he died," I replied, "your father dictated his wishes concerning the leadership of the kingdom. Your uncle Shimon, as head of the Sanhedrin, will read your father's last statement."

Tobit smiled smugly. Etzi looked pale.

"Before my death, I, Alexander Janneus, king of Judea, wish to pardon all members of the Pharisee party," Shimon read in a steady voice. "I grant the Pharisees thirteen seats on the Council of Twenty-three and thirty-seven seats on the Great Sanhedrin. I direct the full Sanhedrin to name my wife Shulamit, Queen Salome Alexandra, as regent to rule in my stead."

Tobit, instantly on his feet, grabbed for the parchment. Shimon, with remarkable agility for his years, wheeled and kept it out of reach. The soldiers, as I had instructed, stepped forward and gestured warning with their swords. "I'm twenty-four and my brother is twenty-six, and you have been named regent?" said Tobit. "That's absurd."

"Your father felt, as do I, that neither of you is mature enough to rule," I said. "When we present this document to the Sanhedrin, I'm sure they will agree. They know that if your elder brother Hyrcanus became king, you would start another civil war."

"The Sanhedrin can avoid the civil war by anointing me king."

"That will not happen," I said.

"I have supporters in the Sanhedrin," said Tobit.

"Not enough of them. As in the old Sanhedrin, the Pharisees again have a majority of the seats. They want nothing to do with you."

"If they try to stop me, I'll annihilate them," vowed Tobit.

"They and I have something you don't have, my rash young son. We have the support of the people. Every man and woman in Judea would fight to the death to have me and the Pharisees rule over them instead of you."

"You? A woman?" scoffed Tobit. "You think you can stop me? Are you going to lead the armies?"

"Our people are sick of fighting. They want to return to farming. But they also have storehouses full of weapons. Your personal guard is no match for the entire people. My garrisons and border stations are packed with soldiers loyal to me."

I had sent messengers to Hanin, Diogenes, Boethus and their sons to come to the site of Yannai's last battle. Having lured my chief opponents away from Jerusalem, I was fairly certain the

Sanhedrin would back my plan.

"The minute your back is turned …," said Tobit.

"Don't threaten me, young man," I said. "My womb may have produced you, but my womb has turned to steel."

"It's always been steel," said Tobit. "Like your tongue."

"I will not hesitate to imprison you and execute you if I hear any reports of troop movements that indicate a plot against my life. Or the lives of members of the Sanhedrin."

"What do you expect me to do?"

"I will assign you a post in one of the border forts, and if you value your life, that's where you will stay."

"So when you die, who's going to rule?" mocked Tobit. "That mouse? He's been standing here for fifteen minutes and hasn't said a word."

"That's quite a good qualification," I said. "Are you capable of holding your tongue for that long? Start now."

"But …"

"The Sanhedrin is assembling now to ratify this plan of governance," I said as I stood and gathered my cloak. "You will march into the Chamber of Hewn Stone ahead of me, take your seat and sign the agreement, or you will take your supper in the dungeon."

CHAPTER 2

My sitting room, with its blue silk couch, its tapestries and flickering wall sconces, and its false window that looked on nothing, had become my command center. "Imprison everyone you can find who was responsible for stringing the Pharisees up on poles during the civil war," I told Caleb. "Diogenes, Hanin, Boethus, Phiabi, and their sons and grandsons. Before the funeral. Quietly."

"I am going to arrest the chief Sadducees," I told Shimon. "Please summon the Court of Twenty-three so that we can hold the necessary trials."

"It's about time," said Shimon.

"Shimon," I said, "everything must be done according to the Law. I want no cause for reproach, either in the eyes of the people or in the eyes of the Almighty."

"We have arrested Ambassador Diogenes," Commander Caleb reported. "Your son Aristobulus has fled the city with his troops. Hanin, Boethus, Phiabi and their sons have joined him."

"Is the Jerusalem guard still posted on the city walls?"

"Yes, My Lady."

"Post guards around the Temple to prevent any interference

with the ceremony to anoint my son Hyrcanus II as high priest."

I asked Commander Caleb to compose a eulogy for Yannai. *I certainly wouldn't trust Shimon to do it*, I thought. Caleb looked as if he would choke, but nodded soberly.

"What else? What else?" I quizzed myself, pacing my sitting room. Miri had hired wailers and ordered the meal of consolation. Though most Judeans hated Yannai, the funeral had to be a grand and beautiful one – a funeral with honor. It was a promise I'd made to Yannai. *Unless Yannai is recognized as the legitimate king, who will recognize me as regent?* I thought.

I ordered Philip, the royal architect, and David, the chief of construction, to prepare a tomb north of the city for Yannai. I designed it in the Hellenistic style, with circling columns and a cone-shaped roof that flares like a dancer's skirt. Around it I planted a grove of flowering almond trees. It is the most beautiful building I have ever designed: a monument to what might have been.

The funeral procession poured out of the city gate toward the temporary burial ground. Each torch wore a veil of fog. I looked like spilled ink in my shapeless black mourning dress, plodding after Yannai's bier.

A long line of soldiers followed the coffin. There were foot soldiers in armor, shields high, tramping in unison. As Yannai had taught them. Cavalry, sitting easy in the saddle. As Yannai had taught them. Soldiers from all the shores of the Great Sea and beyond: bearded Judeans, clean-shaven Egyptians, dark Ethiopians. Swarthy Cypriots, Parthians with braided hair.

"King Alexander Janneus's legacy to us," Caleb told the assembled mourners, "is a more secure kingdom, with defensible borders. The king recaptured all the lands of Solomon's kingdom and more. He gave us Gaza and other important seaports. He consolidated Judean control over the Galilee, the Golan, and Samaria."

Is this brilliant hero the brute I was married to? I thought. I pictured him as I had last seen him: a lumpy yellow ruin.

Captain Beni asked to speak. "King Yannai saved my life," he said. "Twice."

He sniffed and wiped his eyes. "First, he taught me how to fight. Then, when I was in hand-to-hand combat, and my sword was knocked out of my hand, he rode up on his horse and stabbed the man who was about to stab me. He said, 'You've got to keep your eyes open. You never know who will be coming at you from the side.'"

I remembered the day Beni had learned to fight. Afterward, Yannai and I had walked back to the palace in sunshine. I was pregnant with Etzi and still in love.

Four Judean soldiers lowered the bier into the waiting pit. Hundreds of fighters raised their swords in salute: in unison, like silver-winged angels glimpsed through mist. Caleb tossed in the first shovelful of earth. Yannai's comrades leaned on the shoulders of their mates and wept. There was more to Yannai than the drunken brawler. There was the tender lover I had glimpsed once or twice. The playful comrade who loved a good laugh. *Yannai was like a father to these men,* I thought. *Why couldn't he be a father to his own sons? Why couldn't he be a husband to me?*

As the funeral procession returned to the gates of the Temple Mount, priests sprinkled the Jewish mourners with the water of purification. They slipped silently through the heavy gates of the Temple Court to witness Yannai's son Hyrcanus II anointed as high priest.

The mist seeped through my clothes. I shivered and worried. Etzi was not ready to lead the Jewish people. He never would be. Tobit was no more fit than Yannai had been. *Will the people accept a woman as sole ruler?* I asked myself. *And if not, what then?*

* * *

In the black-draped Audience Chamber, I hunched beside Etzi on a low mourning stool. Tobit did not come to mourn his father. Not a good sign.

My heart felt so heavy it was hard to breathe. In the past few days, I had led an attack on a fort. I had organized a funeral, the anointing of a new high priest, and a meeting of the Sanhedrin to name me as regent. Now, for the first time since Yannai's death, I had a chance to feel his loss. Tears sluiced down my cheeks, as if someone else controlled the water source. *Why am I crying?* I thought. *Whatever I had with Yannai was dead after the first few months of our marriage. I have hated him for most of the last twenty-seven years. Isn't this the moment I have waited for all my life? When I can rule Judea as I think best?*

Shimon came in, muttered condolences, sat awkwardly on a cushioned chair. I couldn't stay in the Audience Chamber. I excused myself, stumbled to my bedchamber and bawled like a sick lamb. "He hurt me, Lord," I sobbed. "He hurt everything he touched: our land, our people, our sons. Why did you let him hurt me? To be lifted by love and then dashed like a stone. Why did you let me hope? You, Lord, can forgive. I can't. This fury will poison my heart for the rest of my life."

Scrabbling around in the dirt of my garden after the week of mourning ended, I imagined Yannai hovering somewhere in the world to come, and inwardly shrieked my fury. "We could have had a love greater than Jacob and Rachel. Greater than Solomon and Sheba. You threw it all away."

I began to imagine Yannai yelling back at me. *You made me king,* I could hear him saying, *and then you spent every minute of our marriage trying to make me feel that I wasn't up to the job. You bragged about all the things you accomplished as queen – all the things you said I was neglecting.*

It was true. Some of this misery I'd brought on myself. In twenty-seven years of marriage, I had never learned to hold my tongue.

* * *

I should have expected what came next. But I was blind and deaf. For months, I virtually abdicated my throne. If Miri hadn't come to dress me every morning, I might not have gotten out of bed. When I did get out of bed, I scratched and dug in my garden, wearing the same muddy gardening smock day after day. Bound up in my bitterness and grief, I depended on the Pharisees to lead the kingdom. I listened to their proposals for an hour in the Audience Chamber each day, and trusted them to carry out their plans. They proposed an amnesty for all Yannai's Pharisee prisoners. "Yes, of course," I said, and issued the order.

They proposed to reinstate and declare as law all the ancestral traditions handed down from father to son. "Yes, of course," I said. I let them write the announcement.

They wanted to restart the Jerusalem academy and send teachers to the villages.

"Here are the keys to the royal treasury," I said. "Do as you see fit."

Then the Pharisees did something I never would have permitted.

I knew nothing about it until Tobit arrived at the palace, asking for a private meeting with me.

I had posted guards at the bronze front door of the palace to confiscate weapons from all who entered. I posted guards at columns along the central corridor to search my visitors again. Guards standing beside the carved wooden doors to the Audience Chamber conducted a third search. When Tobit arrived, I was glad for all these precautions.

I sat wearily on the throne. Eight oil lamps in sconces and eight guards with drawn swords flanked me on either side. Tobit stood at the head of a delegation of Sadducee officers dressed in sackcloth and doused with ashes. Wives and children stood behind them, draped in black mourning.

"Your Majesty, we ask for justice," said Jonathan son of Diogenes. "We drove off the Syrian wolf that slavered after your flock. Now the Pharisee shepherds you appointed want to slit our throats. Is this how you reward those who defended our land when others betrayed it?"

"What are you talking about?" I demanded.

"You don't know about the secret trial?" said Tobit. "You don't know about the execution of Diogenes?"

"No, I don't," I said.

Tobit turned to the Sadducee commanders. "We brought this calamity on ourselves. We let the Pharisees in the Sanhedrin convince us to permit a ruthless woman, mad with ambition, to defy the Law and rule over us, when there were some in the flower of their age fitter for it."

Tobit's self-promoting drivel made me want to retch, but I couldn't ignore his news. It was time to rein in the Pharisees. To take back my throne.

* * *

I let my brother Shimon stand and shift on his feet for a few minutes. Let him wonder why he had been called to my sitting room. "We finally have a chance to mold this nation to the Pharisee way," I told him. "I need your help. However, if you insist on acting without my approval, I will do without your help."

"What are you talking about?" said Shimon.

"Is it true that you have executed Diogenes?"

"An eye for an eye, a life for a life. Isn't that what the Sadducees say?"

I leaped up. My mourning silk swirled around me as I paced the room. "Everything was to be done according to the Law," I said. "The Pharisee interpretation of the Law. No executions without two witnesses to the criminal act. No executions without the unanimous consent of the court. Are you telling me that all the Sadducees on the court agreed to execute their leader?"

"Did you plan to keep the Sadducees in the dungeon forever?" said Shimon. "You want the rest of the Jews to feed them?"

"I am trying to heal this nation, not divide it further," I said. "We can't afford revenge. Ask the full court to convene tomorrow at this time, and I will announce my response to the Sadducee officers."

* * *

I gave command of four border forts to Sadducee officers, and relocated their families there. In each I planted a spy reporting directly to me. I put my own officers in charge of the other forts. Sadducee soldiers could not ride from one fort to another without passing by forts staffed by my troops. I took the keys to the royal treasury back from the Pharisees.

* * *

Caleb asked for a private audience. "Your Highness," he said, "you are not safe as long as Hanin, Boethus, Phiabi, Jonathan and their families are alive."

"It's not enough to banish them to the border?"

"You know it's not."

"I would imprison them, perhaps even execute them, but I have no charges to bring against them."

"I would advise you to find some. And My Lady ..."

"Yes?"

"The same goes for your son Aristobulus II."

I knew Caleb was right. But he was asking for something I could not do.

How could I keep Tobit and his troops out of mischief? I assigned them to attack the tyrant Ptolemy Menneus, who was attempting to take over Damascus. The expedition would get Tobit out of Judea. It might prevent Menneus from invading Judea in the future. And it would give me time to think. I had my courier Amos trail Tobit to make sure the troops continued to march toward Damascus. Caleb stood with me at the ramparts, watching the horses disappear into the spiraling dust.

"Your Highness, please forgive my impertinence," said Caleb. "Your guards are devoted to you. But we cannot protect you if you take away our swords."

* * *

I walked back to the palace, sat on the throne in the Audience Chamber. I stood again, bewildered. Why had I come here? Did

I have a meeting? I walked out and came in again. Still utterly blank.

"What was I going to do?" I asked Miri.

"I don't know, My Lady," she said. "Come to your sitting room and rest a bit."

She took my arm. At the door of the sitting room, I wavered. The room blurred. With an effort, I focused my eyes. "It's too much," I said.

"Sit," said Miri. "Rest."

"I need to think," I said. "My decisions determine the fate of my people. I can't blame Yannai or Shimon or Diogenes, or Tobit. If Judea suffers – "

"It will be your fault," said Miri. "Of course."

I shook my head. Much as I depended on Miri to shake me out of my bad moods, this was no time for levity. "I need to go to the Temple," I said.

I prayed until the midnight watch. I had to cling to Miri's shoulder going back to the palace. My eyes didn't work well at night.

I fasted for three days. I brought in painters to whitewash every room in the palace. Even my sitting room. I said good-bye to the little false window with its view of a little false garden. I used to tell myself that the false window was not a graven image since there were neither humans nor animals in the scene. But I was starting over. I knelt before the absent window. *Lord,* I prayed, *when I chose to marry Yannai, somehow I lost my way. I struggled harder to maintain my position, to keep myself safe, to win Yannai's love, than to do Your will. Sometimes I forgot the sacred task you gave me – to guide and protect your people. You have given me another chance. Let nothing obscure my vision. As nearly as I am able, I will follow every jot of Your Law, so that I can persuade Your people to do the same.*

CHAPTER 3

"Finally," said Miri as she brushed my hair, "Judea will see what can happen when the queen rules." She looked at me curiously. "What will you do, now that you are in charge?"

"I have three goals," I said. "I want to heal the land, I want to build a *mikvah* in every village, and I want to make the Law fairer to women."

"I understand the first goal," said Miri, "and I certainly understand the third goal. But what is so urgent about having a *mikvah* pool in every village?"

"The *mikvah*," I said, "is where I learned to pray. In the Temple, the priests lead the prayers. The *mikvah* is the Lord's gift to women: a small, private meeting with the Holy One. When I immerse in the *mikvah*, I understand what I need to pray about. I open my heart. I submit to the Lord's will. I emerge purified, ready to begin anew. When women experience this, when women find a way to draw closer to the Holy One, all Judea will follow."

"Perhaps," said Miri. "But how will you make the Law more fair to women? The laws are written in the Books of Moses, and all interpretation is done by men."

"The same way I've always done," I said. "I will choose a man to help me, and make him think that all the new interpretations are his idea."

* * *

"Why did you summon me?" Shimon asked. "I thought we had become adversaries."

"I need your help," I said. "To heal Judea."

With sun bronzing the new coat of whitewash in my sitting room, I seated him on pillows at the table and offered him a bowl of yogurt, a pita and some date honey. "I'm trying to sweeten what has turned sour between you and me," I said, with what I hoped was a conciliatory smile.

Shimon did not smile. I took a deep breath. "Shimon," I said, "I am on your side. I believe in the Pharisee traditions: purity in food, body, and sexual relations. The Lord commands us to be a kingdom of priests, a holy people."

"You believe in the Pharisee traditions, but you sided with Sadducees in the civil war."

"I sided with Judea, not with Syria."

"You wanted to talk with me. Say what you need to say."

I blew on my mint tea while I waited for my brother to cool.

"We must help each other," I said.

"You want to make sure we fight on your side in the next civil war," said Shimon.

I stared him into silence. "If you attempt to take revenge or sow further division between the Pharisees and Sadducees, I will fight you with all my strength. But please, let's not fight any more. Together, we can do the Lord's work."

"What do you think is the Lord's work?" said Shimon.

"Learning and teaching. We have reestablished the Academy

here in Jerusalem, but it will take a generation before we have enough teachers. Will you travel to the villages to teach the men?"

"I would like to do that."

"When a group of village men is scheduled to serve on the corvée," I said, "we will spend the week before the rotation teaching them Torah. I want them to understand what you have tried so long to teach them. That building our land is a sacred task. That giving one's labor and time is as holy a sacrifice as giving one's flocks."

"You said 'we' will teach them."

"I will teach the women about *mikvah*, keeping kosher, modesty in dress, guarding the Sabbath, the ritual for baking bread – the laws that pertain to them."

Shimon hesitated for a moment. "That seems reasonable. When shall we begin?"

"We will start with Beth El," I said.

Caleb frowned when I told him of my plans. "Your Highness," he said, "this is most unwise. Outside of Jerusalem, you are vulnerable. And without you, Jerusalem is vulnerable. Our people need you. Here. On your throne."

"The people of the villages need me, too," I said. "For too long, their voices have been drowned out by the trumpetings of the powerful in Jerusalem."

"A noble sentiment, nobly stated, Your Majesty," said Caleb. "But you do the people no favor if you sacrifice your life on the altar of your principles."

"I have the greatest respect for your strategic wisdom, Caleb. But this is why I am queen. To lead the people to the Lord's way. If I am not out among the people, why should I be queen at all?"

"Another noble sentiment, My Lady," said Caleb. "Wait until

the time is right."

"I'm an old woman, Caleb. I can't wait."

"What happens if Tobit's soldiers attack?"

"If there is a problem on the road, I will send for you, and if there is a problem in Jerusalem, you will send for me."

"By the time a message gets to me," said Caleb, "you could be dead."

* * *

Large stone houses faced a stone-paved central square. A prosperous village. A middle-aged woman approached Miri, head high, like a noblewoman. She wore a gold necklace and rings, a fine linen robe, a head covering embroidered in silvery thread. "If you please," she said in a low voice, "would you ask the queen if I may speak with her privately?"

I walked with the woman to an empty spot at the edge of the square. "Your Gracious Highness," she said, "I have a question. If you purchase a new golden goblet, must you smash the old stone cup?"

I was startled by the question. "Of course not," I said. "If the old vessel is still clean and serviceable, it would be a waste to destroy it."

"My husband is a military officer," said the woman. "He returned from war with a new wife. Is it fair to divorce the wife who bore your children and waited for your return, because you have picked up a flashy new jug?"

"Unfortunately," I said, "according to the Law of Moses, any husband may divorce his wife if he chooses. With or without good reason."

The woman drew herself up proudly. "If the Law allowed it, I would have divorced him first. I seek only the money I brought into the marriage. Why should he spend it on that fresh little thing?"

"Your husband refuses to return your marriage settlement?"

She nodded.

I walked over to Shimon and Judah. "This woman's husband divorced her, but refuses to return her marriage settlement."

"Is this true?" said Shimon, motioning the husband forward.

The husband was a portly man in a crisp white linen tunic. "I invested my wife's dowry in a ship," he said. "Unfortunately, the ship was lost at sea."

"I don't see him sitting in the square with a begging bowl," said the former wife.

"Have you no other assets, since the marriage settlement has been lost?" Shimon asked the husband.

"Yes," said the man. "But I have a new family to support."

"The marriage settlement is a loan, not a gift," said Shimon. "You may invest it as you see fit. If you lose it, all the rest of your property must serve as collateral."

"But – " the man blurted.

"I'm sure that you can sell enough property," said Shimon, "to restore to your wife the money that is rightfully hers in the event of a divorce."

I flashed Shimon my best smile.

"What is your name?" I asked the woman.

"Yokheved," she said.

"I hope we meet again, Yokheved."

* * *

Before we left the village, I pulled Yokheved aside. "You are an intelligent woman. I have heard rumors of unrest in some parts of Judea. If you come across any information you think I should know, will you send me a message?"

Her eyes glinted. "Your Highness, no one will dare say a word against you while I live. Not even that empty pot who used to call himself my husband."

* * *

Shimon and I kept up our visits until just before the Days of Awe. Where crops had been lost, we distributed seed grains. Where flocks had been slaughtered, we brought breeding rams and ewes. Where grapevines had been burned, we brought fragile cuttings from the vineyards that had been spared. Where cisterns had been smashed, our potters fashioned new ones – and lined a pool to serve as a *mikvah*. I joined with the women to plant grapevines and herb gardens while Shimon planted seed grains alongside the men. In each place we stopped, Shimon taught the men, and I spoke with the women.

The men studied in the village square. The women gathered in one of the dark, windowless one-room cottages. There was one chair – for me. Women sat cross-legged on sleeping mats or leaned against the rough stone wall. A stray sunbeam coming in the door picked out weary lines on their faces.

"We women have a wonderful secret," I told them. "Men think we must go to the *mikvah* to purify ourselves from menstrual blood. That is the reason given in the Law of Moses. What is our secret? The *mikvah* is the one place no one can follow us. Where we don't have to take care of anyone but ourselves. The Compassionate Lord gave us a haven, a place where our souls may come for healing. When you immerse your head and body in the waters, you become a pure and innocent child again, cradled in the womb of the Compassionate One. The *mikvah* is the best place in the world to pray. But this is our secret. All your husband needs to know is that *mikvah* is commanded in the Law of Moses. So you have to go."

* * *

A week before the High Holidays, we ended our tour of the villages. From the open window of the coach Shimon and I could see men swinging scythes in golden fields of wheat. Almond and fig trees and feisty little olive trees bent under the weight of their fruit. Oxen turned grindstones and oil presses. Sheep and goats nibbled the hillsides, udders swollen with milk. In village after village, women surrounded me, calling out, "Shalom-Zion HaMalkah: the Queen of the Peace of Zion."

They held up daughters for me to bless. "We have heard, Queen Shalom-Zion," said one new mother, ruddy from our work in the sun, "that wherever you visit, the daughters are virtuous and hardworking, the grains of wheat grow as big as olives and the olives as big as pomegranates."

There were still vast stretches of rocky, barren, burned-over land, and deserted, ruined villages. But this year, I realized with satisfaction, the harvest would feed all of our people.

Our last stop before returning to Jerusalem was the mountain town of Ramathaim. I was eager to talk with Michael, my husky mountain man, and to meet the woman he called his heart's desire. I was also worried. I had gotten a message from Michael. He wanted to speak to me. He feared that I was in danger.

On the forested slope, we could see a scattering of small but neat wooden houses – a rare sight in rocky Judea. As our chariot clattered up the steep road, I saw a young goatherd. I called out, "Can you point me to the home of Michael the woodcutter?"

He looked at the ground, shaking his head. He pointed to a square of burnt land at the edge of the forest. "Gone," he said.

"Where? When?"

"Nobody seen him or his son since the night of the fire," said the lad. "His wife and baby are living with her sister."

CHAPTER 4

A crowd of white-robed Levites murmured, milling among the rough blond pillars of the Chamber of Hewn Stone.

"We want justice!" said the leader of the Levite delegation.

"Has someone been unjust to you?" Shimon asked.

"The priests," said the head Levite. "When they collect tithes, they are required to give us an equal share. We get a pittance or nothing at all. We polish the sacred vessels and build the fire and do all the work of the Temple, but we are reduced to begging."

"These aren't the first complaints we have heard regarding the priests," I said. "Immediately after the Days of Awe, I will bring in the treasurer and get a full report, and we will correct any injustices."

* * *

Before Yannai's death, he had appointed Zadok son of Boethus as the new treasurer of the Temple. Zadok's sons had become the tax collectors. At my summons, Zadok flung open the carved door and strutted into the Audience Chamber. His bushy dark beard framed a confident smile. "Your Highness, I wish I could help you," he said. "We don't keep the records from which I could assemble the report you would like."

"You have *no record* of exactly how much has been collected, in crops, flocks or coin?" I said.

"Various people handle various collections," said Zadok. "One person accepts freewill offerings to the Temple. Another is responsible for tithes of crops. And so forth. I'd have no idea of the total."

"Bring me the records of how much has been disbursed and to whom. Payments to the Levites and the poor, to the craftsmen who supply the vessels and the oil."

"I'm sure we have notations on each of these things, My Lady," smiled Zadok, "but not in any central place. I could search for them."

"Name the men responsible for collections and disbursements."

"Your Highness," said Zadok, arching his ample eyebrows, "these men were appointed before I was born. I would not presume to question them. Each man does his task. All goes smoothly."

I wanted to grab this arrogant man by his full dark beard and toss him out of the reception chamber. I said, "I will summon you when I need you again."

* * *

This was a priestly matter. I would have to depend on Etzi to investigate. Etzi's left cheek twitched as he stood before me. His eyes flickered from tapestries to windows. *Why can't he look me in the face?* I thought.

"As high priest," I said, "you must ensure that the Temple is pure. Corruption saturated the priesthood while your father led it."

"What can I do about that?" Etzi said.

"I want you to set up a record system," I said, "so that we know exactly how much is collected in tithes, sacrifices, and coins."

"A record system?"

"I want to know who distributes the money, and who receives it. Investigate the priests and correct any abuses you find."

"Investigate the priests?"

My patience was wearing thin. Why did Etzi repeat everything I said?

"I will do my best," Etzi said, as if he already knew his best wouldn't be adequate. I felt bitterly disappointed. I had given my eldest son the bricks, the mortar, the trowel – everything needed to build a magnificent future for himself and for Judea. Why couldn't he, why wouldn't he do it? All my hopes for Judea rested on Etzi's shoulders. It seemed his shoulders simply weren't sturdy enough.

Etzi stood there for a few moments, blushing. "What is it, son?" I said. "You have more to say?"

"Mother," he said, "would you please stop calling me Etzi? I try to get the other priests to call me Lord Hyrcanus. You use that stupid nickname – Etzi – and all the priests make jokes about it behind my back."

"If you dislike being nicknamed 'baby-fingers'," I said, "act like a fist."

* * *

A month later, I summoned Etzi to find out how the record system was progressing. "I haven't had time …," he said.

"Make time," I said.

As Etzi left, I overheard him mumble, "If I'm supposed to be holy, why do you make me feel like rotten meat?"

* * *

After another month, I summoned Etzi again.

"I talked to Zadok son of Boethus, the treasurer …," Etzi trailed off.

"And?"

"He said he would set up the accounting when he had time."

"Do you expect him to find the time?" I said. "You set up the system."

"I don't know how …"

"Why can't I rely on my son to do the job he has been preparing for all his life?" I said. "Leading a nation is hard work. I demand no more of you than I demand of myself."

"But I'm not you," said Etzi. "Why do you expect me to be you?"

"Etzi," I pleaded. "There are enemies who covet your position. You must protect yourself. The only way you will be able to protect your throne when I die, and perhaps even your life, is to take action now against those who would threaten you. For your own sake, and for the sake of the people of Judea."

* * *

"I'm not ready to deed the Temple to the thieves," I told Shimon. "Let's take them to court."

Dust swirled in the village square of Beth Zur. Shepherds and farmers, merchants and vendors waved their hands and shouted complaints. "The grandsons of Phiabi whacked us with sticks to collect the taxes," said a grizzled man with a drooping eye. "The grandsons of Boethus bludgeon us with tree trunks."

His wife shuffled up to stand beside him. "They're monsters," she said. "Each of them could balance the leg of an ox on his little finger."

"They took my ox and my ass," said a man with a tunic worn thin at the shoulder. "I have to harness the plow to my own back. When my wheat comes in, I won't have an ass to carry it to market. How will I feed my children?"

"They snatch from us three times the value of the tithes," said a man with a knotted, broken thong tying his sandal. "Does the Temple get any of that money?"

Shimon and Judah ben Tabbai, vice-president of the court, wrote busily, stopping occasionally to compare notes.

"Look at this jug, stamped with the royal mark," said a potter, hands stained with clay. "Why is royal pottery sold here, in competition with our village craftsmen?"

"Check the house of the landowner," said a tanned shepherd with squinting eyes. "My wife is a servant there. She has seen casks of oil, wine and grain all marked with the royal seal. Where does he get them?"

"With the amount these priests have been collecting," I told Shimon, "the Temple treasury should be swollen as a tick after its blood meal. Yet there's never enough money for the most basic expenses."

"We will pursue these offenses," Shimon promised the villagers. "Dishonest priests rob both the people and the Almighty. Do not let them shatter your faith in the Lord and His Law."

* * *

Shimon and Judah son of Tabbai huddled at the table in my sitting room, reviewing the statements inscribed on twenty-five rolls of parchment. "Do you have the votes on the

Court of Twenty-three to convict the grandsons of Boethus?" I asked Shimon.

"The Pharisees have a three-vote majority on the court," Shimon said. "I think we can hold all their votes."

"The priests collected triple tithes," I said. "And failed to give the Levites their share. That's enough to bring them to court."

Eight witnesses agreed to testify: four tenant farmers in mud-splattered sandals, two shepherds, and two white-robed Levites. I grinned at Shimon. "We make a good team," I said.

On the day of the trial, none of the witnesses appeared in Jerusalem. Even the two Levites could not be found. Shimon offered to hold the trials in the villages, before a three-judge court. Not one of the witnesses was willing to speak.

CHAPTER 5

I had stopped looking into mirrors. Mirrors only encouraged vanity. Besides, I didn't think I would look any better than the last time I'd looked. Miri dressed me and swabbed me with ointments to cover the dark spots and wrinkles.

My headaches were growing worse. My back hunched. My shoulders twisted. I had to squeeze the heavy breath from my chest. I longed to straighten my shoulders, lift my chest, walk with pride. I could only stare down at my feet.

And my feet! My left sole hurt as if a thick stone had wedged itself into my sandal. Great bunions protruded from beside both my big toes. Even my feet had become ugly. Miri teased me for my self-consciousness. "When you speak, My Lady, nobody bothers to inspect your feet."

Stop worrying about trivialities, I scolded myself. *Luckily, you're not Esther. You didn't win your position by good looks, and you won't need them to keep it. Like any mason or farmer, you have a job to do. Do it well. Rule Judea.*

* * *

"I applaud you for trying to deal with the scoundrels in court," said Caleb. "They are still free, however, and still a danger to you. Your son Aristobulus most of all."

"Give me a week to think about it," I said. "I will summon you. We will plan."

* * *

It took me a minute to recognize the well-dressed matron who approached my throne. Of course! This woman, with the gold necklace and embroidered gown, was Yokheved, the divorcée whose marriage settlement Shimon had restored. "I must speak with the queen privately," she said to Miri. "My message is not for most ears."

"Come with me," I said, taking her hand and leading her to my sitting room. "I am so happy to see you again."

"You won't be when you hear my message."

When I was seated, and Miri had brought a chair for my guest, Yokheved said, "Your Highness, a slanderer came to our town. An ugly bear. Hair like a fur coat on his arms and legs, and sticking out of his nose and ears."

"What did he say?"

"I couldn't imagine that even one person would listen to him, but some did. He waved a bloody scarf with the royal crest. He said it was proof that you had murdered King Judah Aristobulus and General Mattathias Antigonus."

"What?" I blurted. After all these years, the accusation caught me completely off balance. "How could anyone believe I would do such a thing? And why?"

Yokheved took a breath. "The man said that you killed both General Antigonus and King Judah Aristobulus because the king discovered that you had committed adultery with the general. He said King Alexander realized that Prince Hyrcanus was the son of your adultery and chose Prince Aristobulus to inherit the throne. But you forged a will naming you regent instead."

"What a twisted tale!" I said. "Thank you for your loyalty in bringing the story to my attention. When you go back to your town, I want you to spread a different rumor. Ask people how this shepherd came to have a scarf with the royal crest. Who stole it and gave it to him? As for the bloodstains, remind them that Joseph's brothers dipped his coat in the blood of an animal to deceive their father. Who would have the motive and the means to send a bloodstained scarf from village to village in the hands of a shepherd?"

I pressed a gold brooch into her hand.

"Thank you, Your Highness," said Yokheved. "I seek no reward, but I will treasure this memento."

"Did you find out the man's name?" I asked.

"His name is Seth. He says you took away his wife."

Seth! Now I remembered that bear. Long ago, he had beaten his wife blue. Eva had never gone back to her husband. She was still a scullery in the palace kitchen. She and her son, Daniel, were still my official tasters.

"What a ludicrous story!" I said to Miri after the matron left. We laughed together.

"My Lady, do you think this rumor poses a threat to you?" said Miri.

"I doubt anyone will believe it," I said. "It's so like those Sadducee schemers, using a malcontent like Seth to spread a slander. I wonder how they acquired that scarf, and where they kept it all these years!"

Yokheved squelched the slander very well. By the time she reported back to me a month later, people were laughing in Seth's face when he showed them the scarf, saying, "How did a bloodstain get on that scarf you stole? Did you sacrifice one of your sheep?"

* * *

Like the cattle in Pharaoh's dream, Judea had seven good years. Rain moistened the land before we had begun to pray for rain. Milk flowed from fat sheep and goats. Blossoms swelled into fruit. Grapes scented the vineyards. In every village I visited, men and women proudly showed me the *mikvah* they had built. They lifted up their children for me to bless. Scores of women introduced their daughters to me, saying, "We named her Shalom-Zion, Your Majesty, after you. Because you have brought peace to Zion."

To celebrate the Festival of First Fruits in late spring, farmers marched to the capital from every district in Judea. They entered the city gate following an ox crowned with an olive wreath, its horns painted gold. My heart warmed with pride. I joined the members of the Sanhedrin, the chief artisans and merchants, as all Jerusalem greeted our farmers. Singing psalms, the farmers marched through the gate to the Temple Mount. One by one, they raised tanned arms to offer baskets overflowing with grapes, figs, and bread baked from the first cutting of the new wheat.

In the eighth year, there was a drought. Bad news followed on horseback. My courier Amos, as round as the barrels of wine he enjoyed, gasped out his report. For seven years, Tobit had sulked in his border fort, drilling his troops in the spring and fall, returning when it was too hot or too rainy to the fine house I had built for him in Jerusalem. He was afraid to challenge a queen so beloved by her people. But now Tobit's troops were a day's ride from Jerusalem. I lay awake all night in prayer. *Almighty, I have tried to be a good woman, to follow Your laws. Spare me from the sin of killing my son. Spare Your people the shame of seeing the son kill his mother.*

I thought of Cleopatra III. She was gone and I was still alive, but my sons hated me as much as her sons had hated her. Why? I had tried so hard to treat them fairly.

Fasting, barefoot, veiled not in the robes of a queen but in the torn sackcloth of a penitent, I hobbled to the Holy Temple before dawn. The sky behind the columns of the sanctuary purpled with first light. At the back of the women's section, I folded my seventy-three-year-old knees. *Lord, I am tired,* I mumbled. *All my years are engraved on my bones. But I still have work to do before I die. Forgive my sins. Let me complete my work.* Leaning on Miri's shoulder to haul my body upright, I glimpsed my bare feet. I must change my clothes, I thought. I should be humble before the Lord – never before Tobit.

I limped down the broad stone steps of the Temple Mount, past pilgrims haggling with vendors about animals for sacrifice. Plunging into an alley dark as a serpent's maw, I stumbled on a paving stone. Miri caught me before I fell. I cursed the camel's hump on my shoulders that prevented me from walking without assistance.

Miri helped me twist my arms into the robe of purple silk. She wrapped the belt with the gold buckle around my waist, secured the head covering and the golden diadem. I could hear Tobit's soldiers clanking and shouting, climbing the hill to the city.

Four porters lifted me to their shoulders on a sedan chair and carried me out through the city gate. With Caleb and half the Jerusalem guard arrayed behind me and the rest posted along the top of the city wall, I faced Tobit and his troops. I wore what I hoped was a gracious smile. Tobit pulled back his helmet, baring hyena teeth. Tobit's soldiers stood at attention barely thirty paces from the Jerusalem guard. Half of Tobit's soldiers were cousins, neighbors, and countrymen of my soldiers. They were like my own sons. How bitter it was to see them arrayed against their brethren and against me! The horses on both sides came from my stables, the armor from my storehouses. The breast-plates, greaves and helmets flashing in the sun were identical on both sides. All the soldiers hoisted the same swords, spears and round shields, waved the same blue and white banners. How could my son think of damning these men to another war with one another?

I forced myself to be calm. "Yes, my son? Please dismount and let me welcome you home. Do you wish to report on your victories?"

Tobit spoke from the saddle. "I believe that at the moment our enemies pose no threat to Judea."

"I thank all your soldiers for their brave and loyal service. You may return to your garrison."

Tobit's eyes flicked nervously from side to side – comparing the strength of my force to his. I thought, *He's wondering whether he has the power to cut off my head right now without endangering his own.* Tobit dismounted, strode closer. In a low voice, ignoring my outstretched hand, he said, "You let the Pharisees run the country. When you die, they will be gone."

"That's why I am regent," I whispered, "and you have to wait for me to die."

"Don't take too long about it," he said, "or I might have to help you."

"You wouldn't dare. I am still the queen."

"You don't have the stomach to kill me, do you?"

"I am still praying that the All-Merciful will change your heart."

"You never stop preaching, do you? No wonder Papa couldn't stand you."

My face flushed as if I'd been slapped. "Don't push too far, my son," I said. "If the Almighty doesn't change your heart, He may change mine."

Soldiers on both sides stirred warily, though no one could overhear. Tobit turned and galloped off, and his men followed. As Tobit's troops disappeared in the dust, I turned to Caleb. "You're right," I said. "Tobit must be stopped."

* * *

Tobit's troops were drilling daily in the border forts with the families of Diogenes and Boethus. According to my spy, they had five thousand swords and lances stacked in a storage area.

Caleb stationed sharpshooters on top of the city wall. They had been ordered to cut down Tobit and the other Sadducee leaders as soon as they appeared. "But it's not enough to wait for the attack," said Caleb. "You must surprise your son by attacking before he is ready."

"Come to me tomorrow," I said, "with a battle plan."

Caleb's plan called for two wings of troops to hide in the hills and attack the fort at dawn from opposite sides. Our spy inside knew where Tobit slept. He had insinuated himself into Tobit's personal guard. He would give Tobit a sleeping draught. Shortly before the midnight watch, he would cut my son's throat. The Sadducees would not have time to set up a new defense plan before my troops attacked.

As Caleb spoke, I was remembering Tobit as a toddler, zooming around the Audience Chamber buzzing like a bee. Clambering from a chair to the windowsill while I held my breath and darted to catch him before he jumped or fell. I remembered him swooping through the public square, pretending to be a hawk chasing the pigeons. Riding proudly on his mare, his legs barely reaching past the saddle blanket, his black curls streaming. I pictured him on his wedding day, smiling at Michal, so proud, lithe and eager. I pictured him lying, like my brother-in-law Matti, smeared with his own blood.

"I can't do this," I said. "I can't start a new civil war. It will destroy everything I have built."

"The war has already started," said Caleb. "The only question is where the next battle will take place."

I shook my head. No. Cleopatra had tried to assassinate her son. I could not.

* * *

Reuben, a village priest I had known and respected for years, limped into the Audience Chamber. At the doorway, he used his staff to knock from his sandals the dust of the journey. He smiled apologetically. He was one of the few priests who had remained loyal to me. "How are your wife and children?" I asked.

"They are well, Your Highness," he said, "though as you can see, my wife and I are no longer nimble. Some day, God willing, I will introduce you to my grandchildren and my great-grand-daughter. But the rest of my news, Your Highness, is urgent, and not so good. Supporters of the Sadducees are spreading a rumor that you framed the Temple treasurer, Zadok son of Boethus."

"How could anyone believe such an accusation?"

"They say you did it to protect your son Hyrcanus II, from

charges of stealing tithes."

"How could any of my people believe that I would countenance such behavior?"

Reuben shrugged. "Neither the priests in Jerusalem nor the priests in the countryside respect Lord Hyrcanus," he said. "Can't you persuade him to take more initiative? Tell him to take a bigger role in Jerusalem. To drill the troops and visit the villages. To welcome us when we come for rotations. He hasn't been to my village in the eight years since he became high priest."

I'm glad you don't know, I thought, *how many times I've tried to persuade him.*

"I will convene the Court of Twenty-three tomorrow," I said, "and invite Zadok to present his evidence, if he has any."

Caleb had been listening intently. I thanked Reuben and sent him to one of the small dining rooms to eat. "Such a gentle, loyal, soft-spoken man," I said.

"The sharpest tongue speaks loudest," Caleb said. "And your son Aristobulus has a sharp tongue. The reports from the harbors are just as bad. Merchants in the port cities mock Lord Hyrcanus. When you stand behind him, they lose confidence in you. They say we need a strong leader to protect us. They say Rome rises while we falter."

* * *

In the Chamber of Hewn Stone the next morning, I did something I had never done before. I sat in the throne at the head of the chamber. "Questions have been raised," I said, "about the financial affairs of the Temple. It is urgent that such questions be answered immediately. Our people must have confidence in the integrity of the Temple and its priests. Zadok son of Boethus, please bring to the Chamber of Hewn Stone the scrolls of records of the Temple collections and expenditures. We will ask three members of the Sanhedrin to examine them."

Zadok stood, his face burning. "Your Highness," he said, "it is impossible for me to bring the records at this time. I will need at least two weeks to assemble them. If you would ask the council to reconvene ..."

"The only records that could resolve these questions," I said, "are the records that you can produce right now."

"But Your Highness – " said Zadok.

"I'm sure the council will understand my reasoning," I said. "I will request that the Sanhedrin consider a new way to manage our Temple finances. Let all collections and all distributions both in Jerusalem and in the villages be made by a group of three men, one chosen by the Sadducees, one by the Pharisees, and one agreed upon by the other two. Let three sets of records be kept of each transaction, one by each member of this group. It may be impossible to untangle what has happened in the past, but we surely can forestall any suspicions for the future."

"This is a most thoughtful suggestion, Your Highness," said Zadok. "When the council meets in two weeks' time ..."

"This is a matter of such urgency that the Sanhedrin must act now," I said. "Does any member wish to speak against the proposal?"

No one did. At least for the moment I had taken the thieves' hands out of the treasury, and stanched the rumors about my oldest son. It was a victory, and I enjoyed it.

CHAPTER 6

Though my daughters-in-law lived within the walls of Jerusalem, I rarely saw them or my grandchildren. Tobit maintained a stony distance. Michal no doubt believed the terrible things her husband said about me. She never attended affairs of state. She didn't bring the children to the palace, even when specifically invited.

Abigail was warmer. After her second daughter was born, she occasionally brought the two girls to the palace. While I sat with Abigail in my sitting room, sipping tea, the two toddlers tumbled over each other like puppies. When they were a bit older, they sat giggling in a corner of the camelhair rug, playing a game with handfuls of tossed sticks. I tried to ask them about themselves – their favorite foods, their favorite games. They answered in monosyllables as if they scarcely knew how to talk. "I am no more talented as a grandmother than I was as a mother," I told Miri after they left.

"Your talent is to rule Judea," said Miri. "How many women could do that?"

These visits from Abigail and her children were rare. Abigail preferred her father's house in Zippori, where she thought the air was better. Etzi visited Zippori when he had time, but never invited me to come with him.

It was seven years before I saw any of Tobit's children. Even then it was only by chance. Three years after the twins, Michal had given birth to a second son, Antigonus, and the following year to a daughter, named – somewhat belatedly – Alexandra. The circumcisions for the boys were held privately. I was not invited. It hurt me to have four grandchildren I had never seen. I tried to imagine what they looked like.

One day, I was walking with Miri – taking a private stroll, veiled, with no entourage to call attention to me. I saw three of Tobit's children following Michal like goslings after the goose. The toddler, Alexandra, was tiptoeing along a stone wall, much as Tobit had done at the same age. Michal turned toward an alley, just in time to see Alexandra teetering on a pile of rubble at the corner of the wall. As if connected to her daughter by an invisible thread, she leaped across the space between them – ten cubits or more – and caught Alexandra before the child hit the ground. I, too, had felt connected to my pretty little namesake by an invisible thread. But I could not run to her without giving up my anonymity.

That thread is what I lacked as a mother, I thought. *That instant, instinctive attunement to my children's welfare. That's why they became the persons they became.* I'd had that connection with Etzi, but somehow I'd lost it. As for Tobit, that thread – which every child needed, which every child deserved, the thread that had connected me to my mother before she died – for Tobit that fragile thread had broken so early. Or perhaps it had never existed.

* * *

I hated what I was about to do. Two years had passed since that chance encounter with Tobit's family in the square of the city. I was about to meet Tobit's children face to face. But not under the circumstances I would have chosen.

When the maidservant opened the door to Tobit's home, Michal was tucking ebony waves of hair into her cap. She dropped the cap, blinked, brushed back her hair.

"My husband is not at home," Michal said. "With all due respect, Queen Salome Alexandra, I am not going to invite you in."

"You cannot show the hospitality due to any guest – even an unexpected one?"

"Guests don't come with an armed guard of ten soldiers."

The face of my namesake, little Alexandra, peered curiously from behind her mother's elbow.

"What have I done to you that you treat me with such hostility?" I said.

"It's not what you've done to me. It's what you've done to my husband."

"And what have I done to your husband?"

"Scorned him, humiliated him, rejected him."

"I did not reject him. When he was a small boy, he chose to leave me and follow his father."

"You deny him his rightful place on the throne."

"That place on the throne rightfully belongs to his brother."

"There is no point in trying to argue with the queen. And especially no point in arguing at my doorstep. If you must speak to me, summon me to the palace."

"That is why I have come. To summon you to the palace."

"You and ten soldiers. Two would have been enough. There is only one of me."

"We must bring your children too."

"No! You can't have them! They have nothing to do with this!"
I stepped forward and Michal stepped back, thrusting
Alexandra behind her. "We will not continue this discussion in
your doorway," I said. "You will step aside, and I will meet with
you and your children in your parlor."

I had never been in Tobit's home. I noted its graciousness with
approval. The cedar paneling, the silvery mosaics, the brown and
red patterned carpets and tapestries, the sand-colored silk drapes,
were as luxurious as anything in the palace. My builders and
weavers had done a good job in providing for my son.

The children clung to their mother, while I seated myself on
a couch covered with camel's hair, soft and tawny as a lion's skin.
Two soldiers stood at my sides. I motioned Miri and the rest of the
soldiers to remain outside the door of the room.

I was touched to see the children together, face to face with
me. Nine-year-old Alexander had chestnut hair and warm brown
eyes, but my eagle's beak of a nose. Antigonus – I guessed him to
be about six – had Tobit's dark curly hair. Five-year-old Alexandra
was dark and dancing. She was so like Michal at the same age
that I had a twinge of guilt. I didn't want to confine that free
spirit. Alexander's twin Miriam startled me. It was like looking
in a mirror and seeing a nine-year-old image of myself. The same
leggy, scrawny self-conscious twisting. The same frizzy brown hair.
The same beak of a nose. The same defiant eyes and proud chin.

"I so rarely get to see you children," I said. "You have all grown
a great deal. But now you will be moving to the palace, and I hope
to see a lot more of you."

Miriam spoke first. "Mama told us we're under arrest. Why?
We haven't done anything wrong."

"It's true that you won't be able to leave the palace," I said.

"But you will have your own spacious wing of the palace, with a courtyard. Even nicer than this lovely home."

"Who are you?" said five-year-old Alexandra. Six-year-old Antigonus shoved his hand over her mouth, but she wriggled free. She stood with hands on hips, head cocked and eyebrows raised. Waiting for an answer. A perfect mirror of her mother.

"I am your grandmother," I said. "My name is Alexandra, just like yours. I am so happy finally to meet you."

"Why are the soldiers here?" said Alexandra.

"Quiet!" said her big brother Alexander, grabbing her arm.

"Let her go," I told him. "She doesn't understand."

"Neither do I," snapped Michal.

I turned to the three eldest children. "I am sad to say that your father and I have had a disagreement. I want him to come to the palace, where he grew up, to talk peaceably with me. I think he will be more likely to do that if you children and your Mama are living with me at the palace."

"Oh, don't be such a hypocrite," said Michal. "Just let your soldiers drag us to the dungeon, so that my children understand what's really going on."

"I will not do that to my grandchildren. Or my daughter-in-law, even if her mind has been poisoned against me."

"Poisoned against you? You are the poison. You sent Tobit off to war when he was five years old. So that Etzi, your favorite, would have the only chance to be king. Despite your scheming, Etzi grew up to be a nobody. All he wants is to be a nobody."

"He has virtues his brother is unable to appreciate."

"So has my father. You like my father, don't you?"

"Yes, I do."

"My father is a very nice nobody. He studies, he gardens. He doesn't try to be what he is not. Why do you push Etzi to be what he is not?"

"Etzi is the rightful king."

"Tobit is a leader. A far better leader than his father. Yet you propped up Yannai, a drunk and a womanizer, for years. Let go. Let Tobit be what he was born to be."

"It's not a question of letting go. Tobit wants to pry the reins from my fingers."

"You can't rule any more. You can barely see. You can hardly walk. Why can't you let Tobit have his turn?"

"A man who can't wait his turn is too impetuous to be a good ruler."

"Why are we talking?" said Michal. "Children, bring your favorite toys. Get your nurses to pack your belongings. There's only one way this conversation can end. It might as well be now."

* * *

When I told him what I had done, Caleb shook his head. "Taking these hostages may be a short-term solution, Your Highness. In the long run it's a mistake."

"Why? My spy says Tobit's troops seem to be preparing to march."

"Tobit seems to have been hesitating, waiting for the right time to attack. You've given him a reason to attack now."

CHAPTER 7

Tobit strode into the Audience Chamber. Even though he'd surrendered his sword to the door guard, the throne guards in their bronze armor held their lances at the ready.

"Where are my children?" Tobit shouted. "Where is my wife?"

"They are safe and comfortable and well fed," I said.

"You're a monster, not a mother. What kind of woman imprisons her own grandchildren?"

"One who fears that without hostages, her son would slay her. Don't worry about your wife and children. They have every luxury. They're probably living better than they did on your stipend. Unless I underestimate the amount of bribes you've gotten from the Sadducees."

"Release them!" Tobit bellowed.

"Their safety depends entirely on you," I said. "They will be in no danger unless you move against me."

* * *

"Hostages or no hostages, I expect an attack on Jerusalem within the next week," said Caleb when Tobit had gone. "If you do not arrest your son – and execute him – you will lose your throne and your life."

"Most villages are still loyal to us," I insisted.

"People whisper that you appear ill," said Shimon. "You must take care of yourself. I need my partner."

"I am tired," I said. "Any woman or man, at seventy-three, needs to rest sometimes."

I went to bed weeping, with the worst headache in a lifetime of headaches. My vision blurred. My eye throbbed. Iron claws gripped the back of my head.

* * *

I was screaming, "My head – my head! Help me!"

Why did no one answer?

A moan like a wounded animal: Was that my voice? Why won't words come?

Hot poultices. Cold compresses. Liquids clogging and choking. Sour and salty, cold and hot, viscous and grainy. In at one end, out at the other, burning shame.

Curtains dim the room. Shimon's rough hand holds my twisted fingers. Miri's strong fingers swab sweat from my forehead.

Tobit and Etzi at the doorway. Tobit grinning and shoving his right fist into his left palm. Etzi biting his nails. "At last you think we've grown enough to rule the kingdom?" says Tobit. "Or has your iron hand become too weak to hold the reins?"

"How can you say such a thing!" says Etzi. "Mother, what are the hopes for a shared monarchy? Tobit has already surrounded Jerusalem with troops. Can't you do something?"

"No, Etzi," I mumble. "You do it."

* * *

I drift among dreams. Ribbons of fire, ribbons of smoke, ribbons of water glimpsed through arches of almond blossoms. Yannai, young and handsome, reaches to pull me through the waterfall, over the threshold to the world to come. *The Lord created us to heal each other,* I whisper, *but we squandered our powers.*

I am ready, he says. *The Lord will give us another chance.*

My eyes burn with tears. I wake to the sting of smoke.

"What burns?" I say.

"Lord Aristobulus," says Miri, "is burning the records of the treasury. And the records of the court."

A sideways tear dribbles into my ear. Miri swabs it away. She dabs at matching tears on her own cheeks.

"Yes, mother," says Tobit, waving a set of keys. "I have the keys now."

"Fool," Miri says to Tobit. "No one can burn what your mother has built."

Shimon looks out the window. "If every scroll burns," he says, "our students can still teach. They know the Law."

Miri's tear splashes on my forehead. A benediction. An anointing.

Shofar sounds. I picture my people gathering at the Temple: soldiers and cobblers, shopkeepers and potters. Women with babies in their arms. *How richly You have blessed us, Lord. You have allowed us to bring Your people closer to You and Your Law. You have permitted us, in our old age, nine precious years of peace.*

I hold out my hand to Shimon. He takes it, and kneels beside me. "See us, Lord," he says. "Hear our prayer. Forgive our sins. Preserve our work. You know us. With all our faults, we are Your servants."

EPILOGUE

●

Shulamit, Queen Salome Alexandra, died in 67 BCE. Her sons Aristobulus II and Hyrcanus II struggled over the throne for four years. They called on Pompey of Rome to mediate. In 63 BCE Pompey conquered Jerusalem. Judea continued as a client state, with puppet kings appointed by Rome. In 70 CE, Judeans fought for independence. Rome incinerated the Temple. Another rebellion in 135 CE also failed. This time, Rome leveled the city of Jerusalem and exiled the Jews. Untold numbers were sold into slavery. A million Jews died in the Roman wars. The Temple has never been rebuilt. One wall remains – not from the Temple itself, but from the retaining wall that enclosed the Temple Mount. For centuries, Jews from all over the world have visited that wall, once known as the Wailing Wall. (In Israel today, it is known as the Western Wall.) Many Jews still pray for the rebuilding of the Temple.

In the battle for the soul of the Jewish people, the Pharisees prevailed. Many of the teachings and rulings of Shimon son of Shetakh and the rabbis who followed him survived. Memorized, they were handed down orally for generations. They were incorporated into the Mishnah and the Talmud, which became the basis of Jewish religious practice and law after the destruction of the Temple. Jews still rely on many of these teachings today. *Mikvah* pools built more than two thousand years ago dot the landscape in Israel and are still being built, and used, around the world in cities where Jews live.

Judaism's daughter religions, Christianity and Islam, adopted the religious framework championed by Queen Shalom-Zion. Prayer, law, and charity, rather than temple sacrifice, became the central pillars of three great religions. Millions of people throughout the world, though they do not realize it, have been profoundly influenced by Shimon son of Shetakh and his sister Shulamit, the nearly forgotten Queen of Peace.

Background

PostModern Hanukkah

The rabbis of the Talmud asked the question, *Mai Hanukkah?* What's this Hanukkah business? I was equally confused when I was a kid. In fact, when I first heard of it, I told my mom, "A girl in my kindergarten class says she's getting a harmonica. Can I have one, too?"

Mom felt so guilty about my lack of Jewish knowledge that she junked the Christmas tree and enrolled me in Hebrew school the next fall. There I learned that Judah Maccabee fought the Syrians so that we could practice our religion. We few poorly armed Jews defeated the mighty Syrian army and after that everything was great. Not exactly. The events in this book took place in Judea in the first century BCE, among the grandchildren of the Maccabees. In order to write about Queen Shalom-Zion, I needed to become somewhat disillusioned with the Maccabees and their descendants.

The story begins with Alexander the Great. He was from Macedonia, a rough kingdom in the northern part of the Greek peninsula, but he loved the classical culture of Athens.

His tutor had been Aristotle. After Alexander conquered the Mediterranean world, his Greek-speaking Macedonian generals ruled the conquered lands. Ptolemy ruled Egypt. Seleucus ruled Syria. Though the common people in each land kept their local languages and religions, Alexander's heirs imported a Macedonian ruling elite who brought Greek (Hellenistic) culture wherever they lived. Hellenistic culture dominated the world much as American culture does today.

SEX and MONEY ruled in the Hellenistic world. In Ptolemaic Egypt, top courtesans, *hetairai,* were celebrities, like rock stars. While the lesser *hetairai* made appointments with their johns by writing with eyebrow pencil on tombstones outside the city, the top *hetairai* made appointments at society parties. Wives stayed home. King Ptolemy II, during a parade in honor of the wine god, Dionysus, stood next to a man dressed as the fertility god Priapus. Priapus sported an enormous erect penis. King Ptolemy IV had a temple to Venus on board his yacht. (Described, along with other juicy details, in John Marlowe, *The Golden Age of Alexandria.)*

Tiny Judea, home of the Jewish people, was sandwiched between Ptolemaic Egypt and Seleucid Syria. Jewish traditionalists like Queen Shalom-Zion struggled desperately to preserve their own Bible-based culture, which was completely at odds with Hellenism. The Holy Torah, the first five books of the Bible, which serve as the basis of Jewish law, stressed belief in one God, modesty in dress for both women and men, and a way of life that demanded discipline and sacrifice from every person. For example, no Jew, rich or poor, was permitted to eat pork or shellfish or to work on the Sabbath – prohibitions that still continue among observant Jews today.

Judea for most of the first three centuries BCE was ruled by high priests. Priests collected tithes of animals and produce from all the people, performed daily and seasonal sacrifices in the Holy Temple as prescribed in the Torah, distributed a portion of the tithes to the poor, and were permitted to eat from another portion of the tithes. They were assisted by the tribe of Levites, who sang hymns and played instruments during worship services and physically maintained the Temple. Some priests became wealthy and adopted the Hellenistic ways of other wealthy elites. The traditionalists considered them traitors.

DECIRCUMCISION AND OTHER ACTS OF SELF-BETRAYAL

High priests of the Jewish Temple in Jerusalem took Greek names. They built a gymnasium where Jewish priests and nobles exercised in the nude, like Greeks. Some wealthy Judeans even went through the painful cosmetic surgery of decircumcision, creating an artificial foreskin out of the flesh of the penis. One high priest declared the pig an approved sacrificial animal and celebrated the festival of Dionysus, the Greek god of wine.

With the encouragement of this Hellenized elite, the Macedonian king of Syria, Antiochus IV, forbade Jewish worship in the province of Judea. Jewish traditionalists and the common people were outraged. Mattathias, a priest from the town of Modi'in, organized a resistance. Led by his son Judah the Hammer (Judah Maccabee), the rebels fought a guerrilla war, not only against the Syrian army of occupation, but also against the Jewish priests and nobles who were trying to Greekify the Jewish religion.

Hanukkah celebrates the cleansing and rededication of the Temple in 164 BCE. But the Judean civil war did not end when Judah and his soldiers reconquered Jerusalem. A power struggle followed. As soon as their right to practice their religion had been restored, the traditionally pious Hasidim, who had backed Judah, wanted to end the war. Judah kept fighting. He wanted to drive out the Syrians and to neutralize the collaborators among his own people. His former allies became his enemies. Jews massacred Jews. Judah was killed by the Syrians when many of his troops deserted.

Judah's brothers (today they are all called Maccabees) kept fighting until all but one of the five brothers had been killed. In 140 BCE, this last brother, Simon, secured a measure of independence. Judea no longer paid tribute to Syria. The Jewish elders and leaders, by acclamation, appointed Simon high priest and prince, even though his father, Mattathias, had been a common priest, not of the high priestly lineage.

Here's the paradox: Though the Maccabees restored religious freedom and political independence for the Jews, they also established a ruling dynasty, the Hasmoneans. In each generation after Judah these leaders adopted more of the luxuries and manners of the dominant world culture, Hellenism. They wore purple cloaks and golden ornaments. They built Greek-style buildings, with columns. They took Greek as well as Hebrew names. Judah Aristobulus, the first Hasmonean to take the title of king, even added Philhellene (lover of all things Greek) to his name. Hanukkah itself is a Hellenistic-style holiday, celebrating a military victory, rather than an agricultural holiday or religious assembly commanded by the Torah. The Books of the Maccabees where we learn the Hanukkah story are as Hellenistic in style as comic books are American. They are not included in the Jewish Bible.

Simon was installed as high priest and prince by a Greek-style representative assembly, later known as the Sanhedrin. Each major city had its own twenty-three-member Sanhedrin to rule on capital crimes. Although we're not sure how much power it actually exercised, the seventy-one-member Great Sanhedrin, with representatives from all Judea, had to give its consent in nationally important matters such as waging war, expanding the walls of Jerusalem, and installation of a new high priest and prince.

By the time of Simon's grandsons, two parties were competing for control of the Sanhedrin and influence over the king and the people. The nobles and wealthy priests called themselves Sadducees, descendants of the High Priest Zadok. The traditionalist rabbis (scribes and teachers who interpreted the Law, not heads of synagogues like today's rabbis) were known as Sages. Though commoners, they strictly followed the way of life commanded in the Bible. The Sages had the loyalty and respect of the common people. Sadducees mockingly called the Sages Pharisees (separatists). Eventually even the Sages referred to themselves that way.

COMMONER TO QUEEN

Queen Shalom-Zion started life as Shulamit, a commoner, from a poor but distinguished family. She was the sister of a Sage, Rabbi Shimon son of Shetakh, head of the Sanhedrin. In the Talmud, the compendium of early legal interpretations on which all later Jewish practice is based, Shimon son of Shetakh and his friend Judah son of Tabbai were the third pair of great rabbis quoted in *The Wisdom of the Fathers*. His rulings on the status of women in divorce are still followed today. When she married High Priest Simon's grandson Judah Aristobulus, Shulamit acquired a Greek name: Salome Alexandra. The name Queen Shalom-Zion was one she earned from the people of Judea, who loved her. She earned it by standing between the crossed swords of the Sadducees and the Pharisees, stubbornly insisting that the welfare of the people came first.

In the thirty years since I first heard of Queen Shalom-Zion, I've done a lot of living myself. I understand now that Queen Shalom-Zion also stood at another crossroads – the crossroads of generations. She was caught between the standards set by her father, the demands and needs of her husband, the judgments of her brother, the demands and struggles of her children. All of which conflicted with her own ambitions. Her challenges weren't so different from ours. But at the same time, she was a woman ruler at a time when most women had the legal status of children or slaves. She managed to hold together a small country, divided within and constantly threatened from without. As for how she managed her own family – you be the judge.

Note: The queen's name in Hebrew is pronounced *Shlomtsiyon HaMalkah,* which means Queen of the Peace of Zion. I have written it as Queen Shalom-Zion to make it easier for English speakers. The queen's brother, Shimon son of Shetakh, like many men of that time, had been named after one of the Maccabee brothers. Both names would be pronounced with the SH sound in Hebrew, but I've called the Maccabee brother Simon to prevent confusion.

Since we have no record of Queen Shalom-Zion's thoughts, I have invented for her a lady-in-waiting, Miri, who has been her confidante and outspoken alter ego since both were young girls.

SOURCES

Most of the scanty information on Shalom-Zion comes from Josephus, a Jewish historian of the first century CE. Most information on Rabbi Shimon ben Shetakh, the priests and the Temple ritual comes from the Mishnah, the first authoritative compilation of Jewish law, and the Jerusalem and Babylonian Talmuds, the collections of commentaries, stories, legal rulings and rabbinic discussions on which most of subsequent Jewish practice relies. For some incidents, such as the confrontation between Jonathan son of Diogenes and the queen, I have quoted directly or adapted from the texts without attribution in order not to interrupt the flow of the story. To integrate the sources with archaeological evidence, I drew extensively on Lee Levine's excellent book *Jerusalem: Portrait of the City in the Second Temple Period*. Also helpful was Elias Bickerman's *The Jews in the Greek Age* and *From Ezra to the Last of the Maccabees*. On the Hellenistic era, I read a number of secondary sources, relying especially on Peter Green's book, *Alexander to Actium: The Historical Evolution of the Hellenistic Age*.

What's real and what's fiction in this story? It's hard to say. Josephus and the compilers of the Talmud as well as Judah the Prince, who collected the laws in the Mishnah, all invent conversations that took place a hundred years or more before they were written down. I suspect that most of the numbers in Josephus and other texts of the period are fiction too – especially the numbers of troops and the numbers massacred. I use them because they are the only numbers we have. For dramatic purposes, I accept the Talmud's assertion that Shulamit and Shimon ben Shetakh were sister and brother, even though most historians today disagree. I include in this narrative some characters, including High Priest Ishmael ben Phiabi, who lived later in the classical period. I attribute to Shalom-Zion achievements such as the proliferation of *mikvaot* (*mikvah* pools) that some historians credit to John Hyrcanus or other rulers.

I take most of the facts of Shalom-Zion's life as Josephus states them. I differ in my interpretation of the motivations behind the facts. In other words: most (not all) of the events in this book as well as the names of most characters come from ancient texts. My portrait of the people who once answered to those names is pure fiction.

ABOUT THE AUTHOR:

Judy Petsonk has written two nonfiction books: *Taking Judaism Personally: Creating a Meaningful Spiritual Life* (The Free Press) and *The Intermarriage Handbook: A Guide for Jews and Christians* (William Morrow/Quill, co-author Jim Remsen). Judy has spoken at women's organizations, synagogues, churches, Jewish centers, universities, and book fairs throughout the U.S. She is married and the mother of two young adults. In previous lives, she was a newspaper reporter and a teacher.

22386181R00155

Made in the USA
Charleston, SC
17 September 2013